# Advance Praise

"Jean Burgess crafts a powerful saga in which an Eastern Shore non-city girl defies tradition and family edict to do something different. What she discovers is not only intellectually challenging and attractive, but spawns romantic possibilities with the considerate Miguel which Margie never anticipated. It's about navigating the process of getting to a new place physically, emotionally, and intellectually…which is what makes the story so appealing and easy to love."

— D. Donovan, *Midwest Book Review*

"This novel captures the joys—and the challenges—of a young woman experiencing a life-changing move to the Big Apple in the 1980s. As Margie struggles to carve out a life for herself, she learns more about who she is and what she needs to "become." The expertly researched historic details of this early 1980s period (who knew there was an April snowstorm dropping one foot on New York City??) magically deliver the reader right into this interesting time and place."

— Mary Kendall, author of *The Accidental Heiress*

*"Navigating Her Next Chapter* by Jean Burgess paints an authentic portrait of city life for a young woman in the early 1980s. The protagonist, Margie, must find her way through relationships, both personal and professional, amidst the rising AIDS epidemic and out of control drug use of the time. As she takes life head on, we also get an authentic and interesting glimpse into the music and theater scene in the Big Apple. Ms. Burgess draws on her own experiences and thorough research to make us feel as if we, too, are in 1980s New York City. *Navigating Her Next Chapter* is a strong and entertaining sophomore novel for this author."

— Carol Cahill – Rockland Library Board Member and former English Chair, Rockland High School, Rockland, Massachusetts

"*Navigating* is certainly an apt word in the title of Jean Burgess's second novel. Her initially naïve protagonist, Margie, not only struggles to map a life and career in New York City amid the HIV/AIDS and cocaine epidemics of the early 80s but also travels the rough terrain that twenty-somethings often face when their aspirations clash with their parents' expectations. Burgess's attention to historically accurate detail and talent for creating believable endearing characters result in a delightfully engaging read."

— Barbara Van Aken, PhD, Sages Fellow (Retired), Case Western Reserve University, Cleveland, Ohio

"This well-written second book is a delightful continuation of Margie's journey as she overcomes her self-doubt about her life's direction. We join Margie after her singing career ends, and she travels to New York to pursue a career in writing music reviews. Margie learns the art of becoming a New Yorker with the help of an interesting cast of characters that become her new family and support system. Jean's ability to describe the people, events, streets, and even the smell of New York allows the reader to share Margie's journey as if they were there."

– Millie Mack, author of the *Faraday Murder* Series

"Burgess perfectly captures the romantic love affair so many have with New York City as they begin their adult lives. She captures the Father/daughter tension, the collection of misfits and lifelong friends who tumble together in our great Metropolis with uncertain beginnings, and the heart break and romance that seem available at every corner. The perfect telling of one woman's journey after she finally 'gets out of the car.' A treat for anyone dreaming of everything that can be theirs."

— Hamilton Clancy, Producer, Director, Actor, Activist, and Founding Artistic Director of The Drilling Company Theater, home of Shakespeare in the Parking Lot......and New Yorker

"*Navigating Her Next Chapter* is an intriguing read. The characters and storyline are well developed and will hold your interest. Since my background is in the field of Substance Abuse and Behavioral Health, I was impressed by the authenticity of the inclusion of the ripple effect of addiction on relationships with family and friends. The author truly captured the essence of the drug culture in NYC during that time period."

— Linda Auerback, CPP, Retired Substance Abuse Prevention Supervisor for Carroll County, Maryland

"Having just found her voice, Margie's now navigating her life through the wonderland of New York City in the early 1980s! From the art deco glory of Radio City Music Hall to the gritty musical ecstasies of CBGB's, day jobs, new writer's workshops, and even the Silver Star Diner, New York plays yet another glorious character in Jean Burgess' second novel in this series. Her protagonist, Margie, careens through the experiences of an every-artist surviving the classic theatrical New York adventure, while stepping fully into herself as a person exploring the possibility of realizing her dreams. With a little help from her friends, family, roommates, bosses, co-workers and all their agendas, *Navigating Her Next Chapter* is the story of her survival in the arts where love, life, and loss all come together in this showing of her escapades. It's a journey of the heart for any burgeoning, current, or reminiscing artist creating a life and aligning their soul."

— Bill Toscano, Director, Designer, Actor, Musician, Technician, Educator and Media Services Coordinator, Bethesda Chevy Chase High School, Bethesda, Maryland

# Navigating Her Next Chapter

# Navigating Her Next Chapter

*A Retro Novel*

Jean Burgess

This is a work of fiction. Although certain story elements, places, events, locations, and incidents are inspired by true and historical events, they are used fictitiously. Other names, characters, dialogues, and events are either the products of the author's imagination or used in a fictitious manner. Any resemblance to actual persons, living or deceased, or actual events is purely coincidental, other than as related to historical events.

Trigger warning: The contents of this novel may be emotionally challenging for its inclusion of scenes of prejudice, homophobia, alcoholism, drug use and addiction, trauma, or death of a loved one.



First Edition

Library of Congress Control Number: 2025949176

Casebound ISBN: 978-1-62720-626-6
Paperback ISBN: 978-1-62720-627-3
Ebook ISBN: 978-1-62720-628-0

Design by Apprentice House Press
Cover photo by Benjamin Lehman / Unsplash
Promotional Development by Trey Sanders
Editorial Development by Pam Mejia

Published by Apprentice House Press

Loyola University Maryland
4501 N. Charles Street, Baltimore, MD 21210
410.617.5265
www.ApprenticeHouse.com / info@ApprenticeHouse.com

*To those of us who have ever faced doubts and fears, who have confronted obstacles that stood in our way, who have finally found the courage to "get out of the car" and inch our way forward.*

# 1

# Immobilized/Mobilized

*March, 1981*

Paralysis gripped me as I sat in Crystal's car on New York's Upper East Side. There I was…slumped down in the passenger seat, terrified to leave her 1979 Camaro, peering out at the manic world of East 65th Street.

The gleaming high-rise buildings soared fifty stories or more into March's gray sky. A constant barrage of honking and sirens assaulted my ears. A taxi driver yelled, "Move it, buddy" at an elderly man with a walker, inching his way along the crosswalk. The loud voices of people passing were punctuated by the clicking and clumping of high-heeled or loafered footsteps. Autos jerking to stops and starts, stops and starts – the busyness forcing me to retreat within myself. I slid further down the passenger seat, seeking refuge. Pulling my wool tweed coat around my neck, I sank into a sense of safety until a woman's voice screeched, "Taxi!" and jolted me out of my secure cocoon.

Reflecting on recent dialogues with my parents prior to making this move, I heard Dad's critical words of discouragement, which only made me more determined to tackle New York City. Back on Maryland's Eastern Shore, in our rural living room, where I plopped down on Mom's favorite gold and brown Early American sofa, Dad warned me multiple times that "a girl from tiny Church Creek would never survive in a monstrous city like New York."

"For cryin' out loud, Margaret. This notion of movin' to New York is even crazier than your harebrained idea of travelin' around the country with a swing band. You're not a city girl," he harped. "We Eastern Shore folk don't do well surrounded by concrete and steel. And all those crazy people – the druggies and criminals and homos and what have ya. A girl like you won't last a New York minute."

*A part of me came here to spite him!*

The truth was in many ways he was right: I was a small-town girl. But unlike Dad, I hadn't let that define me. I graduated from college in 1977; I toured the entire country as a singer with a swing band; and, unlike most of my twenty-six-year-old friends in 1981, I chose career over marriage and motherhood – a fact that drove my father beyond insanity. While the transition from college to band tour to NYC was not without its "Father-Daughter" challenges, here I was making a career move to the Big Apple.

*I just need to get out of the car!*

"Don't be a dork, Margie!" Crystal, my high school friend and future roommate, beat on the windshield. Not only did her high-pitched voice yank me out of my reveries but her smushed face against the glass scared the crap out of me! I cranked down the passenger's side window to hear her apartment update.

"Geez, you're twenty-six years old, you nerd. You can't cower in the car for the rest of your life. Look around, *mon amie*. Perfectly normal people walking around the perfectly normal streets of New York and living to speak of it. What is your problem?" She punctuated her sentences with mocking facial expressions.

"Geez, how about taking a chill pill?" I asked. She could tell from the irritation in my voice that she had crossed a line. *Did that stop her? No way!* She continued to poke.

"Don't get all wigged out, Margie. You are allowed to get out of the car. No one's gonna mug you."

Ever since I met her in high school, I knew Crystal could be a major pain in the butt, but I really couldn't complain. Afterall, she did ask me to room with her in New York. And she drummed up the apartment sublet deal with a cousin or second cousin once removed or something like that. I was dying to break free of living under my Dad's thumb as well as shake my own complacency. I needed to jumpstart my floundering writing career. When Crystal decided she wanted to go to fashion school in the Big Apple, I pounced on her roommate offer. The thing with Crystal was you needed to quickly redirect her and keep your cool when she started to drive you bonkers.

"Okay, Crystal. Spill it. What's the report on the apartment?"

"Oh, right. Got the keys from the Super. Did a quick check. The previous tenants were pigs but nothing we can't fix up. Margie, this is gonna be totally cool to the max. Come on. Pry yourself out of that passenger seat and check out our new digs."

The six-story brownstone apartment, squished between two shimmering high-rise buildings, looked tired and forlorn. The entrance to the tiny lobby sported a large, oval window that no one ever bothered to wash. Fingerprints, smudges, and dusty grime obscured the light. This street level door didn't require a key. *So much for apartment doorman security.*

When we entered the small lobby, Crystal nearly burst into song. "Don't you love these ancient buildings with the teeny tiny mosaic tiles and that old wood smell?"

"Uh…sure." I thought the lobby had a musty odor. Not

stinky, but certainly not fresh or clean.

"The Super gave me two sets of keys." She handed me a pair. "There's one for our apartment door and one for the mailbox." *The tenants may not be safe, but gosh darn it, the mail will be protected.*

Crystal and I began our assent up to the sixth floor, apartment 6C. The climb didn't seem too bad until I realized I wasn't carrying any suitcases or boxes from the car…or future bags of groceries or loads of freshly washed laundry from wherever the hell we'd have to do that! *Good Lord, what have I gotten myself into!*

At last, I stood in front of 6C. As she opened the front door, Crystal announced with her obnoxious sprinkling of French flourish, "Welcome to your new *maison*, Margie." After walking along a long dark hall, we entered the small kitchen with all the usual appliances, however outdated: refrigerator, sink, a tiny gas stove, and, to my shock, a shower stall sitting next to the sink complete with a rickety wooden step to aid the user. I'd never seen a shower stall smack dab in the middle of a kitchen before.

"Okay, shower in the kitchen…so where's the bathroom?" I asked.

"Oh, right. There's no official bathroom. The kitchen sink serves as both the bathroom and kitchen basin. And the toilet's in there. Light's on the outside." Crystal pointed to a door next to the shower.

I hit the switch and opened the door. Something strange caught my eye. Several somethings – small and scurrying and wriggling. Bugs!

"Crystal. There are bugs all over the floor. Ugly, creeping bugs!"

"Oh, right. Cockroaches. It's a New York thing."

"You've got to be kidding me! A New York thing?" I didn't

usually freak out over bugs, but I'd never seen a cockroach in my life. Those were the ugliest insects ever!

"Chill out, Margie. The building Super sprays regularly and we can spray too. It's all part of living in the city." *Not a wonderful benefit as far as I can figure.*

We walked through the kitchen doorway into the sparsely furnished living room, which despite the lack of furnishings, was completely filthy with grime and abundant trash. *Maybe if the previous tenants weren't such pigs, the cockroach situation wouldn't be as bad.*

The same went for the bedroom or what I described later as "a half a bedroom." This extremely small room, directly off the living room, barely had enough space to fit the small clothes rack (our new "closet") and a bunk bed squeezed between the living room and outer apartment wall. Thankfully, a single window offered a bit of natural light and a fire escape for emergencies. *How can a room this small be this dirty!*

"I know, ugh," Crystal said. "The guys who sublet from my cousin for the last two years were total slobs – grody to the max! But the apartment is under my cousin's name, and he had to keep it under Rent Control, meaning 'cheap.' Since his job was reassigned to the West Coast, he found a couple of his frat brothers to sublet it to."

"Rent Control?"

"Yeah. Certain older apartments in New York City have either rent controlled or rent-stabilized leases. It helps to keep the rent prices down, especially for low-income people...like us!"

"All I can say is, thank God I brought cleaning supplies! Let's get to work!"

****

The next morning, I opened my eyes at five-thirty – an hour that should be illegal for waking up. Every muscle ached from all the scrubbing and cleaning Crystal and I had done the day before, not to mention from lugging boxes and suitcases up six flights of stairs. Surprised to hear Crystal in the shower already, I stumbled into the kitchen and searched for coffee makings. Unfortunately, no coffee, but I did find a few tea bags and a kettle, so I began the process.

I yelled to Crystal over the sound of the shower, "Want tea? I'm putting water on now. And why are you up this early?"

"Gotta move my car. And yes, please." That made no sense, but I decided to wait until she got out of the shower to ask for clarification.

About the time the tea kettle initiated its whistle, the water turned off. Crystal's hand popped out of the shower stall, grabbing for her robe hanging on a hook near the kitchen sink. *This kitchen is going to be a freakin' busy spot. I can tell!*

Crystal breezed through the kitchen, the floral fragrance of her Gee Your Hair Smells Terrific shampoo trailing her to the bedroom. "Hey, I picked up muffins at the corner diner and grabbed an application for waitressing while I was there."

"Look at you all ambitious first thing in the morning." Still trying to make sense of her earlier comment, I asked, "What did you mean about having to move your car?"

Crystal emerged from the bedroom in jeans and a black turtleneck sweater with dangling circular red and black enameled earrings. Her red flats pulled the whole outfit together.

"Right. I've got to take my car to Jersey. I made a deal with a friend who's going to keep it for me. He gets free use and I don't have to pay a fortune for a Manhattan parking lot."

I handed her a mug of tea. "Why not park it on the street like you did last night?"

"Street cleaning. If you park on the street, you have to pay attention to the street signs for the day and time of cleaning. If you don't move your car before it starts, you can expect a hefty fine. It's a hassle to the max." She sipped her tea and added, "Besides, no one needs a car in the Big Apple. With the help of buses, subways, trains, and your feet, the entire city is accessible. That's why I love New York! You'll see."

Crystal pulled on a sassy black beret-type hat over her still damp hair and a three-quarter length, boyish cut, red wool coat. *This girl is a living fashion plate!*

"Hey, Crystal. How is it that you can look totally pulled together with wet hair and no makeup? Geez."

She laughed off my compliment as she scooted down the long hall toward our apartment's front door. "It's a *grande* gift!" she called out. "I'll be back soon. Good luck job hunting."

The door slammed shut, causing the tenant from the floor below to start shouting obscenities and banging on the ceiling with what I could only imagine was a broom handle. *Welcome to my first morning in NYC!*

Once the noise from the lower deck subsided, a knot formed in my stomach. I looked around the roach-infested, shower-in-the-kitchen, odd apartment and sucked back a sob. Crystal bopped out the door with the smile of a Vogue model – as if she'd lived here for years – without a care in the world. But I felt like a foreigner on an alien planet.

In that moment of solitude, I crumbled in my chair, overwhelmed with thoughts that I'd made a horrible mistake. *Did I think this move through completely? I'm not the brave, "conquer-the-world" girl I pretend to be. How the hell did I end up here? How can I motivate myself to even move forward?*

When I returned to Church Creek from touring the country

with King Vido's Swing Band, I was shocked that Dad even listened to my plan to move home to work and save money to attend graduate school in creative writing. Yet that's what I did – worked at his general store and picked up a few hours of office work at the Dorchester Art Center, squirreling away my pennies. But as the months turned into one year and then another, my attitude changed – not only about going to grad school but about myself.

I'd become complacent.

I'd always loved our little corner of Maryland's Eastern Shore and life along the Choptank River. Not only did I enjoy hobnobbing with the arts community at the Center, but I was also thrilled when I landed freelance work writing music reviews for the local newspaper. The general store had been an evil necessity, making up the bulk of my income and keeping Dad happy. While working there felt as bothersome and irritating as sand in an oyster, I kept reminding myself of my ultimate goal – graduate school. That was until graduate school lost its appeal to me. Maybe that's what Dad had hoped would happen.

The cost of grad school seemed out of reach. Heck, I had already been writing music reviews and getting paid…even though those were for local papers. Truth was, my writing goals floundered, and grad school no longer held the allure it once had. Instead of reflecting on a new career direction, I kinda shut down.

I kept asking myself: *What's the plan now, Margie? Are you going to live in your parent's house and work at your Dad's crappy store forever?* Those questions began eating away at my psyche, complacency turning to anxiety and resentment, which soon morphed into headbutting between me and Dad. I had hoped that communication would have improved between us as time went on, especially since he initially agreed to my goal of becoming a music critic – a big step for him. *Nope, not the case.* Dad's views on women having careers ranged from bogus to totally bogus. He tolerated a woman working for a couple years as long as her ultimate goal pointed toward marriage and children. And he could be insistent when expressing his views.

In many ways, during the past three years, I learned to conquer many of my fears and to speak up for myself…except when it came to my Dad. It seemed like any time I tried to approach a conversation with him like a grown-up, using logic and critical thinking, it fizzled into a shouting match – mostly him shouting at me. And always the same old blather revolving around Dad's favorite topic.

"Jesus, Mary, and Joseph, you're twenty-six-years-old, Margaret. Had your time to experiment with that band thing. Now it's high time ya find a nice local guy to marry. And what kinda career is singin' or writin' reviews? Time to quit this foolin' around?"

When the opportunity to move to New York with Crystal appeared, I realized I had to do something to snap me out of my complacency and get out from Dad's growing pressure. My hands shook and beads of sweat collected on my forehead when I approached both Dad and Mom with the idea of making the move, but I gathered my courage and asserted myself. Initially Mom, the former teacher, was devastated about me not furthering my education.

"No graduate school? But you had your heart set on going, Margaret." The disappointment in Mom's eyes killed me.

"Originally I did, but I'm thinking a New York internship would be even better for my career."

Dad snorted. "I think it's high time ya get this stuff out of your system, young lady. A woman's real job is in the home."

"Look Dad," I measured my words, reining in any anger bubbling up at his outdated feelings about women. "I put aside my own money for the past two-and-a-half years, by working three jobs."

Mom added, "That's true. She did save her own money. And finding an internship in New York would be an extension of the music reviews she's already been writing for the local newspaper. Isn't that right, Margaret?"

"Absolutely. And Dad, think of it like this: A New York writing internship would give me an even better education than grad school – for free!"

I'm fairly sure that last point – the free part – won him over because he gave his reluctant blessing on the move.

While my decision to move to New York did help to distance me from Dad's constant pressure and life choices for me, I wondered: What was the real reason I wanted to move here? Was it to advance my career or simply to get away from my Dad? And if it was to "escape" having to deal with my father, was that the right reason to make such a drastic move? Wasn't that like running away from an issue rather than confronting an issue head on – even if the issue is your own Dad? *Oh, stop thinking too much, Margie. You're acting like a baby!*

Back to the task at hand, I scanned the Want Ads in *The New York Times* and another paper that Crystal picked up, *The Village Voice.* Job hunting in a huge city like New York proved to be overwhelming and depressing. I immediately realized how limited my skills were and how that was impacting my job opportunities. *Okay, Margie, breathe. Remember, all you need is a job to pay the bills while pursuing your interest in writing about music. Stop wigging out.*

I made a list of what job experiences I had acquired up to this point in my long, long life of twenty-six years. What I came up with included: waitressing at Doris Mae's Diner on Maryland's Eastern Shore, singing with a touring swing band, working odd jobs at my Dad's general store, and answering phones and light typing at the Dorchester Arts Center near my hometown. *Not much to go on.*

On the drive from Maryland to New York, Crystal assured me that having a college degree bumped me up miles ahead of others in the application pile for office jobs. Based on her intel, I narrowed my search to receptionist/office clerk positions. She, on the other hand, had no skills other than waitressing. She stuck with restaurant work for her part-time revenue generator while she attended fashion school. That was the deal she made with her parents. She had stumbled upon an article about The New School's Parsons School of Design programs located in Manhattan and begged her parents to allow her to attend. After initial reluctance, they gave in on the condition that they would pay for tuition, rent, and utilities as long as Crystal found part-time employment to cover all other expenses. *Talk about your great arrangement!*

I, on the other hand, needed to secure full-time employment in order to survive! *Survival! I've been here less than twenty-four hours and I'm already doubting if I'll be able to navigate my own survival in this place.* I got up from the table and wandered over to the kitchen window. To my amazement, two tiny sparrows perched on the ledge.

"How in the world did you sweeties find your way to the sixth floor of this building?" I said as if they could actually hear or even understand me. I'd always found birds to be centering and now, in this strange and unfamiliar setting, here were two small, feathered creatures staring at me. Once the sparrows flew away, I cracked open the window and brushed the crumbs from my muffin onto the outer sill. *Hmm. At least these tiny things have found a way to survive in New York. My inspiration!*

I continued my job-hunting task. After scouring the Help Wanted ads, I applied for three jobs that looked promising. I set up interviews at an insurance company near Wall Street and an apartment rental office on the Upper West Side. Both seemed utterly boring, but I reminded myself that a day job was simply a means to an end.

The third job was for a receptionist at Radio City Music Hall. Crystal's predictions about having a college degree and secretarial skills giving me a leg up proved true during that interview the next day. The woman who interviewed me, Miss Chambers, kept saying things like, "Impressive" and "We don't see that very often" and "That skill will come in useful." The thought of working in a landmark theater surrounded by performers all day had me walking on air, but I had no idea what an art deco gem the building truly was…until a few days later when I accepted my position as Receptionist for the Executive Suites and was asked to report to the 51st Street door of Radio City Music Hall the following Monday.

*First week in New York City and I'm doing alright. Got myself out of the car, moved into an apartment, and found a job. I might survive being a city girl after all.*

# 2

# Explorations Inside and Out

*March-April, 1981*

I spent the first couple of days of my employment at Radio City Music Hall familiarizing myself with my new "office" – an area in the hall outside the elevator on the top floor of the 51st Street entrance to the building. I loved being surrounded by art deco furniture, artwork, and decorations, making my workspace unique and pleasant. I adored my desk – an ebony table with triple bands of rounded silver, serving as legs. To the left, a modern typing table held an IBM Model 75 Electronic typewriter. *A new skill to learn.* Although I'd be isolated from the other offices in this small receptionist area, I preferred the beautiful decor and the non-corporate feel over a stuffy office. I couldn't believe I was a part of this amazing entertainment venue.

On my second day of employment, my immediate supervisor, Miss Beverly Chambers, peeked around the corner. "Are you settling in alright, Margie?"

"Yes ma'am. I love my office area." If she had an inkling of my prior work environment – a dusty general store – she'd understand my gushing enthusiasm. "These art deco designs are amazing. Look at that ebony credenza with the silver trim and this three-dimensional banjo mural hanging over the typing table. I'll be pinching myself working here five days a week."

Miss Chambers' eyes glazed as she casually glanced around the reception hall. "Yes, well…I've arranged for a special Music Hall tour with one of our longest employed pages. Neil will give you a behind the scenes tour of the Executive Suites and the building's production side, areas that the general public rarely see. This will be useful in your position. You'll be doing a lot of trekking throughout the building."

Miss Chambers seemed nice enough, although she acted like a wannabe elite. *And clearly, she is not an Art Deco enthusiast.* As Executive Secretary to the Vice President of Finance, Mr. Eric Mason, I soon learned that she excelled in typing, shorthand, organizing files, and maintaining the rolodex. Mostly, she was the Fax Machine Queen, the latest in technology. Miss Chambers made sure everyone knew about her expertise at sending and receiving faxes. As soon as that annoying fax machine screech revved up in the printer room, we could all hear the clicking of her high heels as she scurried down the hall to retrieve the latest document off its tray. Even more comical were her attempts to send letters, which were often met with busy signals followed by audible swear words from the "trying-to-be-so-classy" secretary. These antics kept me entertained.

Dressed in a dark suit, white shirt, and black tie, Neil arrived in my reception area soon after lunch, ready to begin the orientation tour. Miss Chambers had already told me that, as one of the longest running employees in the page program, Neil had worked his way up from doorman to usher to tour guide to assistant manager in his ten years with Radio City Music Hall.

"Hello Margie. I'm Neil, your guide for the afternoon. I hope you're ready for a great experience."

"I can't tell you how much I'm looking forward to this, Neil."

As we walked through the hallway of offices in the Executive

Suite, I asked, "What can you tell me about the page program? I understand you've been involved for quite a while."

"The page program really started at Rockefeller Center, before Radio City even existed. But after the theater opened in 1932, an usher program was created. It provided entry-level work for young men interested in careers in the entertainment fields, initially as uniformed employees serving as ushers and doormen. By the 1970s, the page program expanded to include females as well as males."

The first thing Neil explained on the tour was the difference between the two sides of the Radio City Music Hall building. The odd thing about the two sides was that the floors on each side did not align. In order to traverse from the administrative offices on one side to the production offices on the other side, I'd either have to navigate a path over or under the massive stage, or take a series of odd stairs or elevator rides.

"Gosh, Neil. I feel like I'm gonna need a map to learn my way around this building. I mean, it is a freakin' block long!"

"I'm sure a smart young lady like yourself will get the hang of it soon enough. Remember what I told you. The building's 50th Street and 51st Street sides are different. That's the trick. You'll be fine."

When Neil deposited me back in the reception area, Miss Chambers sat on the long, cream-colored sofa facing my desk, flanked by two gorgeous, deco torchiere floor lamps in brushed nickel. She resembled a celebrity waiting for an interview. Neil and I gabbed, absorbed in comparing our favorite parts of Radio City's treasures: Was it the marvelous Art Deco studio apartment built for the famous S.L. "Roxy" Rothafel, the visionary behind Radio City Music Hall, or the view from the light booth taking in the sun burst proscenium arch surrounding the magnificent stage?

"I take it you enjoyed the tour," she said.

"Yes ma'am." I turned to Neil. "Thank you for sharing your extensive knowledge and your love of this building."

"Yes, thank you, Neil, dear. You may return to your duties," Miss Chambers said. She was all business…kind of.

I tried to figure out what made Miss Chambers tick. She put on a superiority act, but what was she striving to achieve? She dressed in tailored designer suits with perfectly coifed platinum hair and heavily applied foundation and rouge. Oh, and the nails…always immaculately manicured. She spoke with an affected voice, sprinkling "darling" and "you're such a dear" into conversations, although once in a while her Tennessee twang slipped through. She must have worked extremely hard to disguise it.

As we continued to get to know each other, Miss Chambers had plenty of unsolicited and unwelcomed advice for me about how I should live my life in New York in order to "find a man." From what I cobbled together, she came to the city in her early twenties in search of a wealthy, important husband. I estimated that she was around thirty-five, so prospecting had not been too successful for Miss Chambers. *And yet she continues to feel it is necessary to give me husband finding tips!*

Miss Chambers viewed my interest in writing as "an interesting hobby," but at least she appeared to take a genuine interest in what I enjoyed doing with my spare time. And despite her misplaced attempts to force her "husband-snagging" advice on me, I liked her.

Although I had to dance around Miss Chambers' oddities, my new job proved to be easy. Despite taking a week to conquer

Radio City Music Hall's layout, I did learn my way around, as Neil predicted. I mastered the rest of my receptionist duties on day one. The job description consisted of: Greet visitors and announce them to the executives' secretaries via the phone paging system. That was it. Simple enough. Actually, guests were greeted and vetted by a Radio City doorman before they even stepped foot on the elevator.

On a daily basis, when executives expected guests, the doorman stationed below at the 51st Street door would call upstairs to alert me that a visitor was on their way up in the elevator. By the time they reached the Executive floor and my reception area, I had already alerted the appropriate department secretary, where my instructions were to either escort the guest to the correct destination or to ask the visitor to wait until a representative came to the reception area to greet them personally.

*Radio City Music Hall is a well-oiled machine for sure!*

****

While I familiarized myself with my new receptionist position at Radio City Music Hall, Crystal landed a waitress job at Silver Star Diner on the corner of our block at East 65th and Second Avenue. Her parents would be paying for tuition and most of her big expenses, but this income helped her to fill in the gaps while she attended Parsons School of Design. And how radical was it that she only had to walk half a block? I was not as lucky.

It didn't take me long to learn the reality of city transportation and my morning commute. Radio City Music Hall was about twenty blocks from our apartment. The first two weeks of work I naively thought, "I have to take the bus because that's what New Yorkers do." Taking the bus meant walking two and a half blocks to Lexington Avenue in heels, waiting at the designated stop, cramming into an already overcrowded vehicle like sardines in a can, while praying for a seat, but settling for grabbing onto a pole, getting pushed and shoved as more riders entered and exited for several stops until hopping off the bus as close to 51st Street as possible. I finally figured it out. A way to save money on bus fare and salvage my sanity! I simply left my heels at work, laced up my sneakers, and hoofed it to Radio City Music Hall each morning. From that "ah-ha" moment on, I carried an umbrella daily and became a New York City walker. Miss Chambers turned up her nose, of course. "Dah-ling," she'd say, drawing out the word in her affected manner, "How will you ever attract a wealthy man wearing sneakers?" I laughed off her question. *Fancy suits and designer heels don't seem to be doing the trick for you, Beverly!*

I loved my job, but after a month of sitting around at my upstairs receptionist desk waiting (hoping) for visitors to come to the Executive Suites, boredom took over. To save my psyche from rotting, I approached various department secretaries, asking if they needed help with typing or stuffing envelopes or special projects – anything to help the hours to speed along. Several secretaries sent over financial reports that needed retyping, documents to be proofread, piles of envelopes to be stuffed, and much more. I enjoyed the busy work, and they appreciated the help.

More importantly, Miss Chambers sang my praises to the higher ups. I wasn't trying to show off, but apparently a few of the underlings had a reputation for shirking from their work loads. While it didn't make me the most popular gal in the building, the extra effort got me noticed by the management. Truthfully, boredom was my only motivator.

Having overcome desk ennui, my lunch break became fun-filled adventures. Despite Dad's descriptions of muggers and kidnappers waiting to attack me on every corner, I used my lunch hours to explore mid-town Manhattan on pleasant days. I enjoyed window shopping along Fifth Avenue, gawking at St. Patrick's Cathedral's architecture, and checking out the Theater district – all within walking distance of Radio City Music Hall. On rainy afternoons, I navigated the series of underground tunnels between Radio City, Rockefeller Center, and the subway system, thanks to the "insider information" I received during Neil's tour. The tunnel required an employee ID to enter but provided direct access to a complete "city" directly under Rockefeller Center and beyond, including the Rink level, small retail stores, a delicatessen and other food offerings, a hair salon and barber shop, and a drug store. If you knew your way around, there was even a Post Office under 45 Rockefeller Plaza. When I didn't pack my lunch, I'd splurge on a fried egg sandwich from the deli, a chocolate croissant from the bakery, or a single slice of sausage pizza from the pizzeria – all hidden underground from the masses, a best kept secret.

My mid-town explorations broadened as the springtime weather became warmer. I loved discovering new buildings and monuments because it made me feel more at home in the city. I frequently took my lunch outside on a bench overlooking Rockefeller Center's ice rink-turned-café, surrounded by the Flags of the Nations waving in the breeze. Occasionally, I went on treasure hunts in search of artwork surrounding the center. Inside the doors of 30 Rockefeller Center, I adored the impressive murals by two artists commissioned by J.D. Rockefeller in the early 1930s to decorate the walls of that massive building: Jose Maria Sert's "American Progress," a forty-one-foot-long mural looming over the reception desk in the east lobby, and Sir Frank Brangwyn's four themed murals addressing "Man Laboring," "Man the Creator," "Man the Master," and "Man's

Ultimate Destiny." I filled my journal with amateur sketches of vistas, street scenes, landmarks, and iconic works of art that appeared around mid-town during my wanderings.

As much as I enjoyed traipsing around by myself and secretly defying Dad's dire warnings of "doom and despair for a small-town-girl-in-the-city," there were times when anxiety and self-doubt crept into my mind. Sure, I had an apartment and job – great first steps – but I struggled with how to move my writing career forward. And a new fear had begun to paralyze me lately.

Ever since I moved to New York, whenever I took out my journal to jot down a written reflection, I blanked out – as if the noise and constant movement and frenetic pace were too distracting for me. I'd heard of writer's block but geez…I couldn't even journal? The whole reason I moved to New York in the first place was to jumpstart my enthusiasm for writing again and to explore writing options. What was going on with me? What if Dad was right? Was I a naïve small-town gal getting eaten up in a big city like New York? *Breathe, Margie. You're still adjusting. Don't wig out!*

On workdays when I especially wanted to get away from the traffic, the throngs of people, and pandemonium swirling about, I found my way to St. Patrick's Cathedral, across Fifth Avenue from the Rockefeller Center complex. Inside, the beauty of the vaulted ceiling soaring overhead, the carved marble columns like tree trunks rooted in the earth while reaching to the heavens, and the multi-colored stained-glass windows with the midday light streaming through all created a sense of awe and serenity. But most of all, the quiet, the lovely quiet – hard to find in New York – refreshed and restored my spirit. This beautiful landmark cathedral became my little slice of solitude.

I discovered St. Patrick's as a refuge by accident, or maybe by divine intervention. I had passed it many times during my regular lunch hour walkabouts. But one day, after my routine gawking at the windows of fancy retailers along Fifth Avenue, I found myself climbing the concrete stairs leading up to the cathedral's massive doors. What drew me to enter the cathedral that particular day? Was it the excessive noise of honking taxis and town cars jockeying for position? Was I looking for an escape from the unusual April warmth? Was I fed up with feeling like a human pinball, pushed and shoved by wide-eyed tourists and inconsiderate businessmen? For whatever reason, an other-worldly energy guided me up those steps and into the dark foyer in the back of the sanctuary. I eased my way into the cathedral and nearly gasped at its vaulted glory.

"She is a beauty, isn't she now?" A woman's voice with an Irish brogue spoke in a hushed volume behind me. I turned to see an older nun, perhaps mid-seventies in full habit standing near me. "Good afternoon, my dear. Is it your first visit to St. Patrick's Cathedral?"

"Yes, Sister."

"I'm Sister Kathryn and you are?"

"Oh, Margie…I'm Margie, Sister."

"Aye…and have you come for the sightseeing or personal reflection and prayer today, Miss Margie?"

"Truthfully…a bit of both."

"Well then, here's a wee bit of a suggestion for you. I tell visitors to work their way around the perimeter of the sanctuary and take in all the beautiful sculptures in the various nooks and crannies. Then find a pew toward the front of the sanctuary for divine solitude. It tends to get noisy back here with all the gawkers." She punctuated her advice with a wink and moved along.

I whispered, "Thank you, Sister," but she had already begun

to greet a group of Asian tourists.

After taking Sister Kathryn's advice and settling in a pew near the altar, I noticed that the city's commotion and noise drained from me physically, mentally, and, well…spiritually. My lunch hour visits to the awe-inspiring St. Patrick's not only restored my energy, but also allowed me quiet time to reflect on questions of the soul. Not surprising, really. Although my parents raised me in the Catholic tradition, I had turned away from attending Mass when I became confused by my observations of contradictions – things I saw and dealt with while traveling around the country with the touring band, and especially at home in Church Creek with my Dad. A lot didn't align with what the Church had taught me. I had questions…confusion…even anger. But that didn't mean I rejected all religion or even Catholicism.

The Church was one of several sticking points between me and Dad. I had high hopes that communication with my Dad would improve after I returned from the band tour a few years ago. I saw a glimmer of change in Dad right after I came home – he seemed open to me going to grad school, to freelancing as a music reviewer for the local paper, even to moving to New York, however reluctantly. I wanted to believe that one day we could begin to have adult conversations about how I felt about the Church's teachings and what confused me, about where we differed on acceptance of all races and persuasions of people, and about my career choices versus his traditional marriage and child rearing values. But truthfully, how could I expect him or anyone to treat me like an adult when I constantly found myself floundering in a pool of indecision. One day I talked about graduate school; the next I was iffy about graduate school; then I delivered a pitch about internships in New York City. *Worse than a rock fish flipping and flopping right out of a fishing boat!*

Dad's continued lack of tolerance toward others, especially in his comments about my move to New York, was especially irksome. "Stay away from those New York freaks, Margaret. Ya know, those foreigners and fags." Geez, it was bad enough when I toured with King Vido's Swing Band and he insisted that all the musicians were "drugged out hippies." In his mind, the entire world was filled with horrible people, all out to get him. *And this is a man who attends Mass every Sunday!* No wonder I questioned the Church's teachings.

I did find it ironic that, despite my wandering away from my Catholic upbringing, a cathedral became the very place that brought me the peace and calm I needed to reexplore my connection to my spiritual center in the bustling city.

****

Right on cue at one o'clock on Sunday afternoon, the pale blue princess-style telephone rang in our living room. It had become routine since Crystal and I moved to New York four weeks ago.

"It's probably your Mom," Crystal yelled from the kitchen.

I jogged from the bedroom where I'd been organizing my few pieces of clothing and desperately attempting to figure out how to create office outfits for my receptionist job. I picked up the receiver.

Me: Hi Mom.

Mom: How did you know it was me?

Me: (*Laughing*) Crystal and I don't know anyone else in New York and you call like clockwork on Sundays.

Mom: I suppose that's true. How are things

going? I never asked you about your apartment. Is it clean? Is it in a safe neighborhood? Your Dad and I see all kinds of reports on the news about how New York is unsafe – filled with drugs and all.

Me: Relax, Mom. You already asked me about the apartment, and I told you then that we're in a safe neighborhood.

Mom: Oh good. And you have a doorman for your apartment? Is it secure?

Me: (*Pause*) Uh…You should see how secure the mail is. Nobody's getting near our mail, that's for sure.

Mom: Oh? Well, how's the job going?

Me: Great, but I do have a problem. I don't have many office-type clothes to wear, and I don't have the budget to buy a new wardrobe.

Mom: I've got the perfect thing. I'll whip up a couple of skirt and vest combos that you can mix and match. All you'll need are a few blouses. I can mail the pieces to you in a few days.

Me: You'd be a lifesaver, Mom! Oh, by the way, how's Dad been doing with my move to New York.

Mom: You know your Dad. He's tolerating it. He did agree to the arrangement – temporarily.

Me: Ugh. That's all I need…more pressure!

Mom: What do you mean? Who else is putting pressure on you?

Me: The usual. Me! But I'm sure I simply need to settle in. Once I find a writing internship, I'll begin to feel like my career is moving forward again. In the meantime, thanks for bailing me out on those work outfits, Mom.

Mom: Okay, I need to start sewing. Bye, Margaret.

Me: Bye. And thanks Mom.

I hung up the receiver. Despite Dad's pressure and Mom's fears about me living in New York, I smiled knowing she had my back. *And now I don't have to worry about the "office wear" crisis facing me in the bedroom!*

# 3

# Expanding Our NYC World

*April, 1981*

Things were going smoothly with our move to the Big Apple. Crystal's waitressing job at the Silver Star Diner brought in extra cash until her semester started. Since she worshipped the fashion world, I expected her to sail through her design program.

I settled into my position at Radio City Music Hall nicely. Next on my agenda, I needed to secure a creative outlet to balance my life. A writing partner or group might snap me out of my creativity drought, but I had no idea where to find either in such a huge city. When I lived in tiny Church Creek, all I did was complain and whine that the nearby towns didn't offer enough opportunities for me to write. Now settled into the world's largest city, I felt overwhelmed to the point of becoming immobilized. Worried if the complacency I experienced back in Church Creek followed me to the Big Apple, panic set in. *Deep breaths, Margie. Something's bound to turn up…*

After only a few weeks of living in the city, Crystal decided we needed to throw a party. I arrived home from work on a Thursday evening with take-out. It was our Kung Pao Chicken night. Before I had a chance to put the food bag down on the kitchen table, Crystal pounced with her announcement.

"Two things. First, a package arrived from Church Creek

today. Probably those work outfits your Mom made for you. But way more important, *mon amie*…I've been thinking about this all day. We need to have a party. It'll be totally cool."

"Um, this has been brewing all day, you say." I laughed while deciding how to point out two obvious flaws to her plan. The new thing I learned about Crystal in our few weeks of living together: tread lightly and let her think each idea originated from her. "I love the party concept. Don't get me wrong. But are you forgetting that A) we don't have any furniture to speak of, and B) we don't know anyone in New York?"

Crystal brushed off my concerns with a wave of her hand. "Right. Leave the guest list to me. Besides, it's *très* 'New York' and *très chic* to have plenty of room to move around at a party."

I reluctantly gave in.

****

The evening of the party arrived, and the event turned out better than I expected. Crystal came up with guests from our limited resources: our apartment building and her place of employment. But hey, our tiny universe had begun to expand.

First to arrive: two guys living on the building's fourth floor, whom Crystal had met at the lobby mailbox a week ago.

The younger of the pair introduced himself. "I'm Gordo. I know, I know…an unusual name around here but where I'm from – Laredo, Texas – it was a playground nickname that stuck."

"Does 'Gordo' have any special meaning?" I asked. "It sounds almost Spanish to me."

"Yes ma'am. But y'all will probably laugh. It means 'fat.'"

We did chuckle at that piece of information. Standing about five-foot-five, Gordo was of slender build, not at all heavy. His accent confirmed his Texas roots. At around twenty-four or twenty-five years old, his youthful features were framed by dark hair in tight curls and a thin moustache over his upper lip.

He was accompanied by his partner, Doug, who not only towered over Gordo's slight frame, but also looked to be at least ten years his senior. Doug's muscular body, receding hairline along a wide forehead, deep-set dark brown eyes, and sharp cheekbones created a first impression of meeting a thug. This impression was dispelled by his soft-spoken greeting with a touch of a Bronx accent and his fashion choice of a scarf worn ascot-style around his neck. An interesting and dramatic style combo, for sure.

The next guest, Girard, lived across the hall from us. I'd seen him exit his apartment and jog down the stairs once or twice, rarely looking up. But then, who could tell where he gazed behind the Ray Ban sunglasses he wore day and night? Girard looked like a magazine model – sculpted cheekbones, cropped blond hair, and a muscular six-foot frame. Very GQ model-ish. Crystal had been able to corner him and invite him to our little soiree.

"There's beer in the fridge, guys. Help yourself," Crystal announced.

Our tight budget permitted us to offer cheap beer, chips, and onion dip. We splurged with the addition of Ritz Crackers and a block of cheddar cheese. Along with the food, paper plates and napkins were arranged buffet-style on the kitchen table. Everyone grabbed a beer from the refrigerator and served themselves a plate of snack food before finding their way into the living room.

We didn't have much furniture in the living area, other than a bookcase, an old ottoman, and a folding screen. We had to get creative. With only two kitchen chairs for guest seating, we pulled pillows off the bed and piled them in the corner of the living room to function as seating. Guests placed their plates or beers on the windowsill, bookcase or floor, depending on where they plopped themselves down. While this party may not have been the "New York *chic*" fantasy that Crystal envisioned, it was nice having a small group where we all could be in one place and get to know each other. It all kinda worked.

"What do you do, Girard?" Crystal asked. "No wait…let me guess. You work in retail, something high-end like Saks, right?"

"Nope," he said. "I wait tables."

"Although at high-end restaurants, that's for sure," Doug added with an odd sarcastic edge.

"Oh, you and Gordo know Girard then?" I asked.

"We've overlapped living in this building for…how many years now, Girard?" Doug asked.

"Not sure," Girard responded icily. *Ouch. The tension coming from Girard seeped into the living room air.* Either Girard didn't want to talk to Doug, or he seemed to be concealing details. *Interesting.*

Doug continued, "Well, at least five years since you moved in, right?"

"Yeah, maybe. Anyone need a beer?" Girard got up and moved to the kitchen.

Crystal jumped up to follow him. "Well, I wait tables too, though hardly at a high-end establishment." *Do I sense that Crystal's flirting with Girard? She totally is. She's also oblivious to the chilly exchange between our guests. Typical Crystal.*

With Crystal and Girard in the kitchen, I had an opportunity to ask Gordo and Doug about their lines of work. Doug ran operations for a small Off-Off-Broadway theater in Greenwich Village, although he aspired to be a stage director. Gordo freelanced as a writer, working a day job in data processing to pay the bills.

"Wow, your interest areas are fascinating. I have a bit of theater background, mostly college and community theater. As a Classical Voice Major in college, they encouraged us to audition for all the musicals."

The minute I uttered the words "theater background," Doug's eyebrows arched in renewed interest. "Ever perform any Shakespeare?"

"Alas, no. Sorry to disappoint…Wait! Does *Kiss Me, Kate* count? Lots of Elizabethan banter in that musical. I played Bianca in a college production."

He let out an exaggerated sigh and struck a comical melodramatic, wrist-to-forehead pose. "Alack…Broadway's rip off of Shakespeare's *Taming of the Shrew* DOES NOT count." Gordo and I laughed at the theatrics. Doug followed up. "You do know your musicals, Margie."

"Like I said, I performed in my fair share."

"Ah, Gordo, do I sense an aspiring actor among us?" Doug said.

I jumped in. "No, no. The whole reason I'm here in New York is to work on my writing career. Truthfully, I'm overwhelmed on what to do next as far as writing goes. And by overwhelmed, I mean I'm stagnating."

Gordo straightened in his chair. "I don't figure you'd be interested, but I belong to a small writing group. We get together once a month at Dr. Ava Rodriguez's apartment in SoHo. We got one slot to fill. If you wanna work on a lotta different writing styles, this might be the perfect thing."

Without hesitation, I said, "Yes, yes!," jumping at the chance to work in a critique group. *Could this be the thing I need to jerk me out of my writing doldrums?* Gordo told me he'd make the arrangements with Dr. Rodriguez and get back to me with meeting details and the fee, which was minimal.

In my excitement I didn't realize how late it had gotten or how quiet the kitchen had become. Gordo and Doug helped me pick up a few items in the living room and toss them in the kitchen's trash bin. There was no sign of Girard and Crystal.

"They probably went out for air, is all," offered Gordo. As he and Doug headed to our long hallway to leave, Doug turned and said with great flourish, "Parting is such sweet sorrow."

Gordo laughed, hitting him gently on the arm. "Ignore this Shakespeare nut. He's always spouting off one quote or another." They said their goodbyes and left for their own apartment.

Chuckling as I put away the leftover food, a knock on the door interrupted my chore. More like hard pounding. Thinking Crystal must have forgotten her keys, I shouted, "Hold your horses" and proceeded down the hall. More pounding accompanied my walk to the door.

The second I opened the door, in burst a young woman with vivid pink bursts of color streaked over brown hair, thick black eyeliner around her upper and lower lids, and bright red lipstick. She wore a dull ochre waitress uniform trimmed with a brown collar similar to Crystal's Silver Star Diner outfit and carried a beat-up suede backpack slung over one shoulder. She pushed right past me, exclaiming, "I've gotta pee!" and ran toward the kitchen.

"Uh…Okay," I said.

A voice from inside our closet-sized toilet area shouted, "You must be Margie. I'm Alissa."

"Um…Hi?" Needless to say, confusion took over as I wondered how she found the toilet so swiftly and how she knew my name. "And how do you know me?"

"Oh, I don't." *Well, that certainly did not clear anything up.*

After what seemed like an eternity, the voice/Alissa emerged. "Much better. I was ready to burst."

She had completely changed into a different outfit. *No wonder it took her forever in the bathroom.* Alissa, a woman in her mid-twenties, stood before me wearing a short orange and brown plaid mini skirt with a fuzzy chocolate pullover sweater over jeans that were tucked into a pair of short, black boots. Oh, and around her neck she sported a choker with metal studs and a bracelet to match. *What a transition! It must have been a Mary Poppins' trick watching her pull all these clothes out of her suede bag!*

"So, you're the super straight roommate, huh?" Not giving me time to process what she meant or how I must have been described to Alissa, she plunged ahead, "Where's Crystal?" She peeked into the living room. "And where's the damned party?"

"Gosh, I'm sorry. Crystal took off with Girard. Maybe she forgot you'd be coming."

"What a total bitch," she said half-joking. "Crystal knew I worked the late shift at the diner tonight. She ditched me for a hot guy, right?" *Ah, Crystal's co-worker from the diner. Of course.*

"I don't know if she went for a walk or what. But look, you're here now. Are you hungry, wanna beer?

"You got any root beer?" she said, gazing around at what I figured she thought was our unique kitchen arrangement. "Wow, you guys have made it to the big time with this 'shower-in-the-kitchen' set up."

I handed her a root beer and pressed her for specifics. "What do you mean? We think it's bogus."

"True, but you can't expect these old buildings to be high-end penthouses, you get what I mean? You should see my apartment on East 91st Street. I have a freakin' bathtub in the middle of my kitchen with a hinged board that swings down and serves as my kitchen table. No kidding." She paused to take a huge swig of her root beer before adding, "I'd kill for a shower!" and released a loud belch.

"I can't even imagine," I said, not sure how to respond to her kitchen description or her…er, gaseous punctuation.

Alissa and I chatted a bit about how she ended up in New York from her home in Cleveland. She pretty much left home at eighteen and never looked back. Closed-mouthed about her relationship with her parents, I sensed there was a story there, an unhappy one, but I didn't pry. Despite our completely different backgrounds and goals – I came to NYC with specific aims; Alissa came to NYC with no goals and remained rudderless – we hit it off nicely. I'm sure my father would have dismissed her immediately based on her appearance, but who cared if she had pinkish hair and bold makeup? Aside from the belches, Alissa seemed nice and interesting. It was after one-thirty a.m. when she grabbed her bag and headed home.

I finished putting the last bits of party food away and wondered about Alissa's "…you're the super straight roommate…" comment. Crystal had a reputation of being a party girl back in Cambridge – known to drink a lot, even experiment with pot and who-knows-what-else, and certainly had her choice of boyfriends. Compared to her, I guess I would have been labelled "Sister Margaret." *The main thing is that's all in the ancient past. Crystal is focused on the future now – I hope.*

I started to wipe the kitchen table when I heard the apartment door open. A giggling Crystal skipped down the long hall and into the kitchen. She launched into a barrage of stream-of-consciousness thoughts and questions, never allowing me a chance to respond.

"Oh, great, you're still awake. Sorry I left you with the

cleanup. Wasn't that the most radical party? I knew it would be. And fun. And great to meet people in our building, don't you think? Perfect." At last, she took a big breath.

"Geez, Crystal. Take a chill pill. You're rambling," I said. "Did you and Girard go for a walk?"

"Yep. We walked down by the East River. Did you know there's a park down there? It's super cool, especially at night with the lights, and the lights."

"Yeah, you said that."

"I did? How funny," she said, giggling. "So pretty by the river though. We'll have to go to that park, Margie. You'll love it. And then, guess what? Girard and I came back to his apartment and…oo…he kissed me. He's totally cool, don't you think? I mean, what a hunk!"

"Well, it sounds like you had quite a night. You must be exhausted and it's getting late. You ready for bed?"

"Nah. I feel revved up. I don't think I can sleep for hours! I mean, I'm excited, exhilarated. I met a new guy; we had a great party; way too much pulsing through my brain right now. You go on, Margie. I want to hang out for a while. *Bon soir*."

"Okay then," I said and headed to the bedroom. When I got to the doorway, I turned and said, "Oh, I almost forgot. Your friend Alissa arrived after her shift at the diner. She's nice."

"Oh shit," Crystal said, throwing her sweater on the chair. "By the way," she yelled from the living room. "Girard told me that Doug and Gordo are partners…and I don't mean business partners."

Brushing my hair in the bedroom, I let her comment sink in. Deep breaths were not helping. I brushed harder and harder as I processed the evening's events. Crystal insisted on having this party then took off with Girard and left me with the hostess duties. When she finally returned, she ended up uttering unkind nonsense about two guests whom she barely took the time to know. *Geez! I need to address this.*

I peeked my head through the bedroom door frame. "Do you have a problem with Doug and Gordo being gay, Crystal?"

She looked a bit panicked, like a child caught in the act of being naughty. "Uh, well…Girard pointed it out, that's all."

"Well, then it sounds like Girard has an issue, doesn't it? Look Crystal, Gordo and Doug are extremely intelligent, friendly, and fun. If you had stuck around tonight you would have found that out. Get to know them as people, okay?

Crystal looked down and fidgeted with her hands but didn't respond. I muttered goodnight and withdrew to the bedroom. *A perfectly uncomfortable ending to a perfectly lovely first party.*

## 4

# Navigating Doubts

*May, 1981*

Based on Gordo's recommendation, I received the slot in the writers' group and attended my first meeting in May. Facilitated by Dr. Ava Rodriguez, the group met in her apartment in Manhattan's SoHo neighborhood. Gordo and I took the subway at the Lexington station to the Spring Street stop, practically at her doorstep on the corner of Spring and Lafayette. Climbing one flight of stairs, we knocked and entered her apartment. The bohemian look of the small but neat one-bedroom space embraced me like a warm, fuzzy blanket. The tiny kitchen, open and accessible to the large living room, used a counter that served as an eating/food prep area. The colorful living room took my breath away – filled with books, textiles, and plants. Floor to ceiling artwork pieced together like a jigsaw puzzle included Havana posters of various sizes, presumably prints by Cuban artists depicting dark-skinned musicians in yellow or red shirts or dresses and straw hats, or streetscapes of pink, blue, and cream-colored buildings leading to an azure sea. Under this maze of pictures sat a U-shaped bench, cushioned and draped in rust-colored fabric, the major furnishing in the large living area. Throw pillows of various sizes and textures rested along the two side walls and under the double window facing the front of the apartment. Instead of window shades, a series of plants in thickly knotted macrame hangers created privacy from the street below.

Wearing a black and red print maxi dress, Dr. Rodriguez, or Dr. R. as the group called her, relaxed on a rocking chair facing the makeshift sofas. Once the four writers assembled, she addressed the group. "Let me begin by reiterating our mission for our new member, but also to refresh these ideas for all of us. First, we encourage writers to explore a variety of styles by changing writing genre assignments each month. One month we may write poetry, the next we may focus on short stories or journalistic articles or short plays."

Gordo asked, "How do you like the sound of that, Margie?"

Though I hated being put on the spot in front of new people, my exhilaration about the group bubbled out. "These goals sound challenging and exciting – exactly what I need at this point in my writing career." Everyone nodded their heads. *I guess they all feel the same way!*

Having established our purpose, the group introduced themselves and talked about their current work or preferred genre. I already knew Gordo personally, but was interested to learn more about his writing goals. He mentioned his desire to write about the struggles he faced as a gay man in a committed relationship as well as the prejudices and abuses gay people faced in New York City. *Personal and raw and brave.*

Miguel, originally from Puerto Rico, moved to the United States when he was ten. Standing at about five-foot ten, he had warm brown skin with a patch of dark facial hair on his chin and across his upper lip, making him look older than twenty-four. His outfit also aged him. The black jeans and boots seemed typical enough, but the untucked, long-sleeved shirt in a four-block pattern of gray, white, and black, appeared rather dressy for our casual group meeting. *Maybe he had a date afterward?* I found him intriguing – his musky cologne, his slight Spanish accent, his intelligent eyes shining behind wire-framed glasses.

"Short stories are my main strength," Miguel said in a quiet voice. "I create stories sparked by my city observations and *El Barrio* neighborhood: pigeons in Washington Square Park, trash on the sidewalk, graffiti on the subway cars, or mom and pop businesses." *Interesting and so serious.*

Miguel's wavy black hair partially covered his face, like a veil filtering his soft voice when he spoke. It was hard to know if he was purposely creating a mask to hide from us or if he was simply shy? His good looks, intelligence, and mild manner piqued my interest immediately. What can I say… his quiet mystique drew me in. *What goes on behind those glasses?*

And then there was Gwendolen, who claimed to be a serious poet, sitting cross-legged on the sofa's far end, notebooks and journals surrounding her like a castle wall protecting a princess. She wore a short-sleeved pink and blue plaid jumpsuit with a thin pink belt and pink moccasin-type shoes, straight from the Spring J.C. Penney Catalog. Gwendolen talked incessantly with constant head bobs that caused her blond ponytail to fly around like a horse's tail shooshing flies on a summer day. At twenty-three years old, Gwendolen's favorite topic was mostly herself and she addressed us as if we were her "royal subjects."

"I plan to change the world with my poetry," she announced in her introduction. She read her latest short poem, which she "proclaimed" would clarify all we needed to know about her. To tell the truth, I had a hard time figuring out what the heck the poem was about, but I forced myself to keep an open mind. I found Gwendolen condescending to the max. *You've been with people like her before, Margie. Don't let her get under your skin.*

As it drew closer to my turn to introduce myself, butterflies fluttered away in my stomach. My mind teemed with doubts: *What am I doing here? Gordo has enthusiastic writing goals, Miguel seems to be an artistic writer, and Gwendolen has...I'm not exactly sure yet but she's a poet.* That negative voice in my head kicked into overdrive and continued to feed me with self-doubts about my writing skills. My interests in journalistic writing and music criticism seemed overly...practical. Intimidated by this enthusiastic group of writers, my palms sweated and a knot formed in my belly. *Snap out of it, Margie!* On the other hand, I did come to New York to kickstart myself out of complacency and explore other avenues. *Who knows? Maybe I'll shock the world and become a poet?*

"My interest in writing musical reviews began when I toured with the King Vido Swing Band as a singer. Two band members, Jimmy and Chaz, took me under their wing and taught me about different genres and styles of music," I told the group.

"Wow, you sang in a traveling band. I'd love to do that." Gwendolen interrupted my introduction to make it all about her. "To be onstage with all eyes on me! Plus, my country club-obsessed parents would be horrified." She then became consumed by her own maniacal, high-pitched giggle that sounded like a frightened turkey the day before Thanksgiving.

"Well, that's not really the point. I wrote reviews in my journal while on tour, which led to reviewing bands for the local newspaper back home in Maryland, which led to me making the leap to come to New York in search for bigger writing gigs, hopefully an internship."

"Do you think you only wanna write reviews, Margie?" Gordo asked. "I mean, let's say other writing opportunities came along. Would you wanna go after that?"

Dr. R. chimed in, "A good question for all of us to consider?"

*That was a good question.* Did I want to be the way Crystal must have described me to Alissa, the "straight roommate," a person who never navigated beyond the norms, never took risks, never got out of the car? Or did I want to let go of my personal fears and doubts to follow where my creative juices might lead me, despite who may try to influence my decisions, even my Dad?

"Well, in my case..." I said, attempting to get back on track, "...so far I've written reviews and articles, reported on the who-what-when-where-why, and occasionally talked about how music made me feel. That's about as deep as I've gone. To answer your question, Gordo, I'm open to other opportunities, although I feel that journalism is my strength. But I'm here in this group and in New York to explore new things and see what's next for me."

After introductions, Dr. R. led us in a warmup activity "to stimulate creativity," she said with a barely present Spanish accent hinting at her Cuban roots. It was a simple writing prompt; nothing off the hook unusual. We each received an index card with a two-word starter, like "I want..." or "I can't..." or "I regret..." or "If I...." From this simple prompt, we were to write a journal response. Her dark eyes twinkled as she challenged us to dig deeply, reflect silently, and tap into our inner beings. I loved her instantly. This was exactly the sort of exercise I needed to shake me out of my writing rut.

After that great warmup, Dr. R. introduced the genre assignment for the month. And what was the genre for the first month? Poetry! The very word made me break out in hives and a cold sweat! To say I felt freakin' anxious would be an understatement. I preferred journalism, especially reviewing musical gigs, as I had stressed in my introduction to the group. Why couldn't she have chosen any other topic for my first go-around with this group? *Buck up, Margie. Keep telling yourself: You are a writer*!

For the rest of the time, we read and experimented with different forms of poetry. The afternoon flew by between reading poetry samples selected by Dr. R., quiet writing time when we toiled in our journals attempting to emulate each style, and a short period when a couple of group members bravely read their poems to the group. I was not one of those brave souls. *Typical of me…I'm a big old coward when it comes to sharing my work.*

At the meeting's end, Gordo and I gathered our belongings, said our goodbyes, and strolled in the warm May sunshine to the subway station to catch the train uptown. We climbed down the stairway from street level to the underground platform, confronted by the undeniable stagnant water-urine-dead rat subway smell. *I will never get used to that pungent odor.* Since I had purchased a slew of tokens on our earlier trip, I merely needed to fish out one from my change purse. Once we inserted our tokens and entered the turnstile, we settled onto the platform to wait for our train. On Saturdays, the train schedule was slightly different than on weekdays, so we expected to have to wait a bit. *Weekday versus Weekend schedules…Local versus Express trains. Lots to learn about navigating the NYC subway system.*

As we waited, Gordo and I chatted about the writing group, and I gushed about the experience. "Dr. R. is great. She made me feel welcome and comfortable. And I love how each writer in the group had different writing goals."

"Yes ma'am, she's good at both teaching and writing. I wish she could get a job at New York University but so far, no."

"You mean she's applied before but never landed a position?" I asked.

"Yep. She has a doctorate and teaching experience but she's always getting passed over. I keep wondering if it's the double whammy: She's Cuban-American, and she's a woman."

"Surely, there are women on the English faculty at the university," I countered.

"Not many. Look it up." *So much for the threat of women-libbers taking over the world. It's 1981 and women with doctorates are struggling to get college teaching positions? What gives?*

As I was pondering this injustice, I noticed Gordo's facial expression change. His eyes darted around, scanning further down the subway platform, and his forehead creased with worry lines. In a flash, this jerky guy came right up in my face and yelled, "Why the hell you hangin' out with that faggot?" Taken aback, I didn't know what to do or say. Voiceless and scared.

Gordo grabbed me by the arm and said quietly, "Come on. Keep moving." We walked at a measured pace down the platform toward a larger group of people and blended in, while the guy kept yelling until we were out of his sightline. Clearly no stranger to harassment, Gordo remained silent, eyes straight ahead.

On the other hand, I began to babble. An apology spewed forth for not speaking up, not saying anything to that asshole. Gordo stopped me.

"Margie, you'll learn soon enough that in this city it's safest to walk away and blend in. Safety in numbers, that's what I always say."

"But it's not right, Gordo. Neither of us was bothering that guy. I should have given him a piece of my mind."

"No, ma'am. You don't wanna mess with that corn-fed heifer of a jerk."

"It sounds like you know him."

"It's not the first time he's bothered me and my friends at

this station."

"My God, Gordo. That's awful. All the more reason, I should have stepped in."

"What are you gonna do, slap him silly? Bless your heart."

"I could tell him to mind his own business."

Gordo turned to face me directly as the subway train could be heard racing toward our platform. "Margie, look at me. You gotta lot to learn. You might think that'd be a noble gesture, but you'd only be spelling trouble for me, a gay man. Who'd be the one getting the double beating? Trust me."

"No wonder you want to write about struggles gay people face here in the city."

"That's right."

I asked, "Then I take it you'll be writing from personal experience…I mean about the abuses??

"Right again, Margie. I wanna write about my experiences and those of my community. We need to tell more stories about the harassment and injustices we share. We're all human beings wanting to live our lives, like everybody else."

I saw the pain and passion in Gordo's eyes as he spoke. And of course, I supported his writer's purpose.

"In the meantime, Margie, today's lesson: Safety in numbers on the subway platform, safety in numbers. It goes for women as well as gay folks. You'll learn."

During the subway ride uptown, Gordo and I sat quietly. I stared at the graffiti-covered interior of our train car, reflecting on the platform incident and about other discrimination I'd observed during the past several years. I felt the urge to pull out my journal and scribble down my rambling thoughts.

*Subway Incident*

*Here I am learning to speak up, trying to use my voice when I see transgressions, and now I'm told that there are times, at least in New York City, when I should keep my mouth shut. What Gordo says makes sense though. There's a lot to learn…and not only about this city. I look forward to reading Gordo's writing.*

# 5

# Summer's Looming Threat

*June-August, 1981*

The first thing I discovered about living in New York City in the summertime was the near impossibility of staying cool on the sixth floor of a brownstone with no air conditioning. A fan was essential; multiple fans even better. And creating a cross breeze when both sets of windows faced brick walls – an effort in futility!

The second thing I learned was that summer heat brought out the lunacy in the many crazies who already lived in New York, and most of those folks happened to live in our apartment building. "Broom Man" lived in 5C, directly under our unit…so dubbed because, whenever we walked across our floor, the noise drove him nuts, causing him to beat on the ceiling with his broom handle. "Typing Paper Poster Boy" lived in 3B. He received this title because he plastered his outer door with white sheets of paper upon which he had written Bible quotes. Apparently, his mission: to spread The Word via black marker on stark white typing paper. This would not seem bad until the one day I found his door wide open and sneaked a peek inside his apartment. He had also covered every single wall area, piece of furniture, and even the floor with those typing paper-sized posters. *Too much!*

In apartment 2A an ancient woman who must have been

over a hundred years old lived by herself. She wasn't crazy – crazy, no; extremely old, yes. Crystal and I walked by one day and saw her leering out through an inch wide opening. We both stopped to greet her.

"Good morning," I said. "How are you today?" Silence. The woman stared at us, eyes darting back and forth. The apartment was pitch black behind her.

I raised my voice and asked, "Are you alright? Do you need anything? Maybe groceries from the store?" Again, silence and more staring. Then, suddenly and without warning, she slammed the door. The rumor was that she had lived in that same apartment since the building was constructed in the late-nineteenth century. A wild rumor, but she could have grown up in this building and never left.

We continued down the stairs consumed with concern for the elderly woman.

"Maybe she was deaf or didn't speak English," Crystal said.

"Could be. Do you think anyone checks on her? I wonder if she has any family nearby. Does she have enough to eat? And did you see how dark her apartment looked?"

"Right. And what about that prune-like face…spooky!"

"Crystal! Be nice." The woman's sallow, deeply creased face and white straggly hair did give her an otherworldly appearance. But Crystal always had a way of belittling others. I remembered in high school she and her "cool" friends used to walk past the Special Education classroom, name-calling and laughing. *I guess in many ways she hasn't changed.*

****

While the heat could be a disadvantage to city living in the summer, there were advantages. For one thing, our neighborhood became less frenetic, almost quiet. Perhaps the wealthy all rushed off to their summer homes in the Hamptons. However, midtown Manhattan, where I worked, transformed into a madhouse in the summer. Tourists loved Rockefeller Center, Fifth Avenue, Times Square, and the Theater District – all within walking distance of my work environment.

Radio City Music Hall had its own special show running during the summer of 1981, creating even more congestion during matinee times. *America*, an extravagant revue even by Radio City Music Hall standards, opened on March 13th with a planned twenty-seven-week run through the summer. The creative production team pulled out all the stops for *America* and the public relations office made sure the world knew all about it through advertisements, flyers, posters, and billboards. Any announcement leaving the building focused on the razzle-dazzle:

A cast of seventy-six including the beloved Rockettes.

A ninety-four-foot-wide back curtain bedazzled with half a million mirrors.

A thirty-five-piece orchestra supported by two pipe organs and a synthesizer.

A computerized projection system with over nine hundred images.

A ninety-minute tribute made up of eleven vignettes paying tribute to each state in our nation.

*Radio City Music Hall does NOT mess around when it comes to producing spectaculars.*

On a weekly basis, Miss Chambers pulled me into promotional projects related to *America*. Mailings, assembling unique invitations to V.I.P. guests for pre-opening events, and reviewing supply orders as they arrived via messenger. These promotional activities made the days speed by, even if much of it included mundane envelope stuffing.

Miss Chambers' voice rang out with specific folding and insertion instructions. "Make sure your folds are identical. Every letter must face the same direction as you insert it into the envelop." *A stickler for precision!*

I created a working rhythm: grab a letter from the pile to my right, first fold up exactly one third from the bottom of the paper, second fold down from the top of the paper, grab an envelope from the pile to my left, insert the letter into the envelope facing front.

"Place full envelopes in the bin straight ahead," Miss Chambers continued. "We'll affix mailing labels later."

Although the stack of ten thousand envelopes loomed before me, I didn't mind. Mindless work like that allowed me to mull over writing ideas for our monthly group, play with words for a haiku, or work on imagery for a short story. Before I knew it, the pile disappeared, and Miss Chambers plopped ten thousand mailing labels in front of me. *Oh joy!*

****

Crystal hadn't been around much since starting classes at Parsons School of Design. Working on a Bachelor of Fine Arts in Fashion Design, she threw herself into Draping, Patternmaking, and Design Sketching courses. But she wigged out when she learned that all first-year students were required to take Basic Sewing.

"You have totally got to be kidding me!" she blurted, mulling over the course requirements one evening. "I've been sewing since I was eight years old. I grew up on a Singer."

"Don't freak out about it, Crystal. Your parents are covering your tuition. Take the sewing class, breeze through it, and feel good about starting the program on positive footing."

She grunted in response. "It's beneath me to take a Basic Sewing course, that's all."

Despite Crystal's initial resentment, she settled into the design program and spent a ton of time between classes at the school's studio on sewing projects. Between school, waitressing two evenings a week at the Silver Star Diner, and the times she called in sick at the diner to hang out with Girard, I rarely saw her. Those two had gotten pretty cozy. *Not sure if Girard gets sleazebag or super cool status. Too soon to tell. I do know that Crystal is wild about him.*

****

I planned to meet Doug and Gordo at the diner for lunch one Saturday in early June. When I arrived, they were seated in our favorite booth at the window facing East 65th Street. Three iced teas had already been delivered to the table. As I approached, they seemed to be arguing, a rarity for those two lovebirds.

"I think we should be taking these reports seriously, Doug," Gordo said in an exasperated tone.

"It's eight cases, Gordo. No big deal. Eight gay men happen to all come down with a similar illness-"

"Disease, Doug. The experts say it's a disease! And today's *New York Times* article is reporting cases in both San Francisco and New York." Gordo's voice was rising.

"Okay, okay. Disease. But it still seems to me that the media is hyping this thing up."

"What's going on?" I asked as I slid into the booth facing them.

"Gordo's all upset about this article in today's *Times*." Doug handed me the newspaper. Reading out loud, I highlighted the parts that stood out to me.

> Rare Cancer Seen in 41 Homosexuals…
> Doctors in New York and California have

> diagnosed among homosexual men forty-one cases of a rare and rapidly fatal form of cancer. Eight victims died less than twenty-four months after the diagnosis was made...cause of the outbreak is unknown...The sudden appearance of the cancer, called Kaposi's Sarcoma, has prompted a medical investigation...first appears as violet-colored spots on the body... swelling in lymph node glands...Cancer is not believed to be contagious, but conditions that might precipitate it, such as particular viruses, might account for an outbreak among a single group...no apparent danger to non-homosexuals.

"See right there." Doug grabbed the paper from my hands and jabbed at it. "'Cancer is not believed to be contagious.' This is a bunch of hype so the government can shut down gay clubs and make things worse for anyone who's different. A clear manipulation by the government and the media. I don't believe it's as serious as they're making it out to be."

"What do you think, Gordo?" I asked.

"I don't know what to think yet. But I tell you what. I'm gonna find out all I can. I gotta feeling in my gut that's not too pleasant."

Doug reached for Gordo's hand. "And that's the difference between you and me, Gordo. You worry about everything, and I worry about extraordinarily little."

"Well, somebody's gotta watch over you," Gordo said, leaning into Doug and finally letting a smile shine through.

Alissa approached the table with our orders: flaky spanakopita for me; pastrami and Swiss cheese sandwich with Russian dressing on rye for Doug; and Texas BBQ Burger with onion rings for Gordo. Once she placed all the food on the table, Alissa collapsed into the booth next to me, grabbed my iced tea, and took a huge swig.

"Thanks. I'm dying of thirst. Is it like 1000 degrees in here?"

"I'm comfortable, but anything's better than our apartment," I said. "Why do you think I keep coming in here for my main meals?"

"Idea for a great ad campaign: Free A/C with Your Meal at Silver Star Diner!" Doug laughed as he showed us a quick sketch he drew on a napkin of an air conditioner with the Silver Star Diner logo above.

"Very funny. Watch it or I'll report you to my boss for A/C abuse," Alissa said, jumping up to pick up an order in the kitchen.

"Okay, Margie. The food's arrived. You wanted to meet us for lunch to tell us your big news. What's going on?" said Gordo.

"Here's the skinny: I'm official. I got an internship with *SoHo Weekly News*, thanks to a recommendation from Dr. R.!"

"That's major," Gordo said.

Doug piled on his congratulations as well in his usual theatrical way, paraphrasing Shakespeare. "Be not afraid of greatness, Margie. Some are born great, some achieve greatness, and some have greatness thrust upon 'em."

"And some work in the shadow of other writers on the staff!" I added, laughing. "I was told I'll be working at the right hand of Josh Friedman, the editor. But more likely I'll be working with the underlings."

Alissa appeared out of nowhere with a pitcher of iced tea and slid into our booth again. She had an amazing habit of being everywhere at once, having overheard my news.

"That's totally bitchin', Margie," she said. "*SoHo Weekly News* was one of the first papers to interview The Ramones back in 1978, and they also ran an interview with The Talking Heads. I mean how freakin' cool is that."

"Well, I doubt I'll be assigned to a big-name musical artist anytime soon. I'll need to maneuver my way through the system, starting at the bottom, but this internship is a great opportunity for me to learn."

"Good for you," they all said.

*I truly appreciated the support of my growing New York family: Gordo, Doug, Alissa, and even Crystal, when she's around.*

****

As it turned out, my *SoHo Weekly News* assignments were even less high profile than I imagined. Throughout the entire month of July, the management had me planted in the office to "see what I could pick up from the other reporters." I wouldn't have minded this strategy if it hadn't included a huge amount of time at the ditto machine and being best friends with the Mr. Coffee maker!

After six weeks of "office clerk" duties with nary a glance at any of the staff writers' copy, I summoned the courage to have a chat with the assignment editor, Phil. I figured if I described my writing background again, he might understand my goals better. At least, during my interview, he seemed to hear me when I stressed that I wanted to write about music during my interview.

"You see," I said during my second meeting with Phil, "when I toured as a singer with a swing band in 1978, these two horn players taught me a ton about appreciating all kinds of musical genres, like jazz, bebop, funk, and R&B."

Phil chuckled. "Um, I can guarantee you won't be sent on any swing band assignments in Lower Manhattan. But it sounds like you're open to all styles of music. That's good. Keep that open mind, if you want to write for the *SoHo Weekly News*, okay?

"Sure, right. A journalist has to write without prejudice. I get that."

"Let's see where this goes, Margie. You seem curious, open-minded, and bright. A good combination."

*Not sure how much headway I made with that meeting, but he acted impressed anyway.*

****

The heat of late August meant many New Yorkers spent as much time as possible outside, unless they possessed A/C, of course. The Mall in Central Park became a veritable roller rink-o-rama, crammed with all abilities of skaters from the most expert skate-dancers with shoulder balanced boom boxes blasting out disco tunes to the wobbly beginners hanging on light poles for dear life. In other sections of the park, break dancers entertained visitors with their agile moves and gyrations. Along the walkways, benches were filled with alternating elderly folks feeding pigeons and budding musicians yearning for tips. For two friends looking for quiet and solitude, Gordo and I were forced to hike further into the park for a spot of shade near the lake, where we could catch a sweet breeze.

"Good spot?" I asked, already spreading out a crocheted pink and pale green afghan from my childhood bedroom. *Mom would wig out if she saw me using her hand-made throw on the ground!*

"Yes, ma'am," answered Gordo, his accent in full swing.

We settled in – Gordo with a copy of *New York Native*; me with my journal. I wanted to experiment on last month's writing group topic: Personal Essay, a genre I struggled with since it required honestly reflecting and expressing my inner thoughts and opinions. I was a work-in-progress when it came to the "expressing" part of that process.

Gordo and I silently read and wrote, enjoying the quiet of our lakeside spot when he blurted out, "Listen to this, Margie. It's an interview with Larry Kramer…"

"Wait, who's Larry Kramer?

"Ah darlin', you never heard of Larry Kramer? Writer, film producer? Anyway, a few weeks ago he held a meeting with over eighty gay men in his apartment to discuss what he's calling 'the epidemic affecting gay people.' He's starting to raise money 'cuz there's no public or private funds being raised to fight this damned thing."

"That's great, Gordo. We were talking about that *Times* article last month and how the doctors need money to start finding answers." Gordo showed me the *Native* interview. "But why isn't the government funding research or doing a public campaign or something?" I asked.

"I think we both know the answer," he said. "Nobody wants to talk about gay issues, especially 'a Gay Cancer' – that's what they're calling the Kaposi's Sarcoma, the 'Gay Men's Pneumonia.' It doesn't help that the researchers are calling this thing, GRID."

"What in the world is GRID?" I truly didn't know what Gordo was talking about.

"GRID. Gay. Related. Immune. Deficiency. GRID. Another misleading nickname. That way the world'll think only gay men get this horrible disease. And if it only affects gay men…well then why would the government waste money trying to understand it or treat it or even prevent it! Arg!" Gordo grabbed his face with both hands.

"I agree with you, Gordo. It's frustrating."

I doodled in my journal, mulling over the frustration when suddenly an idea popped into my head. "Gordo, I know this doesn't help anything at the moment, but it's got me thinking. I claim that I want to express myself, to use my authentic voice. But then when it comes to important issues like this, I'm a wimp – I retreat inside myself. But I'm not living in tiny Church Creek anymore, where the biggest controversy is a fisherman cheating during a fishing contest by hiding sinkers in his 'catch of the day.' I need to pay attention to politics, take a stand, read a damned newspaper. I can start right now with my personal essay for the group."

"Yes, ma'am. Now you're talking."

"What if I write an essay about the lack of research funding for this horrible disease, and about how I feel the government seems to be shying away from looking for answers to the cause and treatment, about how *The New York Times* and other media need to make this front-page news rather than hiding these articles in the back pages, for gosh sake!"

"Aw, Margie, darlin'. I do believe that you'd make Larry Kramer proud!"

I filled my blank journal page with random topics that needed further research, feelings that had surfaced during conversations with Gordo, even silly things like images that came to mind. I finished the entry with the following:

> *It's not much, but it's a start. I feel good about this essay assignment. I'm starting to understand that my writing can be more than reporting a bunch of facts and figures. I don't have to be afraid to tap into my own heart and express my feelings in my writing. How freeing!*

# 6

# New York Family Emerges

*September, 1981*

As the trees disguised themselves in their autumn apparel, transforming leaves from dark green to shades of gold, orange, and crimson, our growing New York family continued to evolve. By the end of September, Crystal excelled at Parsons School of Design, which surprised no one since she oozed "fashion-sense" even in her most casual moments. I never knew a girl who could roll out of bed and look as fashion-plate glamorous as Crystal. While I stumbled around the apartment in the morning in an oversized T-shirt, she would glide into the kitchen in a frilly designer night gown, looking fresh and glowing. *Geez...How the hell does that happen?*

While Crystal continued to do well with her classes, the writing group also thrived. Doug stayed busy with the new theater season, and my Radio City job remained status quo. The internship at *SoHo Weekly News* presented the only snafu in my otherwise workable world. I'd been asking, begging, pleading for a writing assignment for weeks with no luck. *Same conversation every time.*

"So, Phil," I'd start. "How's it looking for an assignment this week?"

"Hm?" Phil, a master at pretending he didn't hear his

employees, forced us to repeat our questions.

"Even a small review? It doesn't have to be a big name musical group. A small article would be fine." I heard the whine in my voice, which I hated since it smacked of desperation. *But I am desperate!*

He always ended the conversation in the worse possible way. "We'll see." *Agh! Why do parents use that phrase with their toddlers? It's not comforting. It's infuriating!* Needless to say, no progress had been made on the writing front at *SoHo Weekly News.*

****

On the East Side home front, things were progressing swimmingly. About six months into our New York City adventure, Crystal and I finally completed furnishing our apartment – the real New Yorker way – from items found on the street and a nearby thrift store. *God, my Dad would die if he knew this is the way we struggling New Yorkers did things!* Our street finds included a short stool—to serve double-duty as a plant stand or additional seating for dinner company—and one more kitchen chair. Who cared if the chair didn't match? As Crystal said, "Mismatching is *très chic.*" The important step was to spray for cockroaches *before* bringing any street finds into the apartment. We learned that the hard way!

The thrift shop treasures included a comfy overstuffed chair in a maroon print that complemented the ottoman we already owned, a small pine chest of drawers in need of a good washing and new set of pulls, and a wide bench in dark cherry to serve as a sofa in the living room until we could afford a real couch. The bench, chair, and chest of drawers only cost us sixty-five dollars. I splurged and bought a wooden rack with four hooks to put up in the kitchen. *Instant coat closet.* An additional ten-dollar hardware purchase, but totally worth it! Doug said he'd help us install it…he yammered on about needing to find where the wall studs were or it would fall down on our heads. He built enough sets to know about these things. I completely trusted him.

Of course, having the apartment fixed up meant Crystal's mind started revving up. I knew a Crystal idea was brewing when I came home from work one evening and saw her bouncing with excess energy, waving a list she created.

"I have an idea, a totally rad idea. Let's have a dinner party. A 'Night in Italy' dinner party. I've got it all figured out. It'll be super cool." Crystal's ideas and enthusiasm for...well, anything had become over the top lately.

"Let me reinterpret, to be clear. You want to have a spaghetti dinner, right? Because that's all we know how to cook."

"Oh, you're no fun…but yes. Won't that be totally amazing? We can have pasta and sauce and wine and salad and bread and some sort of dessert. Oo, and maybe we could find Italian music to play on the cassette player. Oo, and-"

"You are super hyper. Chill out, okay." I worried she would hyperventilate the way she rambled on. "We have enough chairs now, but if we invite the regular group, folks will still have to eat with a plate on their laps..."

"Speaking of invitations, why don't you invite that guy from your writing group you always talk about? What's his name, Miguel? Let's add new blood to our group. It'll be fun."

My cheeks burned hot as I flushed with embarrassment. "I don't always talk about Miguel," I said. "But it would be nice to mix things up a bit." *Do I always talk about Miguel? I didn't realize…* I changed the subject and rattled off party suggestions. "Okay, but we don't have a table big enough for a group that large. As long as guests will be okay doing the lap thing. Do you think that will go over…I mean with spaghetti? And we don't have wine glasses…I guess juice glasses will have to do."

"You worry too much. No one will care about any of those details. Stop being such a Betty Crocker."

Succeeding in redirecting Crystal from the Miguel topic, we set a date for our "Night in Italy" dinner party.

****

The crowd arrived for our Italian dinner: Alissa, Doug, Gordo, and Miguel, although no Girard. *Typical Girard no-show!* Alissa made a grand entrance with a new hair color, turquoise, and a six pack of root beer. Doug and Gordo contributed lemon gelato for dessert. Although Crystal plastered a fake smile on her face, her agitation at Girard's absence oozed while we ate angel hair spaghetti with homemade tomato sauce (my mom's recipe) and a side salad tossed with carrots, cucumbers, celery, and topped with mozzarella cheese. And the lemon gelato… completely refreshing. Crystal's assignment was to provide a loaf of Italian bread, but, as usual with her lately, she forgot. We had a Night in Italy dinner without bread! She did find time to scrounge up a cassette tape of Italian music at the thrift shop, adding to the ambience of the evening.

The spaghetti dinner was a hit. I introduced Miguel to Crystal and Alissa, who both nodded and winked their approval when his back was turned. *Please God, don't let my face turn red!* Miguel, though quiet, fit in with our ragtag group. When Broom Man sounded off, Miguel scrunched his face and commented, "*A lo loco,* yes?" We couldn't stop laughing which only made Broom Man pound harder. Even when we tried to be as quiet as possible by taking off our shoes and tiptoeing around the apartment, Miguel was right there with us – stocking feet and all!

After dessert, we relaxed and chatted in the living room, listening to Bruce Springsteen's "Hungry Heart" turned down low. Crystal slipped into the kitchen to make coffee. We heard a knock on the apartment door and realized that Girard had arrived – two and a half hours late! *Figures. That guy does whatever he wants, whenever he wants. But she likes him, for some odd reason.* I refocused on the living room discussion, which had morphed from favorite music genres to life stories.

Miguel had begun to respond to Alissa's question about his day job. "I work at my family's restaurant in *El Barrio,* my neighborhood in the far Upper East Side. It is near the small apartment I share with my cousin and brother. I do all sorts of odd jobs there – cooking, waiting tables, cleaning up."

"We have a profession in common, Miguel. I'm the Queen of waiting tables!" Alissa said. "How long has your family owned the restaurant?"

"They have been working with this restaurant since they arrived in the States, fourteen years ago. First as cooks and servers, then as managers. My mother, father, uncle, cousins – all worked hard and saved their money. Three years ago, the owner was ready to sell to my family. We all pitch in to keep it going."

I thought about Dad's general store and how tough it could be at times for him to keep it profitable. At least Dad inherited the store from his father. Miguel's family moved here from Puerto Rico, starting from scratch. That took a lot of courage and persistence and plain hard work.

Alissa turned her attention to Doug next. She wanted to know how Doug ended up in the city. He proceeded to tell us his life story.

"I'm New York born and raised, if you count the borough of Queens, and who doesn't? Blue collar father. Stay-at-home mother. Older brother who aspired to follow Dad into the fascinating world of plumbing. While I knew my way around construction and tools, I had no interest in the family business."

I was curious about Doug's current career choice. "How did you become involved in theater?"

"Ah, well...'There's the rub' as Shakespeare would say." He took a deep breath before proceeding. "Like many a misfit in high school – the non-athletic kids, the nerds, the closeted gays who were picked on by bullies – I sought refuge in the after-school theater program. Frankly, theater saved my life."

"Meaning?" I asked.

"I mean...daily rehearsals and building sets with that group of kids – theater kids – well, the high school auditorium became a refuge, a home away from home, a place of pure acceptance, a second family...Need I go on?"

"Ah, I get it." I appreciated Doug's candor. "And where's your real family now, Doug?"

"Right here." He gestured to Gordo. "But if you're referring to Mother and Father...they're retired to the swamps of Florida – Tampa, I think. And my brother still plumbs away in Queens, though we rarely speak. I can safely say, our life styles don't exactly mesh."

Doug's voice sounded excessively bright as he threw off that last comment, as if he were suppressing the fact that this separation from his family truly did pain him. I wanted to alleviate his discomfort. *Or am I reacting to my own feelings of conflict with Dad?*

"Gosh, I'm sorry you don't have much contact with your family, Doug."

"Well, Margie. There comes a point in one's life, when, if others are pressuring one to live by their rules and social morals, one must take a stand. It's not easy but it's the only way to fly."

"Ain't that the truth," Alissa said. "And Gordo, what about

you? How did you end up in the city? And don't tell me you grew up in Queens with that Texas accent."

Gordo chuckled before unraveling the story of his childhood, one that he hadn't shared with me. I wondered if the recent one-sided media stories and depictions of the gay community were giving voice to his suppressed experiences.

"Well, I had me a bully of a daddy. And since I didn't live up to the image of a son he hoped for, well ...I figured I embarrassed him from the age of five onward. Never played T-ball or football or sports of any kind."

"And the whole world knows, sports is a religion in Texas!" Doug said.

"That sure is true. Since I preferred to read and write little stories, Daddy constantly called me 'sissy' and 'namby-pamby' growing up. Not 'cuz I was out of the closet or had a boyfriend or anything like that. More 'cuz I didn't fit the image he had in his mind of what his son should be. Or maybe he suspected. Hell...I knew from the time I hit elementary school. But either way, he made my life hell."

"That's freakin' horrible, Gordo. So, how did you end up here?" Alissa asked.

Gordo took a deep breath. "I was seventeen and Daddy had had enough of me, I guess. He came home from the corner bar around ten o'clock. I was finishing my math homework for school the next day. Outta nowhere, he up and smacked me across the face, real hard. Then he kicked me out of the house. Said he never wanted to see my pansy face again. I figure some Texas jerk made a comment to him at the bar that ticked him off. That was it."

"What about your mother?" I asked. "Didn't she try to stop him. You hadn't even finished high school yet."

“Mama? She was scared to death of Daddy and for good reason. He wasn’t only a bully to me. Daddy like to wear those belts with the huge shiny buckles. If you’re an intimidating bastard, that ole belt’s very convenient.”

“Aye, this is hard,” Miguel said, shaking his head. He had been following both Doug and Gordo’s family descriptions closely. “It seems bullying could be a theme for many stories, yes? By words or fists or a belt; by parents or others.”

Surprised by this deeply emotional reaction from Miguel, I asked, “Not wanting to pry, but are you speaking from personal experience?”

“In a way, yes…I can empathize with Doug and Gordo’s stories. When I came to America, I had much emotional and physical bullying at school. The other students did not like those of us who came here from Puerto Rico.”

“That’s sad, Miguel.

“Life in *El Barrio* – in East Harlem – was not an easy place to grow up in. There was harassment from gangs, temptations at each corner, and bullying at school.”

“You seem put together. How were you able to get through it?” Alissa asked.

“Strong parents. When my older brother had enough of the *blancos* bullying him at school, he started skipping, hanging out on the streets. When my father found out…*Ay caramba!*

“What happened? Did your father find him, dragging him back to school, screaming and yelling?” Alissa asked.

“That is what I thought would happen, but my father is wise. He walked the streets of *El Barrio* with my brother, took him through the worst alleys and rundown buildings where heroin addicts shot up. He turned to my brother, saying, ‘Son, I do not want this for you. You must learn to be strong so you can have a better life.'"

"That must have had a huge effect on your brother," Doug said.

"Yes, and also on me." Miguel then turned to Gordo, "My brother and I were lucky to have parents who supported us, Gordo. How awful for you to go through that abuse in your own home and at the hands of your father."

"It turned out to be a blessing for me," he continued. "I left that house with eighty dollars in my pocket and a change of clothes in a backpack. Hitched my way to San Antonio, took the Greyhound to New York, and never looked back. That was seven years ago. This is my home now." Doug reached for Gordo's hand.

"Doug, how did you guys get together?" I asked. "Was it soon after Gordo arrived in the city or much later?"

Doug took a long sip of wine. "Well, the truth is…I found him beat up outside a bodega in Hell's Kitchen two months after he arrived in New York. He was thin, hungry, and a mess. I brought him home to clean him up, but had no intention of starting anything relationship-wise. Hell, I wasn't a 'committed relationship' kinda guy. At that time, my entire social life existed around Christopher Street bars in the Village and one-night stands. I'm not proud of my past lifestyle – the gay clubs, the bathhouses, the wildness – but that's who I was. But when I met Gordo, listened to his story, saw his passion for life…and well, we connected like I'd never connected with anyone before. It sounds corny as heck, but a switch got flipped inside me. I not only wanted to spend time with him, to get to know him better, but I wanted to nurture him, to be a part of his life. After a while, all the other stuff became tiresome."

"Doug was there for me," Gordo added. "And that goes for

the entire gay community…my friends accept who I am and let me live my life. I work and pay my bills and my taxes. I don't hurt anybody and, aside from a few drunk jerks on the subway platform late at night, nobody hurts me. I don't understand why we can't all get along, whatever our religion, gender, skin tone, or hair color.

"Hey buddy," Alissa said. "Is that a crack about turquoise hair?"

They all laughed, and the mood lifted a bit. But I sank into my own thoughts. I wished my Dad could be part of this conversation, to hear how unthreatening gay people could be. Maybe he'd cool it with the ridiculous name calling and spouting off misinformation about groups he knows nothing about – whether gay folks, Blacks, Hispanics, or women!

I refocused on Gordo, reaching over to touch him on the shoulder. "Don't forget…you have a family right here. And you too, Miguel."

"That's right, Margie," Doug said. "According to Willy Shakespeare, 'Family is not an important thing, it's everything.'" *How* does *that man come up with a quote for any occasion? He amazes me.*

The party wound down with Alissa leaving to grab a cab for her apartment. At that point, we all realized that Crystal had split…probably gone off with Girard. *Good thing no one really wanted that coffee Crystal was making.* Doug, Gordo, and Miguel helped me gather and stack dishes in the sink. We chatted quietly, hoping the Broom Man had tucked himself in for the night.

Suddenly, the apartment door flung open with a crash. Laughter, singing, and shouts exploded down the long hall. Crystal danced into the kitchen in all her wild abandon followed by a grinning Girard. And of course, Broom Man added his two cents by pounding on his ceiling below.

"Now you've done it," Doug said directly to Crystal, half joking.

"Chill out, Broom Man!" Crystal yelled at the floor, while I tried to shush her.

"What happened to the party, you poopers," Crystal said.

Gordo and Doug did that "knowing look" toward each other that couples do when they silently tell each other it's time to go home.

"Early day at the theater tomorrow," Doug said. "Tech rehearsals all week. Duty calls." He and Gordo made a quick exit.

"What happened to the party?" Crystal repeated. "Where's Alissa?"

"The fresh air has an interesting effect on you. I see you found Girard," I said.

Crystal grabbed Girard's butt, causing him to jump. "Sure did."

I glanced over at Miguel, who stared at Crystal with head leaning forward and eyes questioning. Perhaps he wondered about the abrupt personality change he saw in her, from pre-Girard's appearance to now.

"It's after midnight. Alissa caught a cab home and the rest of us wanted to chill. I'm gonna clean up a bit and go to bed, okay?" I picked up a few dishes and placed them in the sink.

"Why are you being such a straight-laced nerd?" Crystal's words cut deep.

I froze. The hairs on my neck bristled and tension gripped my shoulders. Dropping the washcloth into the sink with a splash, I turned to face her. "What did you say?"

I think Girard sensed that I was angry because he-who-rarely-speaks piped up. "Come on Crystal. Let's go over to my apartment and listen to music."

And like a lemming blindly following its leader, Crystal trailed Girard out of the apartment, leaving me to fume over her rude comment until the morning. She'll brush it off with an insincere apology, which I'll accept, and life will go on. That was our dance: *She blurts; I get pissed; she feebly apologizes; I forgive. Been like that ever since we were lab partners in high school biology.*

Beyond bio class, we had little in common. Crystal sparkled as "Queen of Cambridge High's Beautiful People" – the jocks, cheerleaders, pep club suck ups. I, on the other hand, earned my badge as "Wallflower of the Year!" I found salvation in the school musicals, choir, and writing for the newspaper.

After I returned from touring with King Vido's Swing Band, Crystal reached out to me. More like clung to me – constantly hanging around at the Art Center or Doris Mae's Diner, where I worked part-time to save money for grad school. All her "la-dee-da" high school friends had abandoned her – gone to college and never looked back – while Crystal opted to stay home in Cambridge with her wealthy parents and did nothing. No dreams of college, a career, travel…nothing. That was until she stumbled upon the advertisement for the Parsons School of Design's Fashion program in New York. Once she got that fashion design idea in her head, I guess she saw me as a means to an end. Her parents would never let her move to New York by herself. I agreed to come with her, hoping that we'd moved beyond "the dance." But I wondered if I still felt inferior to the "Queen of Cambridge High's Beautiful People." *Is that why I always cave to her flimsy apologies when she treats me like crap?*

The sound of Miguel's voice snapped me out of my mental trip down high school's memory lane. Miguel stayed to help me dry dishes as I washed, which was super helpful in our tiny kitchen. "You seem upset by Crystal, yes?" he asked.

I scrubbed a juice glass in the soapy water, rinsed it in the running water, and handed it to him to dry. "A bit. She gets like this on and off. She plans these parties, then runs off with Girard and gets upset when we all don't share her 'let's keep the party going' enthusiasm. It can be frustrating." Miguel looked at me with sympathy then broke into a wide smile. *This guy has a gorgeous smile.*

"Ah, but she makes an interesting character for a short story!"

We both laughed. He had a great point. I admired his ability to always be observing and focusing on the next story. A sign of a good writer. *And great looking, too!*

While Crystal had her lovable and laughable moments, those frustrating episodes were becoming a regular thing. And Girard was leaning more and more toward the sleazebag end of the spectrum, as far as I was concerned!

# 7

# A Writing Assignment at Last

*October, 1981*

It finally happened. While performing my normal internship duties at the *SoHo Weekly News* office – dumping used coffee grounds and scrubbing burn rings from the bottom of the Mr. Coffee pot – Phil approached. *Great. Here I am with soap suds all over the front of my blouse and now he wants to talk!*

The entire conversation took place in the space of less than thirty seconds.

"Hey Margie," Phil started. "Friday the Second. You're covering Pulsallama at Club 57. Nine o'clock. Do good."

Catching me off guard to the max, I simply stuttered, "Uh, er, right, uh, g-good." *Real professional, Margie.* I managed to ask, as he bolted down the hall at his usual clipped pace, "Wait, Phil. What genre of music is Pulsallama Band?"

"Uh, I think it's called no wave. Sorta anti-new wave music. Experimental. Ask Rosie. She can fill you in more. I'm swamped."

I finished "coffee duty" and made a beeline to Rosie's cubicle, bombarding her with a hundred questions. "What is Club 57 like? What's new wave music? What's no wave music? What do you know about this band? Who should I try to interview?" Rosie provided minimal background. I still had work to do and only four days to get my research together.

I decided to walk a bit before grabbing an uptown subway home. I needed processing time. My first big writing assignment! I needed more background info and data, otherwise I'd be completely unprepared! *Breathe, Margie...you're panicking.* Analyzing the problem from all angles, I asked myself: Who was the most immediate resource I knew to provide background about this kind of music? Finally, it came to me: Alissa!

Back in my own neighborhood, I popped into the Silver Star Diner to see if Alissa was working. I spotted her turquoise hair immediately and took a seat at the counter.

"Hey," she said from behind the cash register as she rung up a tab. "Finishing up my last order. I can seat you in Emily's section, if you need a table."

"Actually, I want to talk to you, if you have a moment... when you're off work, I mean."

"Mysterious...," she said. "Give me five minutes and I'll walk you to your apartment." I nodded and stood near the dessert kiosk, drooling over the revolving display of chocolate cake, key lime pie, strawberry cheesecake, tapioca pudding, and Greek pastries.

As we walked the half-block to my apartment, I explained the venue and band assignment, including my situation. By the time we settled in my kitchen and I doled out a can of root beer for each of us, Alissa burst wide open.

"What a bitchin' first assignment, Margie. Club 57 is a major venue for the punk and new wave movement. Trailblazing. They do amazing things there. Smashing together progressive music and God, pretty much any art form that's considered way out!"

"Who should I interview about Club 57?"

"Well...Ann Magnuson, for sure. She's a founder, but she's also a Pulsallama band member. Oh, and Father John, if that's even possible. Too cool if you could get an interview with Father John, Margie."

"A priest?" I grabbed a box of Cheez It crackers from the cupboard and poured them into a pink plastic bowl. I crumbled a few in my hand and sprinkled them on the windowsill for my birds. *I hope the sparrows like cheesy treats.*

Alissa laughed, munching on a fistful of crackers. "You and your birds! But yeah man, a priest. Club 57 is in the basement of a church near Union Square. I think it's like the Holy Cross Catholic Church or Holy Cross National Church, something like that. Father John supports these different creative types. Super cool, huh?"

"All this info is helpful. You're a Godsend. Even the other writer at the paper didn't have this much detail. I don't know how to thank you, Alissa."

"Aw, forget it. That's what friends…and family are for, right?" She winked.

"Seriously, how do you know all this background stuff?"

Snarfing down Cheez It crackers like a starved puppy gobbling its supper, she finally spit out, "I like music so I club hop. It's my thing." Then she slurped the last of her root beer.

"Well, I guess we have one thing in common, Alissa. I like music, too," I said.

And with that, Alissa let out her signature belch.

****

Armed with a slew of background information, I arrived at Club 57 on the night of the Pulsallama show for my first writing assignment. I showed the door attendant my *SoHo Weekly News* Press Pass.

"Come on in, sweetheart." Despite the unprofessional greeting uttered through a thick Bronx accent, I asked him if he'd be available to answer questions later.

"Sure, no problem-o. Ya got any questions, ask away, doll."

Full of confidence and ready to conquer my interview, I walked down the stairs and was confronted by a huge photograph of a giant phallus at the entrance to the club. *I wasn't expecting to be greeted by that!*

Every wall of the club was covered with assorted artwork: a painted mural behind the bar, graffiti, a collage of photos and paintings, draped fabric, framed posters. One area housed a screen, reserved for film performances. The windowless basement club carried a dank underground feeling but that didn't seem to bother the thirty plus "members" in attendance.

Since Ann Magnuson, the spearheading founder of Club 57, would be performing in Pulsallama that evening, I wasn't able to interview her until after the show. I turned to the other staff to cull new details for my review, beginning with the door attendant.

"Club 57 is a 'members only' club. Ya wanna know why?"

"Sure, give me any info you have," I said to the huge hulk of a doorman, who I assumed doubled as a bouncer.

"Being 'members only' gives dem private club status dat allows dem ta serve alcohol."

"Oh, I get it. What can you tell me about the actual Pulsallama show?"

"Da show…it's an all-female, thirteen-piece orchestra – two bass guitars, percussionists, and singers. Dem dames all dress up in 1950s cocktail dresses. It's a gas!"

Finally, Pulsallama began its first set. The doorman nailed the description. I loved the 1950s costumes. The act consisted of band members using strange props like kitchen utensils and pieces of garbage. The band's costumed mascot, a huge llama, danced throughout. The whole performance felt like Theater of the Absurd, concert-style. The music tended toward strong rhythmic beats and pulses, switching between various percussion instruments for each song. One song was heavy on tambourines and shakers; the next incorporated lots of cowbells.

The women layered vocals with snippets in various languages ranging from English, Spanish, and French. Occasionally, they would harmonize or shout or recite narration or create characters. While waiting for Ann Magnuson after the performance, I tracked down a vocalist. She summarized her interpretation of the performance.

"We're poking fun at the American way of life, at silly girl talk and how women try hard to live up to a certain image," she said. *Wow, I must have missed a lot of hidden meaning from the show!*

When I finally caught up with Ann, still in cocktail garb and heavy stage makeup, I asked questions about Club 57's mission and the whole membership thing.

"Club 57 is becoming quite hip," she said. "A lot of people who go to the Mudd Club or Max's or even Hurrah's uptown, end up at our little joint."

"Why do you think that is?" I pressed.

"Because we don't let anyone tell us 'no,' that's why." Ann became animated. "We don't let poverty stop our artists from realizing their dreams, their inner-most creative impulses. One time we built a miniature golf course out of boxes pulled out of the trash and another time we made the entire Club to resemble a Jamaican shanty town, accompanied by our DJ's music. An artist's vision."

"Um…okay." I frantically wrote down each word she uttered, thinking I'd sort through it later. "And what about your own artistic vision?" I asked.

"Look, I'm a performance artist and a musician. The uptown art scene is simply the 'land of no' for most women. But downtown, here in the Village, I saw a lot of woman artists thriving and controlling their own destiny. I wanted the freedom to make my own creative choices."

I didn't know too much about the arts world uptown versus downtown, but I believed her. I saw the contrasts of rich versus poor; male versus female; haves versus have nots all over New York City. I felt sure it applied to the arts as well. I loved what Ann said about controlling her own destiny and wanting the freedom to make her own choices – creative choices. *What a cool woman! I wish I had the strength to take more risks like that in my own creative work.*

When it came to writing the actual review, I pulled from my past. Having had acting experience in college and with community groups, I connected to the theatricality of Pulsallama. Even my time as a singer with the swing band helped put me in the right frame of mind while writing the review. I may not have understood all aspects of Pulsallama's no wave performance, but I enjoyed the creative concept. Most of all, something Ann said continued to resonate in my head: "Because we don't let anyone tell us 'no.'" *I need to hang on to Ann's strength of conviction, especially when the going gets tough.*

****

After our October writing group meeting, Gordo needed to meet up with Doug at his theater, so Miguel and I decided to walk through Washington Square Park to enjoy the autumn warmth before grabbing the subway uptown. The late Saturday afternoon sun streamed through the park's many trees as we circumvented roller bladers and tricycle riders in search of a free bench. We passed an older woman seated on a wrought-iron bench, tossing out seed to a flock of pigeons. The birds and the women seemed to be enjoying themselves immensely, both cooing with equal enthusiasm.

Once comfortable, Miguel and I sat quietly, breathing in the brisk air. I was about to speak when Miguel stopped me. "One moment," he said. He reached into his bag and pulled out his journal, jotting down a few lines. I allowed him time to work, uninterrupted.

When he closed his journal, I asked, "What have you created there, Miguel?"

"Nothing fancy – a haiku observation."

"A haiku came to you out of the blue? Like a sudden inspiration from your muse? Please read it."

He opened his journal and read.

> *Aged woman sits*
> *Feeding pigeons all around*
> *Cooing happily.*

"I can't believe that came to you instantaneously. Do you know how much I struggle with poetry?"

"Well, poetry is not my first choice for a writing genre. I use it to help me stretch my word choices and expression. I prefer short stories."

"Why is that?"

"In that form, each line must work hard to express emotion, character, relationship, conflict, resolution, action. To me, it is like creating and solving a puzzle."

"In our writing group, you've said you are inspired by mundane scenes from around the city – graffiti subway cars, a weathered newsstand, and now even a woman feeding pigeons. But to write a story the way you do, with fully fleshed out characters, your inspiration must come from deep inside, Miguel."

"I think so, yes. But this is hard to explain to anyone who has not lived in *El Barrio*. In my community, in my Puerto Rican neighborhood…there is a spirit, where graffiti on a building is a work of art; where a rundown storefront holds a mystery; where an elderly couple sitting on an apartment stoop is the beginning of a love story. Yes, my neighborhood can also hold dark stories and experiences. They are all the city scenes, all the world."

Miguel never ceased to amaze me – the universality of his writing philosophy, the way he tackled various writing genres with ease, his intelligence, and his humble nature. We'd been finding more reasons to spend time together over the past weeks, like meeting for coffee to review an assignment for the writing group, or visiting a favorite bookstore. I'd grown even more attracted to his serious, gentle manner. I hoped he felt the same way about me, but so far…all our time together appeared more friendship or colleague based.

We chatted about the meeting and our assignment for the month: haiku. Dr. R. stressed that we needed to relax as we approached this new form. "Let go of your fears and doubts. These only hold us back as artists. Be a risk taker." *I know she's right. I also know that taking risks is not my forte.*

"I see you took Dr. R.'s word to heart, Miguel. You took the risk and jumped right into the haiku writing. I admire that."

The conversation about risk-taking led to Miguel's news, which he nonchalantly mentioned. "I received a notice that one of my stories will be published in a literary journal next month."

I couldn't believe it. This was huge news! And Miguel tossed it into the conversation as if to say, "I had pancakes for breakfast this morning."

"Congratulations. How wonderful! Why didn't you announce this to the writing group?"

Miguel flashed a bashful smile. "I do not like to brag. I should not take the credit. Dr. R. was the one who told me about the journal seeking entries for short stories and encouraged me to submit."

"Well, I think it's totally cool. Your parents must be super proud."

Miguel's posture changed dramatically – head tilting to one side, eyes staring down at the pavement. "Not that much. They are confused about my writing, about where this interest may take me. What my parents understand is working hard and earning money. It is not their fault...it is what they know." *Another thing Miguel and I have in common...parents who don't get us!*

I patted his arm to get his attention. "Well, I'm extremely proud of you, Miguel. Being published in a journal is a big accomplishment."

"Thank you. But look at you, Margie – writing reviews for a real New York newspaper. You are getting published too!"

"I guess you're right, Miguel. But a short story published in a literary journal is a big deal."

****

I submitted my first professional review to the *SoHo Weekly News* at two thousand words, including my radical description of Club 57's interior, the Club's membership policy, Ann's philosophy of women artists, and the review of Pulsallama's performance. The final copy, after the editing department picked over it, ended up being published at fewer than a hundred words, buried on the edition's next to the last page. It read:

On Friday, November 2, 1981, Pulsallama

performed at Club 57. Ann Magnuson's all-female, thirteen-piece orchestra is made up of two bass guitars, percussionists, and vocalists. The band members dressed in 1950s cocktail dresses and exaggerated makeup. The act entailed the band members incorporating strange props like kitchen utensils and pieces of garbage, while fighting over a cowbell. A large llama appeared as the band's mascot. Call Club 57 for a list of this month's performances and show times.

*Pitiful.*

# 8

# Navigating the Holidays-NYC Style

*November-December, 1981*

Prior to the holiday season, my friendship with Miguel had blossomed into a closeness that could only be described as a budding relationship. We spent Sunday afternoons strolling through Chinatown or sitting in Washington Square Park when the November weather permitted. Chinatown offered an explosion of colorful and unique window shopping from porcelain to purses to posters, and a variety of lantern-festooned restaurants and outdoor fruit and vegetable markets. Washington Square Park bustled with sounds, smells, and people-watching opportunities, including the melodic music emanating from mandolin players who gathered in one corner of the park, the gentle yips from the leashed pups being guided to the Doggie Area, the gleeful laughter of children dancing around the park's large central fountain, and the recitations of actors who rehearsed monologues in hopes of attracting a small appreciative audience. Miguel and I could never resist the odor wafting from the hot dog cart, always purchasing two with mustard to munch on while we grabbed a spot on an iron bench to watch the world go by.

As the weather grew cooler toward the end of November, we spent our lovely Sunday afternoons at our favorite coffee house,

Caffe Reggio's on MacDougal Street in Greenwich Village. Featuring dark paneled walls, stained glass transoms, long front windows, and textured ceiling panels, the cozy room seated no more than twenty customers. Lingering over our cappuccinos, Miguel and I enjoyed discussing our latest writing assignments or whatever came to mind.

Our relationship moved at a leisurely pace, which was fine with me. I'd been burned by a serious relationship after college in a major way. After devoting my life and future to David, completely ignoring my own needs and desires, he up and cheated on me. The breakup sent me into a downward mental spiral. I truly believed there was no recovery from that dark abyss. Thankfully, I was wrong. Although I'd gone out with a few guys since then, my overly cautious and distrustful heart had prevented me from completely jumping back into the fray, manufacturing obstacles for any budding romance. But when it came to Miguel, something stirred deep in my heart. Thrilled to see him when we were together; constantly thinking about him when he wasn't around – I was excited to see where this attraction was headed.

****

The New York City holiday energy pulsed everywhere I turned, especially at Radio City Music Hall and around Rockefeller Center. The area above the ice rink buzzed with workers preparing for the enormous Christmas tree lighting, scheduled for the first week of December. Lacy white angels, greenery, and dazzling lights popped up around the Rockefeller Plaza. Inside Radio City Music Hall, creative teams, performers, and the Rockettes worked their magic to produce the amazing *Magnificent Christmas Spectacular* for the November 20th opening.

I'd never seen the Christmas show before, but from my receptionist desk I heard the Rockettes rehearsing in the dance studio down the hall. Once in a while, during a break, I'd sneak a peek into the studio to watch the precision dancers as they took instruction from their choreographer, Violet Holmes. The routines, the high kicks, the absolute exactness blew me away, but Ms. Holmes spotted imperfections and demanded more from her dancers.

During tech week, when the performers moved to the huge, one-hundred-forty-four-foot-wide Music Hall stage, I'd climb up to the light booth during my lunch break. High above the six-thousand-seat auditorium's third balcony, I got goosebumps watching twenty-six Rockettes, fully costumed as soldiers in white trousers, red jackets, and tall black hats with gold trim complete with white feathered plumes, perform the famous "Parade of the Wooden Soldiers" routine. *Absolutely amazing! Thank God I get comps to see the entire show after it opens.*

In mid-November Girard flew to Amsterdam without telling Crystal how long he'd be there or why. It seemed funky to me. All she knew was that he asked if he could borrow her suitcase and promised to bring her back a surprise. Crystal freaked out. Not only was she down in the dumps and extremely cranky, but she was also physically down. She didn't sleep well, and most mornings could barely drag herself out of bed to get to her design classes. Instead of waitressing, she called in sick at the diner on Tuesdays and Thursdays, opting to stare at the television all evening until after midnight, though I doubted she comprehended anything she watched. Even though I secretly thought Girard was a major sleazebag, I hoped he'd come back soon.

On Thursday, November 26, Thanksgiving Day arrived and with it the threat of rain. Alissa and I talked the depressed Crystal into dodging raindrops and attending the Macy's Thanksgiving Day parade with us. Once onboard with the idea, Crystal became a woman possessed with excitement. "You're not a true New Yorker until you've attended the Macy's parade in person" became her mantra.

The three of us planned to find a prime spot to gawk at the parade along its Broadway route near Columbus Circle. Crystal and Alissa brewed coffee for a thermos in the kitchen, while I gathered up a blanket from the bedroom. We needed to hurry because the parade started uptown around West 72nd Street, and we planned to plop ourselves near West 59th Street. Bundled up, layering sweaters, scarves, hats, and gloves under rain jackets, we trudged the nine blocks from our apartment to Columbus Circle. Wiggling through the crowd onto a curb, we plopped onto a folded wool blanket. Damp chilly air suggested an impending shower but for the moment we were spared.

The thumping sound of drums and the crowds' attention pulled uptown caused us to stop gabbing and focus. Energy built as skating clowns and New York Mounted Police led parade officials. The banner carriers came into view holding a large drape with the year's slogan: "If You Haven't Seen Macy's, You Haven't Seen New York." A gigantic uniformed marching band followed.

"I've always watched the parade on TV but here I am, up close and personal," I shouted over the crowd cheering for a passing float and another approaching marching band.

"Yep, and sitting in a smelly gutter," Alissa said. "Romantic, ain't it?"

I laughed at Alissa's cynicism. "Oh look, the Sesame Street float and Big Bird." I loved the Christmas song the characters sang, "Keep Christmas With You." Crystal and Alissa shot me a look like I was a sap.

A little later, Crystal gushed, "Ahh. A Strawberry Shortcake float. Those dolls are super cute. I wish they made them when I was a kid. I would have sewn an entire wardrobe for them."

"Oh sure, now who's the dweeb?" I said with a wink.

We were freezing and damp to our bones, but I wouldn't leave until I saw the Rockettes, my whole reason for coming to the parade in the first place. At last, the dancers approached Columbus Circle.

"They're coming, the Rockettes are coming!" I shouted. "They look amazing."

The Rockettes strutted down the street in formation in the skimpiest of costumes, waving to the children. I shivered looking at all that exposed skin. But they were such pros. Heads held high, smiles on each face. They looked absolutely festive in their gold, red, and white diagonally striped, strapless costumes with flirty gold ruffled skirts. Hair was pulled back with a matching bow attached at a jaunty angle on the left side of the head. Gold character shoes capped the Rockettes' uniform look. I hoped that Columbus Circle would be one of the spots where they would perform their routine, but no such luck. In fact, they all climbed onto a float for the remainder of the trip down Broadway to Macy's department store.

"Alright, you saw your Rockettes. Can we go now? I'm freezing my ass off." Alissa didn't mince words.

Despite the thermos of hot coffee, drizzling rain and wind won the day. We decided to head to the Silver Star Diner before Santa's Sleigh made an appearance. In the diner's warmth, we ordered turkey club sandwiches and hot coffee. In honor of the day, we each stated one thing we were grateful for. Crystal claimed to be "totally" thankful for Girard coming into her life, causing Alissa to shoot me an "Oh brother" look. *Apparently Alissa has doubts about that guy, too.*

"Well, I'm thankful to get my ass out of the gutter we

were sitting in," Alissa said. "What can I say? I'm more of an in-the-moment chick. What about you, Margie? What are you grateful for?"

"Hmm...Here's something cool. I've been bugging the editor at *SoHo Weekly News* about when my next writing gig might be assigned. He mentioned that after the holidays there are two clubs I could possibly be assigned to. I never heard of them, though. Maybe you have, Alissa. ABC No RIO and Space 2B."

Alissa nearly choked on her sandwich. "Good God...yes, I've been to both. One's cruddy and the other is cruddier. They're both in the East Village, and by that I mean extreme East Village, baby."

"East Village. That's odd. Shouldn't *SoHo Weekly News* stick to reviewing music in the SoHo neighborhood?"

"Well, look. If you get to choose between ABC No RIO and Space 2B, I suggest we girls take a little daytime field trip," Alissa said. "You wanna know what you're getting into, you get me? Who's in?"

****

Crystal, Alissa, and I met up the next day and took the subway downtown. As we walked through the East Village, Alissa reminded us, "The neighborhoods down here are lined with junkies. It's better to walk in the street than on the sidewalks to avoid stepping on used needles. Put your purses inside your coats, girlies. You're walking into the jungle now." She added a wolf howl for emphasis, which didn't make sense at all. *Did wolves even live in the jungle?* But that was Alissa. Super in the moment.

The first club we visited was Space 2B, a former garage converted to a performance space of sorts, on the Lower East Side. Although the joint was locked up, we peered through a dirty window and got a glimpse of the interior.

"I saw an act here once," Alissa said, "but I can't remember who it was. I do recall performers scampering around those hydraulic lifts that raised cars for oil changes. That's about it. Pretty wild." Alissa was right about one thing: cruddy was a perfect description.

ABC No Rio on Rivington Street in the East Village opened as an artist-run space in 1980. Alissa described the club's appeal as a sort of do-it-yourself, anything goes, and anyone-can-do-it venue.

"The space has a gallery, a theater, and artist's rec room. Pretty much a punk stomping ground."

Amazingly the door was open. With Alissa leading the way, we clomped down a staircase into the basement and descended into the ABC No Rio's venue. Alissa was right again: this club was cruddier than the other. I started to believe that the new wave/no wave groupies liked it that way. Maybe the crappy venues permitted artists to be as "out there" as they wanted – no rules, no barriers.

After getting a good look at both venues, we hightailed it out of those scary neighborhoods. Even Alissa acted freaked out by the grungy sidewalk trash and homeless situation.

"This is worse than ever, man," she said. "Haven't been down here in a while."

Crystal said, "I can't believe you'd even go to these clubs, Alissa. Why?"

"For the experience, you get me? You never know if the band you see is going to blow you away or not." *That could be true in any genre, I suppose, whether punk, jazz, new wave, or a classical quartet.*

As we quickly walked toward SoHo and a safer neighborhood,

I began to question if these venues were where I wanted to hang out. Smelly former garages, graffiti-splattered storefronts that look deserted, garbage-filled neighborhoods swarming with drug addicts and petty criminals. And while I was warming up to punk and new wave music, I still preferred jazz and funk. I recalled a mentoring session (that's what I used to call it) with my two horn player friends from the swing band. Jimmy and Chaz introduced me to the subtleties of the band Chicago, and I remember describing what I heard. Driving down the highway toward a gig while listening to "Saturday in the Park," I had been able to pick out the tonal modulation in the middle of the song. *Good lord, I sound like an old geezer in a 26-year-old's body. "Back in my day, when music was really music…"*

Beside the music thing, there I was putting down the East Village neighborhood, like a stuck-up debutante from the Upper East Side. I mean, I did live in the Upper East Side, but in a total hovel of an apartment with our fair share of cockroaches. I did have the luxury of less garbage and fewer homeless drug addicts lining the sidewalks outside my apartment door, however. Alissa's little field trip succeeded in one big way: I felt grateful for our East 65th Street neighborhood between First and Second Avenues. Close enough to walk to the East River and the Lexington Avenue subway stop. The Silver Star Diner on the corner. A drug store, coin laundromat, and grocery store with delivery service within a block in either direction. Plus, a tiny Art Film cinema and a bookstore within walking distance on Third Avenue. Central Park with the Meadow on the east side or the "Literary Walk" statuary or the lake – all a short trek of a few blocks.

Before catching the subway uptown, Alissa and Crystal slipped into a SoHo art gallery while I opted to sip on hot chocolate at a nearby coffee shop on Spring Street and Broadway. I took out my journal while my cocoa cooled. In our writing group discussions, Dr. R. encouraged us to continue to self-reflect and write about personal conflict as this might influence the direction we took with our writing. She suggested watching for signs where pivoting might be appropriate and to not be afraid to explore and experiment when those feelings arose. I admired Miguel's clear vision about his writing. He understood his writer's purpose and the genres that best aligned with his message. Using my journal, I attempted to dissect my own state of being:

> *A Looming Question*
>
> *I'm not sure if I'm being a coward, a big baby, or truly experiencing a real change in direction but the knot in my stomach and tension in my shoulders is telling me I'm feeling conflicted. A looming question is hanging over me: How strongly do I feel about writing reviews for these genres especially in these unsafe environments? Is this me? Something doesn't feel aligned. Is this simply a new challenge I need to navigate or is this feeling a real obstacle in my career plan?*

I didn't get too far into my analysis before Alissa and Crystal interrupted, ready to head home. It had been a long day and I knew I wouldn't figure out the answers to my conflicting feelings immediately. *Keep breathing and exploring, Margie, as new discoveries arise.*

As far as worrying about which of those two East Village

clubs, ABC No RIO or Space 2B, I might get assigned for my next *SoHo Weekly News* interview was concerned…neither one materialized. *And that's the biz…*

# 9

# Circumventing Dad

*December, 1981*

The garbage strike began on December 1st – a great reason to leave Manhattan for the holidays. Stinky trash piled up on sidewalks, spilling out onto streets, and attracting rats and vermin. In a city where four hundred private waste removal companies collected between 12,000 and 15,000 tons of garbage a day from apartments, construction sites, restaurants, hotels, retail, and other commercial buildings, that strike rapidly became a smelly, messy nightmare. Thank God, the strike ended on December 17th but the freakin' turmoil took quite a while to clean up. I was beyond thrilled to take the train to Baltimore and spend Christmas with my parents. I even scheduled a date in Baltimore's Little Italy with my two former band buddies, Jimmy and Chaz, for a mini reunion.

Since I'd never taken the train out of New York before, Crystal instructed me like a hyper momma hen. "Penn Station can be tricky. There'll be gobs of holiday travelers. After you get your ticket to Baltimore at the reservation desk, watch the departure board for your train name and gate number."

"Okay great. Where's the departure board?"

"Oh hell, you can't miss it," she said, a little too loudly. "It's a huge monstrosity hanging over the middle of the lobby. Here's the catch though: It only works half the time. Sometimes there's a jumble of trains with no numbers or names. Other times it's working fine. The Port Authority's too cheap to put the moola into fixing it. At least that's what my father says."

"Well, what am I supposed to do if it's not working?"

"Right. You gotta pay attention to the announcements over the loudspeaker, which can be a problem 'cuz they can be hard to hear. Also watch people, *mon amie*. When they all start running toward a gate, join them and start asking, 'Is this train going to Baltimore?'"

*She's got to be exaggerating.* "How do you know all these fun facts about train travel to and from the Big Apple?"

"You know…my father's a big-time lawyer. We came into the city for Broadway shows and shopping trips all the time. Until he acquired his own firm and got too busy for anything fun!"

"Hmm. Penn Station seems archaic!"

"Right, well, welcome to holiday travel in New York. Be happy you're not driving out of the Holland Tunnel or over the George Washington Bridge right before the holiday rush!"

"Are you sure you don't want to come back to the Eastern Shore with me? Won't your parents miss you over the holidays?"

"Nah, mummy and daddy have plenty of party hosting to do. Lawyers and business associates and real estate tycoons. They won't even realize I'm not there. They're mailing me a Walkman cassette player for my Christmas present to show 'how much they love me.' Besides, when Girard gets home from Amsterdam, he'll want to keep me here, all to himself." *That's funky. Those two never go out with other couples…It's always just the two of them.* I decided the guy gives me the creeps.

Once at Penn Station, the scene unfolded exactly as Crystal

described. A sea of uncivilized humanity pushing and pulling in their attempts to find their correct gates, dragging oversized luggage without a care about who they plowed over to get to their destination. Grateful that I had plenty of clothes at my parent's house, I only carried a small duffle bag of essentials, making me much more agile to dart among the throng of passengers.

Once I plopped into my seat on the train, I let out a deep breath of frustration, relief, and relaxation. I closed my eyes and identified where I was holding tension in my body:

Stinking garbage spilling over on sidewalks – breathe that neck tension away. Frustration with no new writing assignments at *SoHo Weekly News* – breathe that shoulder tension away. Crystal's increased restlessness since Girard took off – breathe that temple tension away. My own uncertainty with this whole New York City adventure – breathe that stomach tension away.

Finally relaxed, I looked forward to reconnecting with my Maryland roots and a traditional Church Creek Christmas. Visiting my former waitress friends at Doris Mae's Diner in Cambridge, taking long walks along the Choptank River in search of rare wintering waterfowl, and indulging in all the Christmas rituals Mom will have waiting for me – cookie baking, tree trimming, putting up the creche, and maybe even Midnight mass. I closed my eyes and drifted off, lulled by the train's gentle rocking, the sound of its clacking along the tracks, and pleasant holiday images.

****

My visit home proceeded as I had imagined. Mom and I trimmed the tree the day after I arrived in Church Creek. Dad had cut a five-foot Douglas fir on a friend's farm and already placed it in the living room. *Dad and his connections! He probably made a deal with the farmer: a few free cans of soda from the general store in exchange for the tree. What a wheeler dealer!*

After stringing red, blue, and green lights and hanging silver garland, we commenced with the labor-intensive process of hanging the decorations. I pulled ancient glass ornaments and silly homemade popsicle stick artifacts that had "A Margie Art Project" stamped all over them out of a musty cardboard carton. Mom delicately placed each one on the tree in "exactly the right spot." The final task was draping strands of tinsel, a time-consuming and precise production, as Mom constantly reminded me, "No more than three pieces at a time!" This gave us a great opportunity to catch up.

"It sounds like you are enjoying your time in New York, but you haven't mentioned anything about dating. Are you seeing anyone?"

"Nah, who has time? Between working at Radio City, my writing workshop, and now this internship…"

"Word around town is that David will be sailing in from one of his private East Coast cruises to visit his folks for a few days. You knew he charters wealthy couples on his sailboat to the Carolinas, right? Maybe you could have lunch with him."

*David!* Even hearing his name flooded my mind and heart with painful memories. I'm sure Mom's not-so-subtle reminder of my former first love wasn't meant to be cruel, but I kept the David topic in the "Do Not Revisit" file in my brain.

"Yuck. Mom, what are you thinking? Because we were together for a few years when I was in college…Ew. You know how I fell apart when I caught him cheating. Why would you think I'd ever want to spend any time with him?"

"Well, people can change. David has a successful business now."

"Right. A successful business that fulfilled his fantasy. Good for him. But I have no interest in being a sidekick in his life's dream. And he never had any interest in mine."

After a few awkward silent minutes, Mom continued her pursuit. "Well, Frankie's been around the house asking about you. He wondered when you might come home for a visit. Maybe you should give him a call while you're here."

"Mom, you know I broke things off with him before I left, not that there was anything to break off. He and I were never a good fit. Why prolong the inevitable?"

"Margaret dear, you say that about any young man you have two dates with."

*She does have a point.*

I saw no need to mention Miguel, even though I thought he was totally talented and humble and sweet and smart – all qualities I found attractive. But first, we were only friends and writing colleagues. No need to get Mom all riled up yet. And second, I'm not sure how my involvement with a Hispanic man would go over. Not that Mom would be the problem. She had always been open-minded and accepting of people of all cultures and faiths. Dad would be the issue. *No need to dive into that confrontation prematurely.* Who even knew where this thing with Miguel was leading, especially knowing my normal relationship pattern. *Although, there is something special about him – that smile, that musky cologne...*

****

The following day I borrowed Dad's pickup truck and drove into Cambridge to visit my old haunts. First on my list: Breakfast at Doris Mae's Diner, complete with hugs and hellos to the regular watermen and business folks I had served when I waitressed there. Familiar sensations washed over me – the blended odors of coffee, bacon, and sausage hitting me in the face as soon as I opened the door; the cozy warmth of tightly packed seating; and the muted sounds of conversation, dishes clanging, and orders ringing up on the register.

After breakfast, I took a stroll along the Choptank River and sat at my special "reflection" spot, a pile of rocks on the shore where I meditated, journaled, or simply breathed in the fresh air. I spotted four or five canvasback ducks in the distant surf. I love those waterfowl. Despite the frigid breeze off the water, I took time to reflect on the differences between these two, beloved "homes": the Eastern Shore and New York City. The quiet and peacefulness versus the constant energy and noise; the bright stars in the dark sky versus the artificial lights at night; the wide open spaces of country roads versus the closeness of city streets and avenues. Lots of contrast between the two; lots to take from both environments. *Although I've settled into New York, I still wonder which one is best for me?*

By the time I drove home, the sun had begun its descent behind the row of loblolly trees lining the backyard of our tiny house. I pulled Dad's pickup truck into our gravel driveway and watched him struggle with a tangled string of outdoor Christmas lights.

"Need help with that?" I said as I jumped down from the driver's seat.

"Alrighty." *Good, this could be nice father-daughter bonding time.*

We worked together to disentangle the long string of colorful lights, despite the wind fighting our efforts. Dad climbed the shaky ladder and, while I carefully fed him each section, he tacked the lights into place around the front picture window. Meanwhile, we watched Mom inside move from window to window hanging red cellophane wreaths surrounding fake electric candles.

"Mom picked the warmer decoration duty, didn't she?" I

wanted to ease into civil, normal conversation, always a challenge with my Dad. Unfortunately, my attempt failed. As Dad and I spread lights over the two evergreen bushes that rimmed the front landscaping, he made his intentions clear.

"Any idea how long you'll be stayin' in that city, Margaret?" His subtext came through loud and clear: He wanted me to move home to Church Creek and forget the whole "New York City craziness."

"Dad, I thought you were okay about me making the move."

"For cryin' out loud, Margaret. At twenty-six years old, you should be thinkin' about settlin' down. Ya did your travelin' with that band, and took time figurin' out if graduate school was next. Okay, decided against that. But this New York thing…it's too much."

"I don't understand what the issue is, Dad. I've already explained that I'm not ready to get married. I've got a good job and I'm supporting myself."

"Don't be naïve, missy. I know all about the bad people lurkin' in New York. All them drug addicts and homosexuals and murderers." *Oh brother. Typical Dad. He only sees the absolute worst in people and places. Not that he's wrong about the crime. The news is full of those stories.*

I tried to nip this uncomfortable conversation in the bud. "I've yet to meet a murderer in New York, but I'll let you know when I do." Dad snorted and pulled out his flask. "Oh, and Dad, you might be surprised to know that those same folks can be found right here on the Eastern Shore."

At that point, Mom tapped on the window, interrupting our conversation. She mimed that steaming mugs of hot chocolate, fresh cookies, and warm fire awaited us inside. Saved by Mom! I didn't want to begin the holidays fighting. *He's probably worried about me as any parent would be...although I wish he'd lay off the settling down routine.*

Dad and I dropped the argument and headed inside. Once seated in front of a crackling fire under crocheted blankets and munching on yummy treats, Mom launched into her own interrogation about my new life in the Big Apple. She asked about my job, interests, friends, what I liked about the city...the works. I described Alissa, Doug, Gordo, Miguel, Girard, and Crystal as my core group of friends and mentioned how much I enjoyed working at Radio City Music Hall. I talked about how important the writing group and internship were to me. Silently, my thoughts wandered to Miguel – those intriguing eyes behind the wire rimmed glasses, his soft voice, his probing questions about writing and life – and I realized how much I missed him. Suddenly my heart raced with an eagerness to get through the holidays and back to New York.

"Are you hearin' me, Margaret?" Dad's voice burst into my Miquel daydream.

"Sure, I'm listening," I fibbed.

Dad dug in. "Find a receptionist job and one of those writin' groups around here. And then ya wouldn't be exposed to all them bad elements."

"Dad, it's not the same. I've gone over this."

Even more determined, Dad blurted, "Well, I don't like it. It's a bad place with bad people."

"Dad, you know, you've never actually been to New York City. Not every inch of it is bad and not every person is evil. You're basing all of your impressions on hearsay and one-sided news articles."

"I've been readin' the news-"

"See what I mean." I interrupted but it did no good. He

forged ahead.

"I read in the news there's that homo disease spreading in places like San Francisco and New York. Jesus, Mary, and Joseph, I don't want you making friends with any gays, Margaret. They're the worse kind of people – human garbage."

"Dad! That's a horrible thing to say! Mom, you don't agree with that, do you?"

Mom sighed and looked at Dad with disappointment. "Isn't 'garbage' overly harsh?" Not much of a reprisal. Maybe she doesn't have the energy to argue with him anymore.

Dad became defensive and dug in. "It's not comin' from me. It's what Anita Bryant says in her 'Save Our Children' TV campaign and she's a born-again Christian."

I stared at him for a moment and shook my head in disgust. "I thought Christ loved all people, Dad."

With no comeback or fresh ammunition from America's "favorite" anti-gay crusader, Anita Bryant, he punctuated his silence with a long swig from his flask and stomped out of the room.

Mom and I looked at each other and sighed. After I returned from traveling with King Vido's Swing Band, I had seen some signs that Dad had turned a corner with his bigotry. He seemed less spiteful in his conversations. Was it my imagination that he appeared to be listening more? But now, his intolerance along with his insistence that his only daughter needed to be married and popping out babies by the time she hit twenty-five disheartened me. And frankly, it only made me want to return to New York and stick it out, just to spite Dad!

"Please tell me you don't agree with him, Mom."

"You know that I'm your biggest cheerleader, Margaret, but…." Mom moved from the fireside armchair to a spot on the sofa next to me. "Your Dad and I have been watching a lot of news stories about all the crime and…other developments going on in New York. He's worried about you."

"I appreciate that he worries about me. I understand that, but…"

"I think he pictures you living all alone in a dangerous place and…well, he gets all upset."

"But that's the point, Mom. Haven't you been listening to me? I'm not alone. I'm surrounded by a group of great friends – in my building, in my writing group. We watch out for each other, like we're family. Can't you explain that to him? He won't listen to me."

"It sounds nice. I'll try but I'm not sure if your Dad will be convinced."

*She's probably right. I can't imagine his reaction if I told him that my New York "family" consisted of a punk girlfriend with changing hair color, a Hispanic man, and a gay couple! He'd probably have a stroke!*

****

The day after Christmas, I borrowed Dad's truck and drove to Baltimore to meet up with Jimmy and Chaz. Dad pitched a fit that I'd be taking his truck for the better part of a day but what could I do? I sold my 1970 Gremlin when I moved to New York last year. Dad supported the idea at the time.

"Ya can always borrow my truck when you're home."

"That's great, Dad," I remembered saying at the time. "That'll be helpful."

I didn't feel bad leaving him high and dry for one day. He'd probably spend the day at his general store anyway, a short walk across the road from the house.

The two-hour drive to Baltimore dragged on. Due to the

freakin' horrible radio reception in the truck, I resorted to watching the scenery – looking at the Eastern Shore farmland, crossing the Chesapeake Bay Bridge, and seeing Baltimore suburbs taking over the landscape. At last, I arrived in Baltimore's Little Italy, familiar territory, since it was my home base for a good portion of a year during the King Vido's Swing Band tour in 1978.

Jimmy, Chaz, and I arranged to meet at Vaccaro's Italian Pastry Shop, one of my favorite eateries, located a few blocks from the former King Vido Swing Band rehearsal studio. When I first auditioned for the band, I drove past Vaccaro's, attracted by its inviting large black awnings covering the outside seating. Inside, I loved the ambience – a huge board with painted menu items hanging over glass cases packed with mouth-watering pastries, several tables and chairs scattered within the intimate dining area, and the blissful aroma of oven fresh delicacies. I treated myself during rehearsal breaks and time off, lingering over a cappuccino at an outside table whenever the weather permitted.

Although Jimmy, Chaz, and I hoped to meet at a jazz club, unfortunately, many of those music venues in Baltimore had gone under by 1981. Disco reigned supreme. We settled for yummy Vaccaro's pastries and coffee, catching up on our various career paths.

Seeing Jimmy with his red, Afro-styled hair and gangly physique, cigarette dangling from his lips as he walked up the sidewalk next to the baby-faced, muscular, six-foot-plus Chaz was an amusing yet familiar sight. We'd only connected once since King Vido's Swing Band dissolved in September of 1978 after being investigated for dubious criminal activity. Though I had already planned to leave the band and return home to Church Creek, the incident left my two band friends unemployed. As it had been almost two years since we'd last met, I was anxious to hear where they ended up.

After hugs and greetings, we began conversing as if no time had elapsed. I caught them up on my New York City adventures. They filled me in on a few band members. Basic small talk out of the way, I wanted to know about their current band gigs. Had they been able to transition to new bands quickly after the end of King Vido's Swing Band?

"Touch and go for a while after the swing band died. Shit, Chaz and I had to rely on picking up gigs wherever we could find them. It's tough for a trumpet and trombone player these days," Jimmy said, taking a deep drag on his cigarette.

"Yep," Chaz added, never one to say much.

I remembered that the world of big bands was already drying up five years ago. We'd had many discussions about how disco hurt live musicians' livelihoods. I wondered how Jimmy and Chaz had been able to survive.

"Chaz and I thought we'd nailed spots with a band out of Towson called Majestics. It's been around since the 1960s in different formations, with and without horns. It would have been a sweet gig, 'cuz they played out a lot."

"What happened?"

Jimmy stubbed out his cigarette. "They pivoted to a six-piece."

"Without horns," Chaz added with a shrug.

Jimmy lit another cigarette, released a puff of smoke, and tossed his match into the ashtray. "Don't worry, Margie. Ol' Chaz and me always land on our feet. We snagged spots with a similar band called Magic Eight. Get it? Eight pieces with horns."

"Sounds rad. And you play out a lot?" I asked.

"Sure do," Chaz said.

Jimmy nodded. "D.C., Annapolis. Even as far as Ocean

City."

"I'm happy to hear that you found a solid band situation. I worried about you guys."

Jimmy shocked the hell outta me with the next piece of news. "Hey, you remember that that singer, Amy – the one who had the secret fling with the guitar player, Ted?"

"I guess it wasn't such a secret." Of course, I remembered Amy. She and I had bonded while touring with the band. I'd thought of her fondly and wished we had kept in touch.

"Well, she called my boy Chaz a few weeks ago," Jimmy said with a weird grin.

"Outta the blue," Chaz chimed in.

"Wait…you heard from Amy?" It surprised me that Amy would have reached out to Chaz but not me. I had a ton of questions about the former singer from the swing band. "Is she in Baltimore? How's she doing?"

"Living in upper New York state. Seems to be okay," Chaz offered. "Weird she called me though."

"Hell, our first thought was she really wanted to talk to you, Margie, because she kinda pumped Chaz for information."

Chaz confirmed Jimmy's sentiments. "Yep, asked a bunch of questions about you."

"That is odd." I took in this information and wondered what could be going on with Amy. "Did she give you an update about her life – any details?"

"Kinda sounded like Amy wanted to fill you in herself," Chaz said.

A funny smile appeared on Chaz's face. "I've got her phone number, if you wanna call her." *Chaz may not talk much, but when he does, he's full of surprises.* At the end of our visit, I took Amy's number from Chaz. *It all seems so odd…almost mysterious.*

# 10

# Dodging Disaster

*December, 1981-January, 1982*

The new year approached with a rush of tourists jamming the sidewalks, anticipation of crowds on Times Square for the annual "Countdown to Midnight," and my own excited reflections of "what's next?" I'd been living in Manhattan for over nine months with a bill-paying job I enjoyed and an internship at *SoHo Weekly News* that affirmed my career path. *I'm writing music reviews – it's journalism – a major reason I came to New York. So why the creeping doubts?* Damn. I felt myself succumbing to my old dual nemeses: doubt and restlessness. *Snap out of it, Margie. You've got exactly what you came to New York for – a career track to write about music. Quit bitchin' and get on with it!* I didn't know whose voice was yakking at me in my head, but it set me straight…for a while.

In anticipation of our first New Year's Eve in the Big Apple, our regular gang decided to venture to Times Square to watch the annual ball drop. In reality, only Crystal wanted to go, but when she convinced Girard and Alissa, the rest of us agreed too.

"We *have* to go, *mes amies*," Crystal insisted. "I read in the *Times* that they'll be dropping a huge apple this year."

"A huge what?" I tried to visualize what she was talking about.

"That's what the article said. Mayor Koch had the old aluminum ball redesigned to look like an apple. Part of the "I Love New York" campaign. It's supposed to have red light bulbs for the apple's skin and green for the stem. It sounds funky!"

I invited Miguel to join us for New Year's Eve. Our time together had been increasing – aimless walks, coffee house meetings, and writing sessions in a quiet corner of the New York Public Library. While people might have called these outings dates, there had been nothing physical between us. I had begun to admire Miguel for more than his writing and his intellect, though. I respected Miguel's convictions and his ability to speak his mind, something I continued to work on myself.

The truth was…I adored being around Miguel. He radiated gentleness, warmth, and security. Though mostly serious, when he did smile, it reminded me of that moment the sun peeked from the ocean at dawn – thrilling and beautiful and totally authentic. I craved those smiles more and more. Inviting him to spend the New Year's Eve holiday felt perfect, and I rationalized that he was already at ease with our little group. Why not include him?

On the evening of the event, we bundled up in heavy coats, hats, scarves, and mittens to walk almost thirty blocks to the intersection of 42nd Street and Broadway. Zigzagging along Park and Fifth Avenue, we passed ornate apartments and posh hotels with uniformed doormen, bellboys, and taxi stands. We could only imagine the opulently decorated lobbies with efficient elevators waiting inside. At about 45th Street, we were confronted by masses of people mashed together, jockeying to position themselves closer to the all-important "ball-dropping" site. My first impression: Oh, the humanity! We left the apartment at seven-thirty, thinking we'd beat the crowds. Boy, were we wrong.

Even this early in the evening, we could tell the crowd had been imbibing. Despite the presence of police behind barricaded side streets, men and women were already acting rowdy – laughing loudly, falling over, yelling obscenities, pushing for no reason. Add the freezing weather to this scene and, frankly, I rethought Crystal's whole "You-have-to-experience-Times-Square-at-New-Year's-Eve-to-be-a-real-New-Yorker" argument.

After more than an hour of standing still in a giant mass of drunken jerks, I'd had enough. "I have an idea," I yelled above the crowd noise. "How about I go back to the apartment and get things ready for our post-ball-dropping dinner? That way I can watch the event on TV and time dinner to be ready by the time you guys walk through the door. Sounds perfect, right?"

Miguel, Gordo, and Doug jumped at the opportunity to walk back with me while Crystal, Girard, and Alissa stayed to watch the ball, er…Big Apple drop. As our little quartet pushed against the crowd in the opposite direction, Gordo thanked me for the escape plan. "I was trying to come up with a way out, but you beat me to it, Margie. Whew!" Miguel and Doug grunted in agreement, shivering between blasts of wind.

Disentangling from the crowd and walking triple-time against the wind, we chatted about the hypocrisy of the New York City fantasy. Many young people were drawn to living in Manhattan under the false pretense of excitement, bright lights, and big futures. The reality could be quite brutal.

"Here we are freezing our asses off while the rich ride limos to their Fifth Avenue penthouses overlooking Central Park," Doug said as his teeth chattered. Then he moaned, adding his signature Shakespeare quote to cap off the moment, "Now is the winter of our discontent." Quite dramatic…and comical. He has his moments.

"*Ey mano*, it could be worse," Miguel said. "At least we are headed to an apartment with heat. A lot of my people live in cold-water, heatless flats on the Lower East Side and *El Barrio*."

"What?" I couldn't believe that in 1981 that could happen.

"Yes, yes. It was true when our family first moved to the States in the seventies, and it still happens in housing developments for Puerto Ricans and other immigrants in the city. The landlords are supposed to buy the fuel to run the radiators at the end of October but, no. Many landlords are cheap or prejudiced. The building supers are powerless to do anything even though that fuel is needed for heat and hot water. A bad situation. My family moved a couple times in *El Barrio*, but it was mostly the same everywhere because we are Puerto Rican.

"That's horrible, Miguel." I had no idea about the conditions that Miguel had endured. I'm sure his father brought his family to the U.S. for a better life but.... "I'm sorry."

"The apartment that my cousin, my brother, and I share is not terrible. Maybe because it is small, our body heat keeps it warm." He smiled, but we were still shocked and sad to hear his story.

"We need to be thanking our lucky stars," Gordo said.

Three of us arrived at my apartment's outer door, when we realized that Gordo had stopped at the newspaper box in front of the Silver Star Diner to grab *The New York Times*.

"Meet us upstairs, Gordo," I yelled. "We're freezing!"

A blast of radiator heat greeted us as Miguel opened the lobby door. As we climbed to the sixth floor, I said, "We may not have fancy doormen or elevators, but we're lucky it's warm and cozy." We reached the top floor, and I unlocked the door to 6C, leading the group into the kitchen and flipping on the light switch. *Home at last and out of the cold!* Doug punctuated my thoughts by slamming his shoe on the windowsill with a loud thud.

"Cockroach! Got it!"

"There's beer and wine and root beer in the frig. Hang your coats on the hook. And turn on the TV while I start getting things together for dinner," I said, sounding a bit like a drill sergeant setting up a field unit. Gordo, Doug, and Miguel hopped to it and settled into the living room, sipping on beers, chatting, and watching the pre-New Year's Eve coverage on TV.

While I threw together a large salad in the kitchen, I overheard Gordo reporting from an article in *The New York Times.*

"Hey y'all. Here's a bit of harsh reality," he said. "The latest reports on folks with severe immune deficiency came out today. One agency reported two hundred and thirteen cases with seventy-four deaths. Another says the number could be as high as three hundred and thirty and over one hundred dead. Dang."

"Do you think the first number might be for New York only and the second number for the whole U.S.?" Doug asked.

"Who the hell cares, Doug. I mean, damn it. People are dying and the number keeps growing, and it's not getting any better." Gordo took a deep breath. "Excuse my hissy fit." He calmed himself with a long swig of beer.

Joining the conversation, I attempted to diffuse tension by steering away from the emotional aspect and sticking to the facts. "You're right, Gordo. It does feel like all we hear are reports about cases and deaths...not really any positive news about research for cures."

Catching my drift, Miguel added, "I also look for articles in the *Times* about medical research or money for treatment to battle this thing. But I see little mentioned."

"That's right," Gordo said. "The rare articles in the *Times* are buried in the back pages and ever since the papers started calling this the 'Gay Men's Pneumonia' – thank y'all very much – no congressman wants to put any money into helping."

"What a mess," I said, though my words hardly seemed adequate. I knew Gordo and Doug were feeling anxious and frightened.

We were snapped out of our funk by the announcers' silly banter on the television. Dick Clark and a celebrity I didn't know commented on the crowd's size and energy. At least it helped to elevate the mood in the room a bit.

We continued to chat, drink beer, and snack on cheese and crackers until at last Dick Clark excitedly proclaimed the words we had waited for all evening. "Are you ready for the Countdown to the new year?" The sight of masses of cold and sloppy riffraff, screaming and jumping and acting like crazed monkeys at the sight of fresh bananas, brought a wave of gratitude. *Thank God I'm far away from that frenzy!*

"This is it, guys!" I shouted. The four of us huddled around the television to watch the infamous Big Red Apple fall from its high perch over Times Square, ringing in 1982. In unison with the announcer and crowd, we shouted, "Ten, nine, eight, seven, six, five, four, three, two, one. Happy New Year!"

The next few minutes blurred for me.

I smiled as I saw Doug and Gordo embrace and kiss. At the same time, Miguel reached for my shoulder, turning me. He leaned in, quickly pulling me toward him, and kissed me. But what should have been a lovely moment wasn't. I tensed up, my throat constricted, and I immediately sensed a nauseous knot in my stomach. I knew exactly why I reacted that way. It had happened before. *My horrible little secret.*

Suddenly, I couldn't breathe. I could…not…catch…my…

breath!

I broke away from him. "Um…Excuse me. I have to start the water for the pasta." I exited to the kitchen, nearly stumbling in my haste. *Breathe, Margie. Come on…one, simple breath. In through the nose. Good, now out, slowly. It was only a simple freakin' kiss. You like Miguel. Don't ruin this.*

But something snapped in my head and panic set in. *Try to catch your breath.*

While filling the large pot with water and placing it on the gas burner, Gordo and Doug commented about the crazy crowd celebrations on Times Square from the living room. Miguel slipped into the kitchen. "Do you need any help, Margie?" The kitchen air suddenly seemed stifling, although I doubted the heat from stove was the cause.

"Uh, sure. Would you mind cracking the window?"

Miguel opened the window, letting in a blast of cold winter air. He moved next to me by the stove. "Look, I apologize if I was too forward back there. I thought…" His voice trailed off.

The look on his face expressed pain and hurt. My heart sank knowing I was the cause. "Miguel, please, no…" *How do I explain this to him?*

Sensing my floundering, he said, "If I misunderstood the direction our friendship was going, I apologize." *What a gentleman! He's taking the blame for the misfired kiss when it's all on me. But I'm not comfortable explaining my odd reaction.*

"Miguel, I don't think you misunderstood at all. I feel like our relationship is becoming close. And I'm happy about it. I am."

"Then why the reaction?"

Fumbling through any sort of explanation, I attempted to put words into a coherent sentence, failing miserably. "I-I wish

I could explain. It's hard to…I can't…I can't talk about it." I brushed away a tear that had welled up in the corner of my eye. "But it was perfectly…you're perfectly…I'm sorry…I-I can't…"

A bewildered Miguel retreated to the living room to join the others while I kept myself busy with the dinner preparations in the kitchen. A short time later, the front door burst open, and the revelers stumbled in with goofy Happy New Year's headbands and noise makers. Broom Man in 5C did not appreciate the cacophony of merriment and demonstrated his displeasure with his usual broom handle banging on the ceiling. We decided to keep the noise to a minimum, but not before we all shouted, "Happy New Year, Mr. 5C!" Surprisingly, he stopped his banging immediately after our New Year's greeting. *Hmm. Maybe the guy's lonely and that's what makes him grumpy.*

While the dinner party was a success, the disastrous kiss with Miguel put a damper on the evening for us both. No more radiant smiles emanated from Miguel. No more eye contact, as he huddled with Gordo and Doug, quietly chatting. *Have I completely destroyed this wonderful connection between us?* I hoped I could salvage the warmth that had begun to develop between Miguel and me, but I was terrified to dredge up the disgusting story that I'd shoved down for so long. *I don't know if I can let that part of my past escape.*

Despite the mess I made with Miguel, I looked around the room at our funky little gang of New York misfits. We truly were a family unit, and I loved us all – even Broom Man in 5C!

I wanted to believe that 1982 could be bright.

****

During the early weeks of January, the entire Radio City administrative staff focused on preparing for the huge upcoming special event to celebrate the 100th anniversary of the Actors' Fund of America. The entire staff acted like Radio City Music Hall was hosting the Grammy Awards or something! *Absurd. Like that would ever happen at Radio City Music Hall.* They even hired big-name Broadway producer, Alexander H. Cohen, to produce the show and called it "Night of 100 Stars." All I knew was that Sunday, February 14th was fast approaching, and we had a ton of fancy promotional stuff to complete between the first week of January and opening night.

The hectic schedule left little personal time for a social life or writing. And that awkward New Year's Eve kiss had created icicles between Miguel and me. *You need to dig deep, Margie, be courageous and find your voice – however difficult this conversation will be.* It took a bit of wrangling, but I arranged for Miguel to meet me on a Saturday afternoon at Argosy Book Store, one of our favorite shops for old and rare books, located on East 59th Street. *Less chance of bumping into people we might know.*

Walking into Argosy Book Store felt like a comfortable bear hug for anyone who loves books, prints, photography, or old maps. The shelf-lined walls were loaded with modern first editions. Old world paintings hung high above aisles filled with racks holding prints, maps, and atlases. The combination of wood paneling and green glass shades over lamps scattered throughout the store gave it an Ivy League library feel. And that was only the first of six floors! I'd hoped sharing an activity that Miguel and I both enjoyed – bookstore treasure hunting –would help us relax a bit before facing the tough personal conversation.

After browsing through the shelves hunting for unique finds, we retreated to a coffee shop nearby, sitting at a corner table. A lump formed in my throat as I assessed Miguel's demeanor. His defensive arm folded, slumped shoulder posture with hair hanging over his face told me he still hurt. While I didn't blame him,

I'd hoped he'd be receptive to listening. I had a painful story to share with him and needed his full and open attention. *All I can do is try.*

"Miguel, I want you to know that I feel horrible about how I reacted to you on New Year's Eve. The kiss, I mean. But my reaction wasn't toward you, you have to believe me. I need to tell you something. I never shared this with anyone..."

He shifted in his chair and unfolded his arms. *At least he appears to be less defensive.*

"When I toured with the swing band, something happened to me...it was bad." I swallowed hard, gazing out the window rather than looking directly at Miguel. *This is harder than I anticipated. Do I really want to tell him this story? Do I want to tell anyone? I've kept it buried for a long time... What will he think of me? What if he blames me? Or if he thinks I'm damaged goods.*

"Go on, Margie. I am listening."

I took a slow deep breath. My heart thumped in my chest. Tears welled up as I feared facing the dark memories I had locked away. *I need to do this if I want any future with Miguel.* "One night a band member had too much to drink and followed me to the condo where the girls were staying." The horror of that night from over five years ago flashed into my mind, exactly what I was afraid would happen if I unleashed it from that place deep in my soul where I tried to bury it. But I needed to explain my ridiculous reaction to Miguel – I couldn't let this experience continue to have a stranglehold on me. "He wanted...I tried to...I told him to go but...he grabbed me and..." Sobbing, I fumbled through an explanation of the night I was sexually assaulted.

Miguel softened, gently grasping my hands. "*Aw, Cariño.* I'm sorry this happened to you."

"But I didn't pull away from you because you kissed me...

no…It was the sudden movement – when you turned me so quickly. I'm sure that's what set me off – caused me to react like that, to sort of shut down. It seems ridiculous, but that kind of close, rapid movement can…Well, I guess…trigger a weird response in me. I'm sorry."

"Hush, hush." He brushed his hair away from his face with his free hand, looking directly at me with his deep mocha eyes through his glasses.

"I should have told you that night, Miguel, but I froze. I was afraid you'd think badly of me. It's stupid, I know, but I still blame myself for the whole thing. What could I have done to prevent him?"

"No, no, no…you must stop thinking that way. This man is a pig! A woman is a person, not an object." He reached up and gently stroked my cheek. "And I could never think badly of you, that you caused this thing to happen, Margie. No."

"Thank you, Miguel."

"Margie, I would very much like to date you, if you are interested." I smiled at the formality of Miguel's invitation to date and nodded. "But I think the best way forward is to move slowly and talk honestly. We are in no rush. Let us enjoy being together and get comfortable. How does that sound?" Miguel smiled his gorgeous, reassuring smile.

"That sounds like perfection."

We sat in stillness, holding hands, gazing into each other's eyes as the rest of the room melted away, as if we were the only two people in the world – in a calm aura of affectionate energy. After a while, the waiter returned to check on us, breaking our "trance." We giggled, becoming self-conscious of our presence in the coffee shop.

Miguel raised my hand to his lips and kissed it. "I was afraid

I had lost you, and I did not understand why."

"I felt the same way, Miguel. I'll try to be more open with my communication. Thank you for being willing to listen today."

The waiter reappeared with a huge slice of New York style cheesecake. Miguel and I looked at each other, confused.

"I think this is a mistake," I said. "Neither of us ordered this."

"It's on the house…my treat," said the waiter. "You two seemed like you had a lot going on. I figured you could use a delicious treat. Here's two forks. Enjoy!"

*You don't see that happening every day in New York!* Miguel and I renewed our "relationship status," sealing the deal over a delicious, creamy slice of cheesecake. And I couldn't think of a better way to do so.

****

Mid-January brought a major push to design, print, and deliver "Night of 100 Stars" invitations for important dignitaries and celebrities. There were also posters to design, print, and distribute; media kits to assemble and distribute; and the list went on. For weeks, the conference room resembled a manufacturer's assembly line with Miss Chambers pulling workers from the secretarial pools of each Radio City Music Hall department. Definitely an "All Hands On Deck!" enterprise using pages and staff alike. We stuffed envelopes; we assembled media folders; we stuck address labels on packaging; we wrapped; we stacked; we counted; we compared lists; we checked and doubled-checked!

I had to admit the "Night of 100 Stars" invitations sent to New York's bigwigs were super innovative. The details were printed on thick cardstock cut to look like the front of a tuxedo shirt, complete with a real bow tie attached. We then wrapped the printed piece in tissue paper, placed it in a glossy black shirt-size gift box, and secured the box with a gold elastic ribbon. Each shirt box had a pre-printed sticker on the back, designating the name and address of the invited guest. Radio City Music Hall pages were tapped to hand deliver these elegant, shiny tuxedo shirt invitations throughout the city. *How impressed will the V.I.P. recipient be when a Radio City page shows up in uniform at their office with one of these cool invitations?*

In addition to "Conference Room Assembly Line" activities, Miss Chambers asked me to act as a runner between the production and the administrative sides of the building. Routinely, there were important messages that needed immediate attention, but the production personnel weren't always available via phone – maybe they were on stage or in the costume fitting room. The memos included budget-related information, like if Mr. Mason approved a stack of production expenses for the "Night of 100 Stars" show. Likewise, the production expenditure requests continued to filter up from "the desk of Mr. Cohen." I about fainted when I had to hand deliver a budget request for "8,000 square feet of star-speckled bright red carpet" to Mr. Mason, which Mr. Cohen envisioned spread along four blocks of the Avenue of the Americas.

*Are you freakin' kidding me? The Big Apple truly IS the land of excess!*

# 11

# Jockeying the Haves and the Have Nots

*February, 1982*

Gathering the staff in the conference room for a last-minute project on Wednesday before the "Night of 100 Stars" event, Miss Chambers made an announcement. "Margie, I'd like you to attend the event as an onsite runner." She announced this in front the entire team of secretary/assembly line workers who had worked their butts off for the past several weeks. "Mr. Mason felt you showed outstanding effort." *Oh great. Now this entire group thinks I'm some sort of a "Mr. Mason" brown nose.* Not known as "Miss Popularity" at work, and not working to attain that title, my proximity to the Vice President of Finance and his executive secretary made me *personae non grata* among the junior secretaries and aides. They were friendly but kept their distance, probably afraid I wielded influence or something. Which I did not!

"Thank you, Miss Chambers," I said, avoiding eye contact with anyone in the room.

Walking home in the five o'clock darkness that crept over Manhattan on winter evenings, I sorted through my conflicting thoughts, attempting to release the tension in my stomach. On the one hand, I'd be lying if I said I wasn't excited to see what all the fuss had been about the "Night of 100 Stars" event. And what an honor that Mr. Mason noticed my work ethic during the past weeks. *Who cares if a few petty secretaries at Radio City are mad at me? It's not like I had anything to do with whoever got picked to attend the event. And...Holy Crap!* I suddenly realized I faced a crushing problem: What to wear to the star-studded event!

Thank God both Alissa and Crystal were lounging in the apartment living room listening to Blondie's "Rapture" when I arrived home. I threw my purse on the kitchen table and nearly attacked them before even uttering, "Hello."

"You've got to help me. I'm desperate."

"Woah. Hold up. What's going on?" Alissa asked. "Did you get caught stealing from the Mob?"

I looked at her in disbelief. "No. Why would you jump to that conclusion, Alissa?"

"Sorry, reflex...what's going on?"

"My boss wants me to attend this huge 'Night of 100 Stars' event on Sunday and I don't have anything fancy to wear. I also don't have the cash to buy a cocktail dress or gown. What am I going to do?"

"Don't wig out, *chérie*," Crystal said. "I have a bunch of *très chic* stuff you can use."

"Oh, and I know the perfect place. This funky little thrift store off Columbus Circle on the West Side. They're open late. Let's go."

Splurging on a taxi, the three of us headed across town to Alissa's favorite thrift store. What a goldmine! I snagged a classic black crepe shift with thin shoulder straps.

"Timeless," Crystal said.

Alissa added, "Although I wouldn't be caught dead in that, you look great." A backhanded vote of confidence, but from Alissa I accepted it as positive.

"I have the perfect accessories and a jacket to complement that dress, Margie," Crystal said. "I think we can finish our 'Dress Margie Project' back at the apartment."

Raiding her collection in our tiny bedroom, Crystal completed the ensemble by loaning me a gorgeous pink peplum jacket with padded shoulders and a single onyx button. She scoured her jewelry box and found matching onyx earrings. To finish the look, I dug out a pair of black kitten heel pumps from under our bunk bed.

"Wow, I don't look half bad."

Crystal laughed. "If only Miguel could see you in this outfit. He wouldn't be able to keep his hands off you!"

I shot a goofy look at her. "You know Miguel and I are only dating, taking it slow. Don't be a nerd."

Crystal's grin widened. "I don't know…dressed like this, Miguel would not be able to resist you. Cindy Crawford might need to watch out for her modelling career." We all broke up laughing. "Seriously…you look *très beaux,* Margie. Classic!"

"See. Loosening up is good." Alissa said, admiring my outfit. "We got your back."

****

The date of the "Night of 100 Stars" event arrived. My official responsibility for the evening consisted of running messages to the various stars prior to their performance entrance. Frankly, all the stars had their own assistants, leaving me to stand in the back of the orchestra, looking useless. However, my post gave me the perfect vantage point to watch important celebrities and New York City dignitaries, like Mayor Koch, Tony Bennett, Peter Allen, and Dick Clark, filter into the auditorium in all their formalwear and entourage glory.

At the show's opening moments, thousands of white lights

illuminated the proscenium arch, traced the stairs on either side of the stage, and dotted the arches hanging on traveling cables, which enabled the set pieces to descend and ascend. A New York skyline glowed on a forty-by-ninety-foot muslin backdrop, specially woven into one piece for this event. *Impressive, even by Radio City's production standards!*

My favorite act of the evening featured the Rockettes. After the thirty-six dancers did their precision kick routine, they were joined in a dance by Edward Asner, Warren Beatty, Sid Caesar, Robert De Niro, Peter Falk, Jackie Gleason, Dustin Hoffman, Burt Lancaster, Jack Lemmon, Walter Matthau, Robert Morley, Paul Newman, Al Pacino, Sylvester Stallone and Lee Strasberg. The audience giggled watching these, shall we say, less-than-precise celebrity dancers attempting to keep up with the world famous Rockettes, particularly when it came to the kick line.

Other outstanding musical numbers included Mary Martin singing a few bars of "I'm Gonna Wash That Man Right Outa My Hair;" Ethel Merman, "There's No Business Like Show Business;" and Alfred Drake, "Oh, What A Beautiful Morning." *How freakin' cool is it to hear Ethel Merman in person singing a song I've listened to on an album over and over? Mom is never gonna believe this!*

The glitz, the glamour, the full-length fur coats, not to mention the thousand-dollar-a-ticket price for over two hundred special seats and the four-million-dollar production budget for the show – radical amounts of money spent on a single night. At least a portion of the ticket money went to The Actors' Fund, a charity that helped support performers and production workers with emergency financial assistance, social services, healthcare and insurance counseling, housing, and assisted living care.

On the other hand, I reflected on Doug struggling to manage an Off-Off Broadway theater, where young artists barely eked out a living by pursuing their writing, acting, design, or stage crafts. Most worked two or three jobs to support their creative passion. Most would kill for a full-length fur coat – to pawn for next month's rent. *New York is truly a world of Haves and Have Nots.*

****

Despite our wool coats, hats, scarves wrapped around our faces, and double pair of mittens, Gordo and I froze as we walked from the subway station to our writing group meeting in February's near zero temps. The finicky radiator that heated Dr. R.'s apartment decided to go on strike. Keeping my long scarf wrapped around my neck, I shivered as I took my seat next to Miguel, snuggling closer than usual to signal affection *and* to steal his body heat. Besides, he smelled incredible. I loved his musk cologne.

"Thank you for being my human heater," I whispered as I pulled my writing assignment from my canvas shoulder bag. He watched me, a gentle smile spreading across his lovely face.

Any other day Miguel's smile would warm me to my core. But that day, my shivers continued. I planned to share the play I wrote for that day's assignment – a first for me. Playwriting was not my usual thing. In an effort to stretch my writing ability, I began experimenting with genre. For whatever reason, the dramatic form, especially as a way to express what I had been reflecting upon lately, had become effective for me. It was as if I saw a film running in my mind's eye and character dialogue was the only way it could be expressed.

Ever since working on and attending the "Night of 100 Stars" event, an idea had been nagging at me – the intense wealth of a portion of New Yorkers versus the many who struggled to get by. After that night, it seemed that wherever I looked – each neighborhood, park, business district, entertainment area – this dichotomy repeated itself.

I used dramatic expressionism to capture what I observed around me in New York on a daily basis: garbage overflowing from trashcans onto the sidewalks as business folk hurried to their high paying jobs; homeless people sleeping on subway grates while women in fur coats step over them on their way to a matinee to watch the Rockettes dance with precision in glamorous costumes at the fabulously restored Radio City Music Hall; the expense of an 8,000 square foot, star-speckled red carpet for wealthy V.I.P.s to trample over to attend a one night event. Basically, the world of contrasts that *is* New York City.

My short play attempted to encapsulate this duality. It featured a single character: a youngster. Homeless people and wealthy women served as two opposing Greek choruses, spewing social commentary. As I wrote it, my premise made perfect sense. Now I wondered if the concept would hold up. *Is my play too far out there? What if the writing group doesn't get it? What if they laugh me out of the room?*

Usually in our writing group, the author reads his or her piece to the members and asks for feedback. But since a play was a unique contribution, I asked the members to read my script out loud. I assigned Gordo, Miguel, and Gwen to read the three roles. It not only helped me to hear the distinct voice of each character, but I could also watch the readers' faces for signs of acceptance or rejection of my piece. As they read, my doubting mental chatterbox kicked into overdrive. *Have I failed miserably? Should I throw in the towel and take the next train back to Church Creek? Maybe resume my career as a waitress at Doris Mae's Diner? Give in to Dad's pressure to find a husband and settle down… God, snap out of it, Margie!*

During my mini psych out, I almost missed that Dr. R. had begun her critical feedback. Despite being nervous about how it would be received, Dr. R. was impressed with the play.

"Your approach – *excellenté*. This format is quite unique, and the topic is a departure from your past work, Margie," Dr. R. said. "What moved you in this direction?"

I carefully gathered my thoughts before speaking. "I was inspired to explore this topic by Miguel's writing, the way he looks at life around him for inspiration. You challenged us to find an emotional connection deep inside ourselves. This feeling of being appalled at the extreme contrasts I've been observing since moving to New York has been bothering me a lot lately. I wanted to explore it, to find a way to express it through the written word."

Miguel praised the use of two diverse choruses to reflect on the social conditions. Gwen asked why I chose a child as the central figure. Before I could answer, the group launched into a debate about the purpose of using a child, which was interesting for me to hear. I sat back, taking it all in.

Finally, Dr. R. interrupted. "Well, Margie. Your play has generated discussion and conversation, a feat any playwright strives to achieve. I would say, you have a hit!"

As Gordo, Miguel, and I exited the writers' meeting, Miguel stopped me before we parted ways outside Dr. R.'s apartment. He gave me a hug and whispered in my ear, "Great job. I see your heart and soul in this play. You sent a message, a personal message. That is what writing should do." Then he kissed me gently on my ear. Wow. My knees went weak and a tingle raced through my chest to my solar plexus. *What was that? Some Miguel magic?* We separated and gazed into each other's eyes, lingering. Then he pulled away, yelling back as he jogged down the middle of street, "I'll call you later."

While Gordo and I picked our way through the ice patches toward our subway stop, the sensation of Miguel's teasing ear kiss and lasting gaze continued to send chills. I barely heard Gordo say, "Your play's exceptionally good. Would it be okay if I showed the script to Doug?"

"Uh…Sure, Gordo," I said, still thinking about Miguel, who became more fascinating by the second.

****

A couple weeks after the writing group's play reading session, Gordo asked me over to his apartment to talk with Doug about my play. Curious to hear Doug's feedback, I jumped at the opportunity. Doug's experience as an Off-Off-Broadway theater manager could be helpful.

I knocked on Doug and Gordo's apartment door and heard, "Enter!" shouted in stereo. The sound of a whistling tea kettle greeted me, and I spied Gordo carrying a tray holding three Fiestaware Mango Red cups and saucers, tea bags, and spoons. A matching creamer and sugar completed the tray ensemble. *These guys' hosting skills are off the hook!*

"Let's get comfy in living room," he said.

We proceeded into the living room, beautifully decorated with an overstuffed loveseat in olive green and two chairs upholstered in printed floral with hues of cranberry, cream, and green. Plants hung in front of sheer curtained windows framed with bookshelves on either side. Wearing a cozy sweater and signature ascot, Doug sat in the loveseat pouring over my script, which he had laid out on a small coffee table.

Gordo cleared his throat. "Um, I need bit of room for the tray, Doug."

After getting comfortable in the living room with our hot

tea, Doug surprised me, not with feedback but with a proposition. "I read your play, Margie. Several times, as a matter of fact. Here's the deal: Our theater in the Village is looking for fresh works for our New Play Showcase. We have an open slot this spring. I'd like to produce your play for the showcase."

I nearly knocked over my teacup. "Are you freakin' kidding me?"

"Now before you get too excited, you should know that you won't be paid. But having a play showcased is a good chance to see your play on its feet, gauge the audience's reaction, consider revisions. As our boy William said, 'The play's the thing,' although he *was* referencing a way Hamlet could determine that his father was murdered." I chuckled at Doug's unique ability to weave in a Shakespeare quote into any situation, whether appropriate or not. "And you never know who might be in the audience."

"Margie, this is a great opportunity to see if playwriting's the kind of writing you wanna be doing," Gordo said.

Doug laughed at Gordo. "That's one way to put it. What do you think, Margie? You interested?"

I didn't think twice. "I'm all in."

Doug explained the process. "You'll be needed for auditions in early April. Then there's three weeks of rehearsals. The playwright attends rehearsals to be available if questions come up."

"Like what type of questions?" I asked. I may have performed in a bunch of well-established plays and musicals, but I'd never been part of a new play development process.

"There are times an actor might want clarification about a certain line. Or during a break, the director will pull you aside and ask if a scene is coming together the way you envisioned it."

"Oh, cool." I loved the idea of collaborating with the actors and the director to make my words come alive. *This workshop project sounds radical.*

"Another thing you might expect during the rehearsal process is possible script changes," Doug added.

"Why would I need to change the script?" I asked, surprised that he would suggest that possibility.

"Well, with a brand-new play, a playwright or the director might see or hear a moment that's not working on stage – a line that doesn't sound right, a move that might have looked good on paper but is impossible on stage and needs an extra piece of dialogue to cover it – that sort of thing. That's why having the playwright at rehearsals is important."

"Hm. That does make sense. Any kinks would have to be worked out. Thanks for this opportunity, Doug."

"Thank you for this cool new play, Margie. Are we good for opening night on April 30th?"

"Sounds exciting." *Wow, I'm going to have my play produced!*

# 12

# Worlds Crashing to Pieces

*March, 1982*

Feeling as if a knife had been plunged into to my chest, I gasped at the disastrous news! *SoHo Weekly News* shut down on March 15th, which meant I watched my internship wash down the gutter with all the other New York City rotten debris. The shutdown's details hadn't changed the fact that my career had derailed (again). I lived in a crappy, roach infested sixth floor walk-up apartment, worked as a receptionist, and had no new writing prospects. Well, I did have an April showcase for my play. *Wait, what am I thinking? Do I really think I'm a playwright now? How bogus is that?*

In addition to my music journalism career falling apart, Crystal seemed to be having her own personal weirdness going on. Truthfully, she'd been elusive for the past couple months. While it was nice that Crystal had planned the big group get-together for New Year's Eve, I hadn't seen much of her since January1st. She spent her entire break from Parsons School of Design with Girard. I didn't know what they did together, where they went, or who they spent their time with. The rest of our little clan rarely saw them. It made me sad at times. While Doug, Gordo, Alissa, Miguel, and I bonded into a sweet little family, Crystal had less and less interest in being involved. And the irony was that Crystal was the one who invited Doug and Gordo to that first party after meeting them at the lobby mailbox; Crystal was the one who worked with Alissa at the diner; heck...Crystal was the one who asked me to room with her in New York in the first place! *Sad and ironic.*

As the one-year anniversary of our New York City adventure approached, I reflected on the milestones Crystal and I had achieved: finding and settling into an apartment, landing jobs to support ourselves, taking our first career steps – all cause for celebration. Though we were never super tight, I had hoped our "roommate status" might have led to a closeness, similar to the intimate "family" feeling I'd developed with the others. Yet, despite occupying the same apartment, Crystal seemed to be drifting away.

On a Tuesday morning in early March, I scurried around in the bedroom, pulling a pale grey corduroy vest over my pink blouse to complete the skirt ensemble, a birthday present courtesy of Mom and her sewing skills. The package had arrived on the second of March, the day before my birthday. Enclosed was a goofy Ziggy card with a message that read: Happy 27th with love from Mom...P.S. I couldn't resist this fabric sale! *Typical Mom.* I did appreciate the new spring addition to my work wardrobe. As I finished dressing for work, I heard a knock on the door. *Seems early for visitors...* A rare morning that Crystal was even at the apartment, I heard her conversing with someone. While I finished dressing, adding a silver necklace and matching earrings to my ensemble, Crystal rushed into the bedroom and frantically tugged her suitcase from under the bed.

"You seem upset. You okay?" I asked.

"Girard needs to pack. He's going back to Amsterdam. Again!"

"Ah…That seems sudden."

Crystal glared at me and dragged the large suitcase to the apartment door. *That is one angry girl!* When Girard went overseas, he never left his agenda, and it drove Crystal crazy. One week? Two weeks? Three weeks? Who knew?

****

I arrived home from work with Chinese take-out on the evening after hearing that *SoHo Weekly News* had shut down. *March 15th will forever be etched in my brain as a crap day!* In my mind, I could already hear Doug jumping on the date and orating a line from *Julius Caesar,* "Beware the Ides of March, Margie. A soothsayer bids you beware the Ides of March." *Not helpful, Doug!*

Hopeful that Crystal would be home to share in my misery, I entered the apartment to find her crashed out in her pajamas on our new foam fold-out sofa, listening to the TV news about John Belushi's overdose death, still front and center in the news cycle, even though it occurred ten days ago.

"Hey, how was design class today?" I asked as I gathered serving spoons and plates.

"Didn't go…kinda tired and depressed. Can't concentrate." *Hmm. She missed class a couple times last month. I wonder what the attendance policy is at the Parsons School of Design?*

"Well, you do seem tired. Maybe you'll feel better once you've had a bite to eat. I brought take-out from Ming Lo's."

"Sh-h. I wanna hear this." Crystal jumped off the sofa and glued herself next to the TV. She appeared super irritable about this John Belushi news.

I dished out a plate of takeout, plopped an egg roll on the side, and brought it into the living room. "Here's a bit of your favorite…Sweet and Sour Chicken," I said, handing her the plate.

Crystal suddenly flew off the handle. "Can't you see I'm super bummed out about John Belushi. I'm not hungry. Why are you always trying to shove food down my throat?"

"What are you talking about? I brought home Chinese. What's the big deal? Eat, don't eat."

*Crystal drew in a huge breath, composing herself.* "Right. I'm tired and upset about the news, and I wish Girard would get back from Amsterdam."

"Ah, I get it." I forced my voice to sound concerned because I still didn't understand what she saw in that inconsiderate sleaze. "You miss Girard."

The next thing I knew Crystal dove into a rant about how Girard was supposed to be back from Amsterdam Monday or Tuesday, and she couldn't figure out what could be keeping him. She completely wigged out, pacing back and forth between the living room and kitchen, like a trapped tiger searching for an escape route.

"He's probably left me for a beautiful European woman. He's so gorgeous. How can I compete?" she said, looking at herself in the mirror over the kitchen sink. "Oh God, look at me. I'm a major disaster." She suddenly turned and confronted me. "Why didn't you tell me I look this bad? These dark circles under my eyes, my skin looks horrible, I'm itchy all over, for God's sake. I'm disgusting. I've got to..."

I jumped in. "Hold on, Crystal. Breathe. How about sitting down and eating a healthy dinner first? When was the last time you ate a meal that wasn't a bunch of snack food?"

Crystal's emotional pendulum swung again. She sat down with an exhale and grabbed the plate of Sweet and Sour Chicken I had prepared. While tearing open a packet of soy sauce for her egg roll, she blurted, "I was thinking today, what if I buy a plane ticket and fly to Amsterdam, you know, as a surprise for Girard. The look on Girard's face will be amazing. Plus, I need to make sure…Yeah, I'm going to do it. I'll get a ticket tomorrow."

Of course, that was a horrible idea, but I needed to proceed with caution. "You could do that, Crystal. But are you sure you're thinking clearly? You haven't been sleeping well, and you look like…well…hell. And think of this…you said he's due back in the states any day, right? What if you board a plane to Amsterdam tomorrow, and Girard is flying home the same day? You'd be passing each other over the Atlantic and not even realizing it."

Crystal glared at me. "You really are a killjoy, Margie." Then she got agitated again. I braced myself for another round of "Boxing with Irrational Crystal."

A knock on the door snapped Crystal out of her latest cranky mood swing. She ran down the long hallway and opened the door. Screams of high-pitched delight pierced my ears. "Girard!" The two came into the kitchen as I slurped semi-warm Egg Drop Soup.

Crystal's mood swung into perky overdrive as she pulled Girard into the apartment. Clad in yet another new pair of Ray-Ban sunglasses despite the evening hour, he deposited Crystal's suitcase in the kitchen. They clawed each other for a minute or two before Crystal announced, "Girard and I are splitting to get steaks on First Avenue. See you tomorrow." Pouf. They were off. *Oh, and hello to you too, Girard. That guy never has a friendly word.*

After eating my fill of Moo Shoo Gai Pan, I packed up the leftovers and stored them in the fridge. I dragged Crystal's suitcase that Girard had oh-so-politely left in the middle of the kitchen to the bedroom, shoving it under her bed before heading over to the Silver Star Diner for a slice of their amazing New York style cheesecake for dessert. I hoped I'd catch Alissa on shift. I needed to pick her brain.

The restaurant was nearly empty at eight o'clock on a Monday evening, perfect timing for snagging Alissa for a chat. Between bites of delicious, creamy cheesecake topped with fresh strawberries (only in the Big Apple can strawberries this yummy turn up in March!), I described the previous Crystal scenario to Alissa and asked for her take.

Under her newly dyed blood red bangs, she released a huge exhale and stared at me with an exasperated look, one that I've learned to mean: "You're about to get lectured, you get me?"

"Alissa, what is it?"

"You really don't know what's going on here, do you, Margie?"

"Clearly I don't, but you're going to fill me in, aren't you?"

"Ya know I love ya, but you're the most lamebrained chick I've ever met."

I laughed. "I've been called worse. Now tell me what I don't know."

Alissa launched in. "From what I've seen, Crystal's using." I was silent, processing, not sure what she meant exactly. She continued. "Knowing Girard, it's cocaine. The whole city knows Girard uses cocaine. We all guess that's what all those trips to Amsterdam are about, you get me?"

"Wait, so he flies to Amsterdam, parties there for a few weeks, and then what? I don't follow."

Alissa patiently tried to tie up the loose ends for me. "Girard flies home with coke that he buys on the cheap – enough for himself and his current girlfriend to last a while. Maybe even a bit to deal in the States to fund his next trip, you get me? I don't know for sure and I don't wanna know."

"Isn't he putting himself in a dangerous position? How in the world does he get cocaine through customs?"

"No idea. Maybe he figures airport security for drug smuggling is more focused on flights coming in from Miami or Houston or LAX."

"That could be right. All the articles in *The New York Times* are reporting that the cocaine problem is stemming from drugs coming through the Bahamas and the Dominican Republic."

"Hey man, all I know is what I hear on the street. And word is that's exactly why a 'source' in a completely different part of the globe might work."

I continued to process this information and make sense of Crystal's part in it. "But if that's true...do you think Crystal knows? Maybe she was worried he'd get caught, and that's why she was agitated when he was over a week late getting back from Amsterdam?"

"Well, probably more like she needed a hit of powder. Face it, Girard's her private dealer and he was overdue. She probably used up her stash, you get me? Was she acting kinda twitchy and moody and super tired?"

*Oh my God, that's exactly how she was behaving, especially the last couple of days. Crystal does have a cocaine problem.* "Yes," I said softly. "How do you know so much about this, Alissa? All the signs, what to look for."

"Been there before, that's all. Done the rehab thing. Took a bunch of tries but I'm clean now. Still, each day's a struggle. Lost most of my friends 'cuz they all use. I told all this to Crystal, but she's not ready to hear it."

*Wow. I don't know how to respond to this bombshell. Alissa...a recovering addict?* I did notice she never drank wine during our little dinner parties, always opting for root beer. I figured she really liked root beer! *I* am *a lamebrained chick!*

Not sure if my silence made her uncomfortable, but Alissa appeared to withdraw. I stopped asking questions. I felt idiotic and out of my element when it came to the world of drugs and addiction, and had no idea how to help. I also wanted to smack Girard for dragging Crystal into this mess. But I rationalized that Crystal was her own person. She could have said no, walked away, and recognized Girard for the creep he was. On the other hand, maybe not. Even in high school, she excelled in being the "life of the party" – enticing older guys to buy her cheap wine, experimenting with weed, earning a reputation as a "fast girl." *Maybe becoming dependent on cocaine is part of the package.*

This whole episode was totally too much for me to figure out. *Could it be true? Girard flies off to Amsterdam to party and then smuggles cocaine to the United States to keep Crystal and himself supplied...until the next time. Is that all there is to this? Is he putting Crystal in danger of getting busted?* This was a world I couldn't begin to understand.

In the meantime, I never had the chance to tell anybody about my dilemma: No more internship at *SoHo Weekly News*. Crap! Crystal's mess seemed a lot worse than my music journalism career drying up. *Here's hoping the second year of our New York City adventure will be more fulfilling…and not devastating for Crystal.*

# 13

# Worlds Coming Together

*March, 1982*

Despite dealing with the stark realization of Crystal's situation and the closing of *SoHo Weekly News,* at least I had two positive things going for me: Miguel and I were solid, and I looked forward to working on my play at Doug's theater. In early March, Doug invited me to a production meeting with the designers at the theater to hear their early ideas about the set and costume designs for the play. Doug and I arrived early for a quick venue tour.

In another study of contrasts, this tiny storefront theater on East 4th Street in the East Village was about as big as the Rockettes' rehearsal studio at Radio City Music Hall. Doug led me through the Workshop Theater's lobby, pleasantly decorated with posters of past shows. The lobby's furnishings consisted of a small table, where I assumed tickets were sold. He held open a single door leading to the auditorium of sorts – more like a large room with thirty or forty folding chairs facing an empty space framed by long grey curtains. The "stage" space measured approximately twenty feet deep by twenty feet wide.

"I know, it's not the fanciest of theater spaces, but it's our home." Doug's face radiated pride as he strode to center stage and struck a grandiose pose. I had to chuckle at his theatrical sensibility – his stance, his grey corduroy blazer with bright red ascot at the neck, the way he pointed to stage right and left as he announced, "These grey curtains on either side of the stage provide another five feet of 'backstage' space."

"Tight quarters," I said. "No wonder you're always on the lookout for smaller plays with flexible casts!"

"Correct. And if the stage didn't convince you...follow me!"

Doug led me behind the stage area where two small dressing rooms and a bathroom resided. "Picture if you will...actors squeezing into these two closet-sized rooms changing into their costumes and fighting for mirror space to apply their makeup!"

"You have made your point, sir...smaller casts are better for the Workshop Theater."

After the tour, Doug introduced me to Viv, the costume designer, and Pete, the set designer. We pulled auditorium chairs into a circle and prepared to discuss ideas for my play. As Producer/Director, Doug's first order of business was to articulate his show concept, covering both the financial and practical restraints.

Doug addressed us in a cheerful, though professional tone. "Greetings, team. Let me summarize my concept for this show with a single word: Minimalistic." Viv and Pete groaned, leaving me to wonder what I missed.

In his heavy Brooklynese accent, Pete responded. "Dat's your concept for every damned show, Doug!" They all laughed. *Okay, I'm onboard now. The theater's small and apparently so is the budget.*

"Well, you know what Shakespeare wrote in *Hamlet*, 'More matter with less art,'" Doug said with a wink, resulting in more groans all around.

"Right-o. Knowing dat, Viv and I jumped da gun and created some prelims. Youse want we should share our designs?"

"Absolutely, Pete." Doug and I nodded simultaneously.

"Set-wise, I'm thinking we use a city skyline silhouette, since we have exactly such a backdrop in storage…"

Doug interrupted, "I like that already – reusing stock scenery."

"Right-o. Knew youse would. Then minimalistic set pieces and props to depict scenery as needed, like garbage bags filled with foam and stacked together, or large cardboard boxes for the homeless city. Lightweight to move on and off stage quickly."

Doug nodded and added, "Can you get us a couple of sketches?"

"No problem-o. Wait till youse see what Viv has for costumes. Show 'em, Viv."

Viv pulled out a few rough sketches in watercolor washes and laid these on the floor between us. "Going along with the minimalistic concept that we knew Doug would suggest, I came up with the idea that both the Greek Choruses – the Wealthy Women and the Homeless Men – would be dressed in black turtleneck tops and black pants. Then we'd layer on a single costume piece to suggest their role. For example, the Wealthy Women might wear a fox stole or sequin jacket or tiara and boa, while the Homeless Men might wear a raggedy scarf or torn jacket."

I loved Viv's costume ideas. "What did you have in mind for the child, the main role?" Doug and I had decided that due to the limited number of rehearsals, we would cast a young-looking adult rather than an actual child for this production.

Viv's eyes lit up. "I had an exciting idea for the child. Since I wasn't sure as I read the script if the child was male or female, I thought to myself, 'What if we made the child both male and female?' I could costume the child as both." *What on earth is Viv talking about?* I let her explain her concept a bit more before jumping in.

Viv held up an absurd looking sketch. "My idea was to create a dual gender character – half male and half female – dressed in an overall outfit of half shorts and half skirt. Get it, boy/girl! Oh, and hair could be straight on one side and a short pigtail on the…"

"Hold up!" I had given Viv a chance to explain her "vision," but I needed to assert myself before this got further out of hand. "There's an important point here. The child character IS NOT half boy and half girl. I can see where the character may be read as a bit neutral. But what you are describing would completely distract from the 'Everyman' quality I'm hoping for." We all sat silently, eyes cast downward, reflecting. I needed to clarify my vision before things derailed and not act like a wet noodle.

Finally, Viv spoke up. "You're right, Margie. I let my imagination run away." She tucked the boy-girl design back into her portfolio. "That design *would* completely distract from the play's message."

I smiled, inwardly releasing a sigh of relief. "How about something that could read both boy or girl? A simple look like a tee shirt under denim overalls with sneakers and short hair?"

Doug piped up, "Minimal and cheap too!" While we all cracked up, I also considered that I had much to learn about navigating this new terrain – the rehearsal production space. Looking back a few years ago, I would have never found the nerve to speak up and offer my opinion or assert my desires in an environment like this. *It's interesting how these skills evolve and pop up exactly when we seem to need them most.*

****

A few days later, Miguel called with a romantic invitation. He suggested we meet at the Museum of Modern Art on 53rd Street between Fifth and Avenue of the Americas. In addition to the Picasso and Monet exhibits, my favorite spot in the museum complex was the sculpture garden.

Our relationship had grown unhurriedly and beautifully over the past several months – since that New Year's Eve debacle. We had been intentional about taking our time to build trust, moving at a snail's pace physically, communicating honestly, and allowing the bond to blossom in its own time. I appreciated Miguel's considerate gestures, like suggesting we meet at one of my favorite Manhattan museums.

We greeted each other at the MOMA entrance with a long embrace, neither one of us wanting to let go. Enveloped in Miguel's arms, I buried my face in his neck, breathing in his aroma and soaking in the energy that existed between two bodies caressing. As we separated, Miguel slid his right hand to the small of my back and guided me toward the sculpture garden. I loved that feeling – security, warmth, respect – all in a simple physical gesture.

Bundling up against the cool March weather, we sat in wire chairs among the pools of still water, barely budding trees, and glass fronted buildings that surrounded the garden. The quiet oasis became the perfect antidote to my especially frustrating week of Crystal's freak out and the *SoHo Weekly News* shutdown. Miguel always knew how to boost my spirits.

"What a wonderful idea, Miguel. Thank you."

"You had a bad week. I wanted to make it better. That is all."

"Seeing you makes things better."

Miguel lifted my gloved hand and kissed it. "Tell me about your week."

"After losing my internship, I'm not sure what will happen next as far as my journalism career." He caressed my gloved hand softly as we listened to a fountain gurgling and splashing at the garden's far end.

Grateful for the way Miguel and I were able to come back together after the New Year's Eve mess, I reflected on his many unexpected traits – how he had been completely understanding about my past trauma, how he had been willing to move ahead slowly, how he patiently nurtured this relationship. In the serenity of MOMA's sculptures and surrounding water melodies, my thoughts meandered to our first intimate night together.

After an evening of my poor cooking and a few glasses of wine, I gently grabbed Miguel's hand and led him to the bedroom. I wanted to be with him but felt unsure – afraid, no… terrified that I'd freak out and screw up the great relationship we had been building. I think he sensed my conflict.

Miguel caressed both sides of my face in the dim bedroom and kissed me deeply. "You are beautiful, Margie." Gazing into my eyes for a moment longer, he calmly leaned in toward my ear, kissing it gently before whispering, "I have a thought."

After an awkward climb to my top bunk, I laid on my side with Miguel lying behind me, both of us fully clothed. With his arm around my waist and his hips pressed firmly against mine, I relaxed against his body. He softly kissed my hair, occasionally stroking my neck. We snuggled and whispered and dozed and kissed and breathed in each other's essences the entire night.

The following morning, I turned to Miguel and poured my heart out. "Last night…I can't tell you how much…this is exactly what I needed, Miguel. I feel closer to you."

"I told you before, I am in no hurry. I enjoy being with you. I care about you and what happens to you."

"You are perfection…and thank you."

The sound of a squawking blue jay overhead brought me

back to the MOMA patio. I looked over at Miguel and smiled at how rosy his cheeks had become from the brisk breeze. He seemed to be deep in thought, although that was a normal look for him. A serious thinker.

"Margie, I have been wondering. How much did you enjoy writing those music reviews – honestly?" Miguel's question surprised me. He had a way of being quite direct, like an archer's arrow to the heart.

"Well…of course I love writing about music. That's what I had been doing even before I came to New York."

"Ah, but New York…do you not find that New York has an energy?"

"Energy? What do you mean, Miguel?

"I am trying to explain…for a writer, an artist…the energy in New York is electric. What you may have been doing before might have been good, yes, but the creative pulse here may drive you to explore much more. Right?"

"Hmm. The energy of the city? So even though I enjoyed writing music reviews and journalism before…"

"Yes, but what do you feel now?" he asked. "What I am saying is that since you have joined Dr. Rodriguez's writing group, you have been exploring other kinds of writing, yes?" I nodded and he continued, "And you are a talented storyteller, not only a fact-teller. Your short play, for example, shows that flexible creative voice."

"Thank you, Miguel. That means a lot to me. But I still… I'm not sure how comfortable I am with other genres of writing. I feel grounded in journalism. I still feel like creative writing is too risky for me."

"Ah…but writers must not be afraid of risks."

We continued to sit in silence, listening to the gurgling

fountain, the occasional chirping sparrow, or the soft voices of another couple across the garden. In my head Miguel's words echoed: "Writers must not be afraid of risks…" Was I tapping into the creative energy of New York or too busy listening to my self-doubts? *Who am I kidding? Taking risks is one of my biggest fears.* If what Miguel said was true, then I had a lot of work to do as a writer.

# 14

# Plotting a Different Course

*April, 1982*

Rudderless without a charted course since the *SoHo Weekly News* folded a month ago, I watched my journalism career drift out of sight. Not that I gained much in the way of writing experience from that quasi-job. I learned how to make a killer pot of coffee and occasionally wrote articles about musical acts that ended up reduced to press releases. My biggest takeaway: I needed to improve my negotiation skills, should I ever get a similar opportunity. I outlined new goals in my journal and used these as daily mantras: "Set parameters. Sell your strengths as a writer. Show yourself to be a woman willing to collaborate. Stop being a sap." *Sounds great in my journal. Let's hope I can actually do this in an interview...if I ever get another interview.*

My parents were super disappointed that I wasn't planning on coming home for Easter on April 11th, but the timing couldn't have been worse. Auditions for *Haves and Have Nots* had been scheduled for early April and then bam! We went right into rehearsals. I made a commitment, and I planned to follow through. Plus, I secretly didn't want to go home. I admit it. The whole New York thing had grown on me – my friends, my growing relationship with Miguel, my safe Radio City Music Hall routine, the showcase for my play. *Could I actually be turning into a New Yorker?* But it ran deeper than that. If I enjoyed New York, if I discovered new writing options, if I had friends who weren't to his liking…I'd have to confront my Dad – exhausting to consider.

Dad didn't understand my interest in playwriting at all, especially if it interfered with his plans. He made sure to drive that point home during my pre-Easter, "sorry-I-can't-make-it" phone call.

> Dad: Margaret, this play thing…it's a bunch of malarkey. Why waste your time writin' plays? Aren't ya doin' journalism?
>
> Me: It kinda unfolded as part of my writing group, Dad. We're encouraged to explore all types of writing as a way to grow.
>
> Mom: (*On the other extension*) That sounds reasonable. How's the internship going? And the job at Radio City?
>
> Me: The job is fine, the internship not so fine. *SoHo Weekly News* folded. There is no more internship.
>
> Dad: What in blue blazes! Now you're livin' in that God-awful city to be a writer and all ya have to show for it is some sort of play? And ya don't even have an internship? Good Lord, Margaret. Talk sense into your daughter, Mother. I'm hangin' up.
>
> Me: I don't understand what he's upset about, Mom.

Mom: Well…you have to see his side a little bit. You do seem a bit all over the place.

Me: What do you mean?

Mom: I'm talking about when you came back from touring with the band, all you talked about was wanting to go to graduate school, which I supported one hundred percent. Then you changed direction and decided to move to New York, telling us that an internship would help your music review writing even more than graduate school. And now you're saying that playwriting has caught your fancy.

Me: Mom! I'm still looking for another internship and this play is simply another way of expressing myself through writing. But he won't even let me explain.

Mom: He's been on edge lately. I guess he wants you home…

Me: Look, thing's aren't bad here. My writing group is great, I have a nice group of friends, and I'm paying my own way. I'll get another internship.

Mom: He has certain ideas…

Me: This I know, Mom.

****

For the next few weeks, I sat in on the auditions and rehearsals for my showcase of *Haves and Have Nots* at Doug's theater, the perfect distraction from thinking about the demise of my music journalism career. Falling back on my community theater experience, my memories of the theater world's traditions flooded in. I enjoyed sitting at the director's table as actors stood on the tiny stage area and auditioned using my words. Knowing my opinion mattered when it came to casting filled me with pride. Due to stage and budget limitations, we reduced the chorus size to three Wealthy Women and three Homeless Men, bringing the total cast size to seven, including the Child role.

On April 6th, the day of callback auditions, a freak unseasonable blizzard hit metropolitan New York. The result: almost a foot of snow – unheard of in Manhattan – rendering the entire island and surrounding area incapacitated. Traffic screeched to a standstill, schools and businesses closed, even government offices quit early. Needless to say, the theater followed suit and callbacks were rescheduled, throwing the entire three-week rehearsal schedule off for *Haves and Have Nots*. An ominous start for what Doug kept labelling my "potential career-changing" project!

After the drifting calmed down and the sun melted the snow a couple days later, Doug and the producers re-grouped and scheduled the callback auditions for April 9th, Good Friday. When the selections were finally announced the following week and many of theater's regular actors were eliminated from consideration, a sense of angst overwhelmed the energy in the building.

However, once the casting news (and grudges) settled, the entire team of actors and crew threw themselves into rehearsals the following week, making up for lost time. Doug proved to be an excellent director, entering each rehearsal with a plan but creating an open space where the actors felt free to experiment with the text I had written. Mesmerized by the process, I was thrilled, watching my words come to life even more vividly than I had imagined. Occasionally, during breaks, Doug asked me about an actor's interpretation, a visual staging he had created, or a transition that needed clarification. With Doug's spot-on insights and respect for my script, I loved working with him as a collaborator and a friend.

At last, April 30th arrived. Opening night! I greeted my friends for the big night, loving that Gordo, Miguel, Gwendolen, and Dr. R. from the writing group attended to cheer me on. Miguel handed me a lovely bouquet of pink roses with a warm kiss. Even Miss Chambers, my supervisor from Radio City, came to show her support, which cracked me up because she looked a tad overdressed in her white crepe suit accessorized with a gold and pearl choker and matching earrings. Quite a portrait of contrasts, posing on the theater's metal folding chairs, I appreciated her trekking to the East Village to become a theater cheerleader. And Alissa made sure she got the night off from Silver Star Diner to attend. The one person who didn't show up…Crystal. She'd been a complete mess lately and getting worse by the minute. I didn't let her chaotic life ruin my big night, though. *Push her out of your mind and proceed, Margie.*

The show, while not perfect with only three weeks of rehearsal, had great acting moments. Doug's direction was highly creative. He was able to plug into my themes of contrast by creating distinct stage pictures with the seven characters. The set designer chose to avoid the obvious black and white motif to demonstrate contrast, choosing instead shades of taupe and gray set against gleaming royal blue and emerald green in jewel tones for the minimal props and set pieces. *Interesting choices.*

An exciting evening highlight: Mr. Allen Tarkington, producer for Red Barn Summer Theater in Plymouth, Massachusetts, sat in the audience taking notes. Apparently, Doug invited Mr. Tarkington to the showcase because he had worked at that theater the previous couple of summers. Mr. Tarkington asked Doug to introduce him to me after the show.

"Ah, pleasure to meet you, Margie. Won't take much of your time." I craned my neck to look at Mr. Tarkington hovering over me. Dressed in a tweed jacket with a pipe in his lapel pocket and carrying a black fedora, he smiled warmly as he extended his free hand to shake mine. "I'm sure you have several friends and family to greet," Mr. Tarkington continued. "I wanted to chat about your insightful short play."

"Yes, please. I'd appreciate any feedback," I said.

"Good. Well, then, in a nutshell. I adored your use of dialogue, the way you incorporated creative ideas to support your theme, and I particularly liked your use of directly addressing the audience at times – breaking down the fourth wall. It created intimacy that many playwrights are afraid to explore. Good job, young lady."

"Thank you, Mr. Tarkington." He flipped his fedora onto his head, turned, and left. Doug winked at me and suggested that Gordo and I meet him in half an hour at Caffe Reggio to celebrate and discuss Mr. Tarkington's mini review.

A coffee house may seem like an unusual spot to celebrate, but the intimate, quiet atmosphere of Caffe Reggio was the perfect place for us to unwind after the hectic three weeks leading up to opening night. Besides, the official cast and crew party would take place after the final performance on Sunday evening. Caffe Reggio, off Washington Square Park, was a short walk from the theater and a favorite New York University student hangout. At ten thirty p.m. on a Saturday night the place was deserted.

Doug found Gordo and me sipping cappuccino at a corner

table when he poked his head in the café doorway. He gave Gordo a quick kiss on the cheek and sat down across from us. I teased him about his important post-show administrative tasks requiring his attention.

"Did you get those folding chairs realigned properly before you locked up the theater, Doug?"

"Very funny, Miss Playwright Celebrity. Seriously, what about Mr. Tarkington's feedback? I'm glad he was able to attend. I invited him to see my direction of the show initially, but I also wanted him to see your playwriting ability, Margie."

"Gosh, Doug. I appreciate it, but it's my first play ever. What do you think will come of him seeing it?" I asked.

"Look. All I know is Mr. Tarkington is always in the market for new playwrights. What's the harm? Why not plant "the Margie seed" in his mind?" Doug paused while he seemed to be thinking. "I have an interesting idea. You ever written plays for young audiences, you know, like Children's Theater?"

"Of course not. Like I said, I'm new at this playwriting thing."

Gordo laughed. "Uh oh. Doug's got that 'Something's percolating in my brain' look. You better watch out, Margie."

****

The following morning, I stumbled out of bed at half past ten, my nostrils filled with the wonderful aroma of fresh coffee. I entered the kitchen and Crystal handed me a cup of freshly brewed java – presumably as a peace offering.

"Before you say a word, I can explain. I was heading to your show thingy. I promise I was. But as I headed out the door, I got a call from Girard. You aren't going to believe where he was." She paused, expecting me to guess. Barely awake, I simply stared and shrugged. "He was in the city jail! Can you believe it?" Sadly, I could, but I remained silent. "He needed me to come bail him out. I grabbed my purse and flagged down a taxi and there you go." Crystal stopped talking as if that was the end of her story.

"Well, what happened?"

"Oh, right…It was all a misunderstanding that happened at the restaurant where Girard worked before he went to Amsterdam. Something about a credit card, but it's all taken care of."

My brain tried to process Crystal's words, but the story didn't make sense. I wanted to ask more questions, but a knock on the door interrupted our conversation.

"It's probably Girard…we're off to breakfast on the West Side." Crystal ran down the hallway and yelled, "Catch ya later, *mon amie*." *And…she's gone.*

I pulled on a pair of maroon sweatpants with a matching sweatshirt and reached under the bed for a pair of sneakers to slip on. Though I headed over to the Silver Star Diner under the pretense for getting breakfast, I especially wanted to see if Alissa had any more up-to-date news on the Girard excitement. Alissa always had more up-to-date news than I did. *She's a gossip magnet.*

The diner was packed with the Saturday morning brunch crowd. I waited near the cash register, attempting to get Alissa's attention. *That's what I get for sleeping in. Doug and Gordo have probably already eaten and gone home!*

Alissa approached, handed me a menu, and started in. "Let me guess…Girard said it was a misunderstanding about a misplaced credit card. Am I right?"

"Yes, that's exactly what Crystal said. How did you know?"

"There's a table in the back, okay? We gotta be discreet."

I made my way through the Saturday morning crowd,

avoiding tables full of omelets and coffee cups and orange juice, to a small booth near the swinging kitchen door. While it was the least desirable spot in the diner, I did get Alissa's point about discretion.

Plopping a mug on my table and pouring hot coffee into it, she said in a hushed voice, "This isn't the first arrest for Girard. It's a scam he runs. Some of us think it's how he gets the bucks to travel to Amsterdam. I didn't want to tell you before…I thought it would freak you out."

"I'm not following. What am I missing?"

"It's a waiter scam, you get me? He waits tables at high-end restaurants. He scopes out one of his tables where there's lots of booze flowing. If the man of the hour pays by credit card, great. Girard runs the card and 'conveniently' forgets to return it. After that customer leaves the restaurant, for the rest of the night, the tab for any table that pays in cash gets run on the lifted credit card and Girard pockets the cash. All night long! And then he quits the next day and books a trip to Amsterdam. Unless he gets caught…"

"What happens then?"

"First, he gets his latest squeeze to come post bail. Then he pours on the charm and claims it was all a big mistake and gag, gag, gag."

"How do you know all this?"

"Believe me, the restaurant industry is a small, gossipy world. Even in the Big Apple."

The ding from the kitchen bell pulled Alissa away to pick up a breakfast order. I sipped my hot coffee and worried about Crystal's naïve involvement with Girard. *What a sleazebag! And she doesn't see it. I hope this is a short-lived phase for her, but she seems to be in deep.*

Thinking about all the changes that had occurred in the short time that Crystal and I had lived in New York.... jobs and school and internships and boyfriends and a theater showcase. We'd been here for a bit over a year and time seemed to be in overdrive in this city. Pressure built within me as I forced myself to plot out a future career course, swinging between continuing my search for another journalism internship or pursuing this playwriting direction. Or wondering if I should steer down a different career avenue altogether. And then there was my Dad breathing down my neck with his expectations for what my life should look like. Each decision came with risks and fear of the unknown...creating emotional swings to the point that I began to feel immobilized.

*Snap out of it, Margie. You're acting like that first day in New York when you couldn't even get yourself out of the car!*

# 15

# Finding Rage

*May, June, 1982*

At our May writing group session, Dr. R. announced that she would be out of town for our June meeting. She offered an interesting prompt for our next writing assignment and encouraged us to reflect deeply, to probe our feelings.

"What enrages you?" she asked. Confused, the group glanced around as Dr. R. continued. "You are clever writers, sure. You have the technical skills to weave together themes in an interesting way or to use symbolism or lyrical phrases to enhance your messages. This is excellent. But for this assignment, I ask for more…I am asking you to tap into a deep emotional response – rage – and find ways to communicate that personal expression through the written word. Your end result can take any form – personal essay, poetry, short story – whatever you feel will best express your deep feelings. Today, let us start with a fifteen-minute journal exercise – brainstorming a list of topics, issues, people, words, images – jotting down anything that enrages you, that evokes a strong emotional response. Ready, begin."

Miguel, Gordo, and Gwendolen jumped right in, scribbling away in their journals. My mind went blank. *Write, Margie. What pisses you off? Hmm. Crystal, lately. But she doesn't "enrage me." No, that's not what Dr. R. is talking about.*

I thought back to a time when I toured with King Vido's Swing Band, and I found out that the female band members earned a hundred dollars a week less than the males. I was pretty upset about that injustice, although I wasn't mad enough to do or say anything about it. *Typical of me.* And I didn't like it when certain people abused other people for being different, whether because of their skin color or sexual orientation or religious choice. My Dad was the worst when it came to displaying his prejudices. In fact, my Dad got me pretty riled up in general – the way he tried to shove his values down my throat. And what about his refusal to listen to me? *Okay, now I'm making progress.*

But lately, I had been even more angry about what I had been seeing around New York. I had begun to express that frustration in my short play, showing the vast difference between people with money and those without. Maybe I was missing how that difference related to the world at large. *Is that what this assignment is getting at? Looking at global issues that tap into deeper emotional responses, starting with rage?*

"And that's time." Dr. R.'s voice interrupted my stream-of-consciousness process. For the rest of the meeting, we each shared our preliminary ideas. While the others seemed to be fine-tuning a topic for their personal essay or whatever, I still floundered.

"Not to worry," Dr. R. assured me. "You have two months before the next writing workshop. Read, watch the news, look around you, journal daily. I have confidence that a topic will rise to the top and connect in an emotional way."

Gordo waited by the door while I said goodbye to Miguel and made plans to get together the following evening for a dinner date. He needed to stay behind to discuss a writing opportunity with Dr. R.. Miguel gently grasped my shoulders and pulled me close, kissing me deeply before saying goodbye. I left Miguel to catch up with Gordo.

"Hmm. Things are getting pretty cozy between you and Miguel, I see," Gordo said as we maneuvered down the narrow apartment stairs.

"Yep, it's nice. He's nice. What I mean is, we're..."

"Why, my dear Margaret. I do believe you are a-blushin'," Gordo said in a silly, exaggerated Southern Belle dialect.

I punched his arm. "Shut up, you nerd!" Laughing, we reached street level and pushed open the apartment door onto Spring Street.

"I'm starvin', Margie. How about we head over to Joe's Pizza for a slice before going back uptown?"

I thought pizza was a great idea. I wanted to probe deeper into his idea for this next writing project. The skies had begun to cloud over, threatening rain. We picked up the pace and high-tailed it across the several blocks from Dr. R.'s Spring Street apartment to Joe's on Carmine near Bleeker Street.

With our typical New York pizza order in hand – two greasy, thin-sliced wedges slapped onto a white paper plate (the way God had intended!) – we snagged two spots at the side counter facing a wall of pizza images and photos of – who else? – Joe Pozzuoli. An immigrant from Naples, Italy, Joe put his sweat and tears into creating this establishment in 1975. *Who doesn't love an American Dream success story?* Folding our pizza slices in half like true New Yorkers, Gordo and I bit into a perfect blend of tomato sauce, mozzarella cheese, and Italian spices baked onto a not-too-crisp thin crust. I waited until he nearly finished eating before asking about his initial idea for our writing project.

"So, Gordo...what enrages you? For the assignment, I mean."

Wiping his mouth with a napkin from the dispenser on the counter, he collected his thoughts before he responded. "I wanna write about feeling helpless when the world seems to be turning its back."

"What do you mean, exactly? Are you talking about parents turning their backs on their kids?"

"No, ma'am. I'm talking about this stupid disease that nobody wants to talk about. What cruel reporters are calling 'the gay plague' or that ridiculous GRID nickname."

"That *is* horrible."

"But we're starting to hear of cases where other people are affected. There are theories that it's not only caused by sex between males but also by addicts' shared needles. Right now, those reports are inconclusive. The point is: What does this mean?"

I shook my head in silence.

"What this means for me is hearing daily stories like about a friend from our community – someone we bumped into a few months ago – who had a few Kaposi's lesions on his hands and face. Next thing we know, no one's heard from him for a while. We come to find out...he died...probably alone." Gordo paused, looking away before beginning again. "What enrages me? That no one seems to be doing a damned thing about any of it."

I wanted to be gentle because Gordo was agitated, rightly so. "I guess the medical community needs more time to figure it out?"

"Margie, this thing's becoming an epidemic. It's killing a lot of people. By December of last year, one hundred and thirty were already dead, but no one cared. The government doesn't wanna put any money toward research because *The New York Times* has already painted it up as a 'Gay' thing. I'm scared and I'm angry."

"I can tell. And you're right. The press is underplaying the story. This sounds like the perfect subject for you to write about for our assignment, Gordo. Maybe a personal essay?"

Gordo fell silent, disappearing into the deep recesses of his mind. I admired his strong convictions, his emotional connection to the topic. I wondered, though, if there was more going on, something he was holding back. I agreed that the disease was horrible and more should have been done, but as usual, I saw myself as an observer of life rather than a "take life by the horns and wrestle with the issues" kind of person. *I need to connect with the world around me more.*

****

On a sizzling Saturday in June, I stood outside Gordo's apartment door dressed for the heat: red shorts with a matching belt, white tank top, and red Pro-Ked sneakers. "Hey Gordo, you sure you don't want to go the anti-nukes protest in Central Park with us? Last call. We can still catch up with Crystal and Alissa."

With the sound of fans blowing in the background, Gordo stood at the partially opened door in his undershirt and neon green gym shorts with matching headband. Beads of sweat dripped down his chest. "Explain to me again why y'all are suddenly jumping on the anti-armament advocacy train again – especially during a heat wave!

"I hear you, Gordo. And truthfully, I think Alissa and Crystal are in it less for the anti-nukes message and more for the musical entertainment. I'm going as a curious observer. You interested?"

"Thanks, but I wanna wait for Doug to call. It's his only free afternoon. You know how life is at summer stock – rehearsals, performances, or sleeping. Very little personal time."

"Well, tell him we said hello. We'll fill you in about the protest this evening."

Doug had left for his annual summer stock directing job in Massachusetts four weeks ago, and Gordo looked forward to those weekly phone calls. I knew he missed Doug immensely, so I tried to include him in activities as much as possible, although I wasn't sure an anti-armament protest in Central Park would interest him. Alissa and Crystal had been counting the days until June 12th, once they found out Bruce Springsteen would be among the entertainment lineup. And since I was still searching for a topic for my writing assignment, I decided to attend as an investigative mission.

Alissa, Crystal, and I navigated our way through the crowds forming on Fifth Avenue, when we noticed an older gentleman in a wheelchair being pushed by two private nurses. The nurses were chanting along with the crowd gathering in Central Park: "No Nukes! No Nukes!" The man in the chair, red plaid shawl placed over his legs despite the hot day, looked up at us and said with glee, "Wild! It's really wild, isn't it?" This event appealed to all age levels!

Arriving at Central Park's East 66th Street entrance, we wove our way through masses of people, using the sound of amplified voices to lead us toward a flatbed truck positioned in the Meadow. No way could we get close to the impromptu stage. The news had estimated upwards of 500,000 people in attendance but…whoa! It seemed like there were more bodies than that. People mobbed the park. Busses arrived with signage from all over the United States. Children, college students, moms and dads, businesspeople, and elderly folks carried homemade posters with slogans ranging from "I Hate Nuclear War" to "A Feminist World Is A Nuclear-Free Zone" to "No More Hiroshimas." Despite the slogans demanding an immediate end to all nuclear arms programs and a call for the resumption of disarmament negotiations, as well as a few other bizarre requests, the entire rally was peaceful.

Even from our distant view of the stage, I felt honored to be in the presence of Rev. Dr. Martin Luther King Jr.'s widow. Watching Coretta Scott King walking confidently to the microphone to kick off the presentation and address hundreds of thousands of attendees sent chills through my body. I could only imagine all the hardships that she had been through in her life.

"We have come here in numbers so large that the message must get through to the White House and Capitol Hill," she said as the crowd cheered. Tears of sadness and anger formed in my eyes as I realized that this event, this movement was much larger than my own small world. *Why does the message of peace have to be this difficult?*

Between rally speeches, we were entertained by the likes of Jackson Browne, James Taylor, Bruce Springsteen, Linda Ronstadt, and Joan Baez, who reintroduced old peace movement songs. Singing along with Joan Baez to "We Shall Overcome" moved me in a profound way. Phrases like "Oh, deep in my heart I do believe" sung in solemn unison by thousands of people brought a sense of hope from the message that the future world might stand a chance to live in peace.

Between musical acts, I wanted to build on the uplifting, positive feeling generated from the music. I wandered through the crowd and struck up random conversations, continuing to look for inspiration for my writing project. Each person I encountered seemed willing to share their personal stories.

A Black woman in her mid-thirties carried a sign that read: "Spend Less on War – Spend More on Her" with a photo of an impoverished child. I didn't understand the cause and asked her to explain.

"A lot of African Americans feel like money going to nukes could be better spent on poor communities, you dig? And it's not only Blacks who feel this way. I know a lot of Hispanics who are pissed at President Reagan's military policies like supporting death squads in El Salvador. Less money for military; more money for domestic issues." *Whoa! There are a lot more layers here than I realized.* Again, I felt angry that this woman's story and that of her community's was being buried.

At one point, an elderly Asian woman held out a pastel pink paper crane to me. The delicately folded crane rested in both her frail, wrinkled hands. In broken English, the woman said softly, "Origami crane." I looked into her dark soulful eyes. I'm sure she saw my confusion. "For you. Long living, peace." The sincerity of her gesture flooded me with calmness. I gently received the gift and thanked her. As I turned to walk back toward the stage area, I noticed a police officer on duty wearing a necklace of folded paper cranes over his uniform. *How beautiful. The crane, the Japanese symbol for peace and longevity, adopted by the disarmament movement.*

I don't know if it was hearing Coretta King's speech, singing along with the anti-war songs, receiving a peace crane from that sweet Asian woman, or a combination of all the people I spoke to, but the Peace Rally touched me. It was much more than the opportunity to see Bruce Springsteen, although that was radical. It had an energy – no, more of a spirit. A large number of diverse people with similar yet different opinions about a global crisis gathered in the bright sunshine on the fresh spring grass and coexisted beautifully in that moment in time. *Inspiring!* All those people pulsing together with the same simple desire. Exactly like the Asian woman said, "Long living, peace." *Isn't that why every single person came to the park today? To express that desire? Isn't that what we all want? It's damned simple, and it hit me upside my head with a thud. It's as if my emotions went beyond a pendulum to a full circle – I'm angry that the world is so hostile while the answer is beautifully simple, which makes me angry that the world doesn't embrace its simplicity!*

As the blazing orange sun sank over the West Side of Manhattan, I met up with Alissa and Crystal at the appointed place and we began our hike home. But I was consumed with a fiery passion about the day's experience. Crystal and Alissa chattered away about Jackson Browne's performance, while I lost myself in deeper reflections.

Crystal interrupted my thought process. "What's going on with you, Margie?"

"Hmm? Oh, inspired by the day, that's all. I think I got what I need for my assignment. Not exactly what ticks me off…well, yeah…it enrages me that we can't have world peace when the answer is as simple as accepting a gift, person-to-person, and letting it grow from there."

"What the hell are you talking about?" Crystal asked.

I pulled out the origami crane. "It starts with the simplest gesture – one person gifting another a lovely, folded crane. Energy is exchanged filled with trust and calm and peace, right?"

"Okay. We're following…kinda," Alissa said.

"Is it possible to carry that same peaceful energy to families? Between parents and children? Where ideas can be communicated and accepted? How about between tribes, countries, superpowers?"

Crystal scrunched her nose. "Sounds *très* doubtful."

"Maybe, but why can't we believe that the energy of the gifted crane, the promise of calm and peace, can be enough to start dismantling any wall that divides people and cultures and religions – whether figurative or literal, anywhere in the world?"

"What the hell are you going on about, Margie? Did you

smoke some weed while you were roaming around?" I shot Crystal a sidelong glare.

Alissa piped up. "I'm getting you, Margie. The idea's a little out there, but I get you."

"My point is: I found the solution to my writing assignment problem, and I'm going to write a peace play to address it!"

# 16

# Navigating Writing Genres and the LIRR

*July, 1982*

I sat at the writer's group attempting to listen attentively to Gwendolen's poetry collection about the many things that enraged her. I tried…really. But truth be told, my heart thumped, my palms sweated, and my brain's negative chatterbox planted seeds of self-doubt into my psyche. I didn't mean to be selfishly thinking only about my own play in response to the "What enrages you?" challenge. But insecurity coursed through my mind, body, and spirit about this project. I hadn't shared any bit of my work with other group members – not Gordo, not Miguel, no one. That's how secretive I'd been about my play.

"You're next, Margie." *What was I thinking writing this play? They'll never understand what I'm attempting to get across? I wish I could sneak out of here…*

I vaguely heard Dr. R. queueing me up. Inside my head, that negative voice continued to spew its venom: "What makes you think you could write a play with serious overtones? Dad was right. You have no business thinking you're a playwright. Mom even said it too. You jump from one thing to the next. The group's going to laugh you right out of this room." My inner voice yammered so loudly that I almost missed Dr. R. when she called on me a second time to introduce my piece.

"Sorry…I was…well, okay." I took a deep breath to calm myself. "I've prepared a play called 'A Wall, A Ball, and An Umbrella.'" Gwendolen chuckled at the title. *Great start… they're already laughing.* But the others waited to hear the rest of my introduction before registering any reaction. "This play is inspired by the recent Anti-Nuclear Armament protests that are cropping up all over the world. It's mostly inspired by my new understanding about the need to stop all the divisions that tear our global community apart."

Instead of me reading the play to the group, I assigned Miguel to read the part of the young boy and Gwendolen to read the young girl. I read all the stage directions. The play told the story of two groups of people, The Dots and The Stripes, whose countries were divided by a wall. At lights up, a child from The Dots played alone with a ball on one side of the wall, while a child from The Stripes amused himself with an umbrella on the opposite side. When the ball accidentally flew over the wall to the "enemy's side," the two children were forced to confront the situation. At first, their ingrained suspicions of each other, taught to them by their parents, kicked in. Eventually, as they collaborated on a solution, the children realized that they were not so different after all. The play ended with a beautiful moment where the two children not only find a way to play together, but also use the umbrella to shelter themselves from the rain by holding it over the wall.

*A simple yet universal theme. But is it too simplistic? Does it get my point across?* Self-doubt kicked into overdrive again.

To my great surprise, Miguel, Gwendolen, Gordo, and Dr. R. provided great, positive feedback. They clearly understood my understated approach, my use of innocent children as the catalyst for a peace message, the symbolism of the divisive wall, and why I steered clear of using colors to denote the two societies and opted for The Dots and The Stripes. Miguel and Dr. R. offered a few excellent suggestions for tweaking the dialogue when the two children first talk over the wall – to strengthen the anger aspect. Gordo seemed especially impressed with the play and asked me for a copy.

As I packed up my writing materials, Miguel put his arm around my shoulders and gently pulled me toward him, kissing me on the cheek. "Ah Margie. This play, though uncomplicated and innocent, spoke universal truths. You have tapped into new paths as a writer."

"Thank you. I think I have."

Gordo and Miguel talked nonstop about my play all the way to the subway station and on the train ride uptown. My thoughts floated, distracted with ways I could revise the work. It wasn't until the train stopped and we climbed the stairs to street level at the Lexington station that Miguel snapped me out of my stupor.

"Margie, have you heard a thing Gordo and I have said to you?"

I squirmed, trying not to look guilty.

Gordo came to my rescue. "It's okay, darlin'. We get it. You wanna get home and start working."

We stopped on the corner of East 68th and Third. Before beginning his walk uptown to the apartment that he shared with his brother and cousin, Miguel embraced me and gave me a sweet kiss. "Work hard on your play. I will call you later tonight and check on your progress." Then he whispered in my ear, "Maybe we can have another cozy sleepover?"

"Yes, I'd like that." I loved how thoughtful and patient Miguel had been about our gradually progressing physical relationship.

Most guys would have bailed at this point. It helped that we shared a love of writing to hold us together. For me, he'd been great as a person to talk to whenever the past reared, causing me to tense up. Those episodes happened less and less, thanks to Miguel.

Back in my apartment, I jotted down a few reflections in my journal before beginning my play edits. I wanted to capture my feelings from the moment.

> *Emotions After Writing Group Reading of A Wall, A Ball, and An Umbrella*
>
> *I was surprised and thrilled by the writing group's reaction after today's play reading. Got great feedback and took tons of notes for edits on the play. It still freaks me out that I've now written two plays. Especially this one. What a radical thought...that I could write a play and it could express what's going on in my head and heart. Despite the nagging pressure from Dad that I should only be focused on what we originally agreed to - publishing journalism-type articles - I can't help feeling excited about this new direction. You never know where your writing will take you...*

****

As if having my play accepted by the writing group wasn't enough, the following week I received a call from *The Village*

*Voice*, an alternative newspaper known for its coverage of politics and the New York arts scene. I had applied for an internship months ago, but figured it was a bust since I hadn't received an interview. My brain buzzed with possibilities from this new venture: better quality assignments, maybe jazz gigs to review, *maybe* even getting my work published this time around!

I had hoped to meet with Robert Christgau, Senior Editor and music critic for *The Village Voice*. I'd read a lot about his style, and he seemed sincere about music criticism. Instead, a less senior editor named Joe Reedy interviewed me. He asked about what genres of music I liked and warned that the readers would expect reviews about trendy music, but that he wasn't totally against occasionally inserting unique reviews.

Remembering my experience with *SoHo Weekly News*, I asserted myself early in the interview. Maybe I was still riding the high from my positive writer's group critique or maybe I was getting cocky. Looking back, I could have blown the entire interview.

"Mr. Reedy…," I began.

"Joe. Please call me Joe. We're pretty informal around here."

"Okay, Joe. I'm extremely interested in this position with *The Village Voice*. I feel that our philosophies about music align. But…um…well, as you know from my resume, I did write for the *SoHo Weekly News* and…well, I wonder if you'd consider hiring me as a part-time writer rather than an intern. I believe I can do a good job for you…"

Joe clasped his hands together in front of his chest, elbows resting on the arms of his chair, and stared off. He sat quietly for several minutes. *Oh crap, I went too far. He's probably going to tell me to hit the bricks.*

Finally, he said, "I hear what you're saying, Margie, and

here at *The Village Voice* we do believe that writers should be paid for their work. Hm. I'd have to run this past Robert...Mr. Christgau...but I have a proposition for you. I'm going to offer you a trial assignment, a review of a gig, and we'll see how that goes. If Mr. Christgau and I like it, then you're hired as a part-time writer. How does that sound?"

Although ready to burst into song, I forced a restrained smile and a nod, swallowing down a scream. Instead, I said, "That sounds radical!"

My excitement ebbed when Joe and I walked to the outer office, and he handed me a "trial" assignment. I'd be traveling all the way to Roslyn, Long Island to a venue called My Father's Place. The band sounded familiar: The Ramones. I scanned the info sheet: Punk band. No new album this year. Rumors that band members struggled with drug and alcohol addiction. *Great...not even close to my preferred genre.* Regardless, I jumped at the chance to demonstrate my writing skills. I remember once when the hard-boiled Allan Wolper, Managing Editor at *SoHo Weekly News,* glanced over an article I'd been tinkering with between making pots of coffee and mimeographing copies. He said to me, "The only way to break in at a news rag is to show em' what you got, and you ain't half bad. Lots to learn but you got chops." If Wolper thought I had chops...

"I'm definitely in," I reaffirmed to Joe, noticing that no other reporters were clamoring for the opportunity to take the Long Island train out to Roslyn on a Tuesday night to cover whoever-the-heck The Ramones were. At least the venue, My Father's Place, had an interesting history, according to the cheat sheet.

As if I hadn't already pushed the boundaries, I asked Joe if I could have two press passes for the Ramones gig, reasoning that I'd be more comfortable traveling that distance late at night with a friend. He agreed.

*A paid internship of sorts at* The Village Voice *should get Dad off my back for a while. Whew!*

****

"Absolutely positively." Alissa nearly screeched her reply to my invitation. "I'm more than in. I'm making that happen. To see The Ramones? I'm for sure coming with you!"

"Wow, okay. Hey, I notice you use that 'Absolutely positively' phrase a lot lately, Alissa. Pretty upbeat for you." I teased, sprinkling breadcrumbs on the window ledge for my birds.

"Yeah, got it off The Clash's new album, Combat Rock. Have ya heard the single 'In a Car Jam'?" I simply stared at her. She cracked a half-smile.

"Absolutely positively not," I said. We laughed as I grabbed two root beers from the frig and handed one to Alissa before joining her at the table. I needed to fill her in on the details for the Tuesday evening Ramones performance – the timeline, the transportation, the press passes, the venue.

Before she left for her diner shift, Alissa said, "I gotta idea. What if I help you dress more for the part?"

"What do you mean?"

"I mean, it might be harder to get interviews from punksters like The Ramones when you're dressed like Marie Osmond, you get me? I'll come over early with a few outfits, accessories, makeup…and work my magic. What do ya say?"

"I don't know…"

"It's not like I'm gonna dye your hair. You want to get good interviews for your review, right?"

"That's true. Oh, what the heck. Let's try it."

"Great," she shouted as she walked down the hall to leave. "I will absolutely positively see you here on Tuesday…early!"

****

Late Tuesday afternoon, before making the trek out to Long Island, Alissa arrived with an armful of clothes and a bag of makeup. First she tried to work with my super fine hair, adding a weird hair gel – sort of like Dippity Doo – to make my hair textured, which resulted in a totally greasy mess. Then she pulled my hair into a high ponytail on the top of my head. Ridiculous! Finally, during a moment when I wasn't paying attention, she pulled out scissors and lopped off a huge section, creating spikey bangs!

"What the hell, Alissa!"

"Relax, all we need to do is…" She combed and teased and sprayed and, to my surprise, I liked the look.

"Not bad. Could you cut off some length in the back – a little bit! And give me a few layers on the sides? But don't go crazy."

Alissa went to work, snipping and cutting. Before I knew it…a whole new me!

Next came clothes and makeup. Alissa brought several outfits from her own closet. We zeroed in on a short black skirt, a black mesh top over a black tank top, a beaded choker, plenty of metal and leather bracelets, a single dangling earring of silver and black beads with a red heart, and black flats. She applied heavy black eyeliner on both the upper and lower lash lines, lots of blue/gray eye shadow, and bright red lipstick. *A whole different me! Not that I planned to adopt this look permanently, but what the heck. A fun diversion.*

Thank God Alissa knew all about the Long Island Railroad and how to circumvent Penn Station. She led us directly to the purchase window for our tickets and the ramp taking us to the LIRR trains. *I picked the perfect friend to buddy up with for this assignment.*

On the hourlong train ride to Roslyn, I shared my pre-gig research with Alissa, asking her to fill in anything she knew about the band. While I spouted off from my notes, Alissa listened – face expressionless.

"I found information about The Ramones' last couple albums. Here's a cool bit: Johnny was pressured by the record company to get more air play on U.S. radio stations. And a fact I dug up: Their 1980 album, 'End of the Century,' wasn't representative of their aggressive punk style. Oh, and their 1981 album, 'Pleasant Dreams,' moved them from punk toward heavy metal."

"Uh…You're gonna say all that? Have you ever read a *Village Voice* review?"

"Yes, I've read their reviews. What are you getting at?"

"You may not want to wig out too much on the before and stick with the now."

"Be here now…probably good advice, Alissa. I'll think about it."

We arrived at the My Father's Place venue – an unassuming, single-story, white brick building with red awnings sheltering undersized square windows and the entry door. Overhead, painted in simple lettering: MY FATHER'S PLACE. *Nothing flashy about this venue.*

Once inside we entered a banquet hall. "I swear I could be at prom night all over again," Alissa said with her usual bite. But she wasn't half wrong. "Get a load of those chandeliers hanging over the audience area." She gestured toward two monstrous lighting units, dripping with crystals – the most eye-catching feature in the room.

"Let's get a closer look at the stage," I said.

Squeezing through tightly placed rows of small round tables

with red or gold upholstered chairs, we made our way to the front of the room. A makeshift stage consisted of a twelve-inch-high platform, about fifteen feet wide by fifteen feet deep. A curtain behind the platform created a backdrop for the musicians. *Kinda low-end for such a fancy room.*

The minute the performance began, the crowd went wild for The Ramones. The musicians masterfully "worked the stage," directly facing the audience and walking forward to the stage's edge as a way to increase the audiences' concert experience. The crowd ate up the loud, crunchy music – not my preference, but as a reviewer I set my personal tastes aside. The fans loved it. After the concert, I tracked down Johnny and jumped into asking him questions from my prepared list.

"Thanks for the time, Johnny. Great show. I loved the way the band was able to engage the audience, drawing them in."

"Thanks. That's intentional," he explained. "I'm not a fan of guitarists or other musicians who perform facing the drummer, or amps, or other band members. That's not why we're up here."

"Johnny, in previous interviews you've expressed disappointment about The Ramones' 1980 'End of the Century' and last year's 'Pleasant Dreams' album in terms of the direction the genre was going. Are you making changes to reverse course?"

Johnny started by saying, "Yea, I've said it before. 'End of the Century' was completely watered-down Ramones. It's not the real Ramones." The second he was about to expand on his point, a group of fans mobbed him. *No way can I ask a follow up question now.*

It was after one-thirty in the morning by the time we left. Grateful to have a friend on the long train ride back to the city, I found myself in a reflective mood, questioning the whole evening and, even more, where I saw myself at this point in my career. *Is this fun? (Sort of) Do I enjoy this music? (Not that much) Do I like writing about it? (It's a writing job) Do other people think it's cool? (Yes, very much.)*

While Joe liked my review of The Ramones, I got the feeling he never intended to print it. It was more of a trial, like he said. He thought my background work was good, but encouraged me to dig deeper with my writing, explore the artists more, not be afraid to ask questions and poke at interesting possibilities and unique angles. Perfect feedback. He offered me a freelance position where I'd be paid per assignment – better than nothing – but no guarantee of how often or of the type of assignments I might get. I liked that *The Village Voice* editors gave their writers freedom to develop their own style. That felt liberating. But I still struggled with the direction of my own writing. Did I want to write music reviews about music genres I couldn't relate to? Was that fair to the musicians? While I knew I should be celebrating the freelance offer from *The Village Voice*, I felt conflicted. And I couldn't ignore the knot forming in my stomach at the thought of explaining all this to Dad. *Will this new writing job live up to his expectations?*

To add to my self-inflicted pressure, my writing interests were pivoting to playwriting. Through characters, dialogue, and unique plot situations, I had discovered a new voice, a different way to express my views about the world around me. For the longest time I imagined myself reviewing music…that was until playwriting presented itself as a new vehicle. Life had a way of making sudden turns, darting here and there rapidly, like a barn swallow scooping up insects at dusk.

# 17

# Surprises: Good, Bad, and Fab

*August-September, 1982*

At the end of August, Gordo and I planned a "Welcome Home" celebration dinner for Doug on the day he returned from his summer stock job. We splurged on a roast at the Second Avenue butcher shop and prepared Doug's favorite broccoli casserole. I threw together a fruit salad with fresh peaches, plums, and blueberries from the market on Third Avenue and sprinkled tiny marshmallows on top, Mom-style. Gordo handed me a fancy embroidered tablecloth and a floral centerpiece to begin to set the table in their apartment living room.

"Doug's gonna be surprised," Gordo said. I knew how much Gordo missed his partner these past few months. His excitement for Doug's return radiated like an aura around his entire being. *Now that's true love.*

While I smoothed the tablecloth and placed the centerpiece, Gordo carried in a tray with silverware, red Fiestaware plates, and wine glasses. "Fancy-shmancy. No paper plates or Dixie Cups," I teased.

"I want it all to be perfect. I know, I'm a dork."

"I think it's lovely, Gordo."

At that moment, the front door opened.

"Greetings!" Doug's tired voice announced his arrival. He

clamored through the doorway looking like a cartoon bellhop – his backpack draped over one shoulder, his canvas tote slung over the other shoulder, and his gigantic suitcase dragging behind him.

Gordo hopped up to assist. "Damn, Doug. Let me help you with all that!" They dumped the luggage into the bedroom and stole a few minutes to reconnect in private, while I put finishing touches on the table.

Once we all reassembled, I opened a bottle of wine and we relaxed in the living room, munching on brie and crackers while the roast finished doing its thing. The loving couple settled close together on the sofa. Doug had plenty to tell us about his summer adventures – the good, the bad, and the "oh so fabulous," as he put it.

"One of the better summers for me – career-wise," he started. "Of course, I directed all the plays in the Children's Theater series, as planned. But here's the fabulous part: Mr. Tarkington assigned me to assistant direct two main stage productions, collaborating with a director from here in New York.

"That is 'fabulous,' isn't it, Margie?" Gordo beamed with pride.

"What does an assistant director do, Doug?" I felt stupid having to ask, but I was totally in the dark, having mostly performed in non-professional theaters.

"While the director develops the overall production concept, the assistant director will record what is being communicated during rehearsals, like the director's notes to the actors or blocking changes. There may even be times when the assistant director will rehearse with actors on a specific scene that needs extra work."

"Ah, then you'd have to communicate closely with the

director, right?"

"Correct, M'lady."

"Oo. I get the honor of a French form of address," I teased. "Now get back to your story, sir."

"The point is now I've got an extraordinary connection with a professional New York theater director. Like I said...one of the better summers for me."

Gordo and I lifted our glasses to toast Doug's successful season – just as the timer for the roast rang. I scurried around the kitchen, refilling wine glasses, grabbing the fruit salad and broccoli casserole, and placing the butter dish on the table. Meanwhile, Gordo plated a slice of beef and a baked potato on three dinner plates and passed them to me through the kitchen doorway.

"Smells delicious," Doug and I said in unison.

While Gordo and I pigged out on second helpings, Doug didn't seem to eat much. He could have been tired from the bus ride. Gordo kept pushing the issue.

"You sure you don't want anything else to eat. Plenty of broccoli casserole. Margie and I have both had seconds."

"I know," Doug said grinning. "You 'hath eaten me out of house and home.'"

I laughed. "Ah. There's our quote of the evening."

"Of course," Gordo said. "You didn't expect Doug to get through an entire dinner without a bit of Shakespeare, did you?"

Doug interrupted our teasing. "Margie, I wanted to be sure to tell you how impressed Mr. Tarkington was with your anti-war play. He said he wished he could use it, but it wasn't right for the typical summer theater audience."

"Wait. Hold on a minute. What do you mean, my anti-war play?"

"The umbrella one that Gordo shared with me...oops, was that supposed to be a secret? Uh oh."

Still completely confused, Doug explained about the Playwright-in-Residence who had been hired to write plays for the summer theater's children's series and how he turned out to be dud. *Okay? Still confused.*

"Here's what happened: This Playwright-in-Residence guy was not great. Okay, actually his material was horrendous – too avant-garde for kids. I mean, who did he think he was, Samuel Beckett? Man, Mr. Tarkington totally lost it. Almost fired the guy mid-summer. I can guarantee that arrogant playwright will never work at Red Barn Summer Theater again.

"Okay, but what does that have to do with my peace play, especially since Mr. Tarkington said it's not right for summer theater."

"The point is that you, Margie Stevens, budding playwright, have received the attention of a theater producer – Mr. Allen Tarkington. It's called opportunity. Now you, Margie Stevens, need to respond to that loud knocking sound." And to punctuate his words, Doug rapped me on my noggin a few times.

"Ouch. Okay, I catch your drift. You caught me by surprise, that's all. So, you showed him my play and he liked it, but not for the summer theater crowd. Hmm. I suppose I could play around with themes for kiddie plays." I racked my brain wondering what in the world I could write that might interest children. "Can you give me an idea of what goes over well with the child audiences at Red Barn Theater?"

"Sure. I'll tell you exactly what Mr. Tarkington is looking for. No experimental, avant-garde crap. Stick with the classics or fables, but it's okay to modernize them. Oh, and the thing he loved about your showcase play was how you had the characters talk to the audience. Direct Address is what they call it. Anytime you can combine that with audience participation in a children's show, that's gold. If you can throw in moments when the actors talk to the kids in the audience – I mean in character, of course – Mr. Tarkington loves that stuff."

"You know I'm not a professional playwright, Doug. I'm a newbie."

"Wait, I've got a great idea. There's a Children's Theater series at the SoHo Playhouse. Why don't we catch a matinee this weekend? You can see how this style of theater is put together. What do you say?"

I struggled to keep a straight face as I responded. "What can I say, but 'All the world's a stage, and all the men and women merely players.'?" He punched my arm playfully and both he and Gordo burst into laughter. I might have chuckled along with them, but inside I asked: What in the world was I getting myself into? I wasn't a playwright – of Children's Theater or any type of theater. And, good Lord, what would Dad say about this? He'd have a fit and a half if anything came of it. *On the other hand, Margie, what could possibly happen? You have nothing to lose, right?*

"Okay, let's check out a matinee," I said. "And I'll see what New York creative energy I can tap into."

"Great Margie, because Mr. Tarkington's not only in the market for a Playwright-in-Residence for next summer, but he also requested to see more of your plays. He's got connections. You don't want to pass up this opportunity."

"Doug does make a dang good point, Margie," Gordo said.

*Yikes!*

****

Doug and I attended a performance of *Sleeping Beauty* at the SoHo Playhouse in the West Village the following Saturday.

Doug beamed as he expounded, "You're going to love this theater, Margie. It's been in existence since 1962, although I'm not sure if it was always at the 15 Vandam location between Varick Street and Sixth Avenue, where we'll be going to today."

Arriving at the theater, I immediately noticed the differences between the storefront site that Doug managed and this venue. The SoHo Playhouse's outer façade exuded elegance. Framed by large posters of current and upcoming productions and stately lighting sconces, an arched entryway with six marble steps greeted theater goers as they approached the recessed doors. Despite the overhead signage, carved in granite, reading "Huron Club" and hinting at the former building owner, this entrance radiated theatrical flair.

After purchasing our tickets at the lobby's box office window for the two o'clock matinee, we entered the seventy-eight-seat proscenium theater. The stage was not much larger than Doug's storefront theater, approximately twenty-three feet wide by twenty feet deep. Looking up at the electrical grid, I assessed that the SoHo Playhouse had much more lighting equipment than the Workshop Theater.

The small auditorium began filling with excited, squirmy, bouncy, giggly, and extremely vocal children! *Crap, this is going to be a disaster.* I turned to Doug for his reaction, but his face indicated no worry or panic.

"Doug, how will the poor actors ever manage to control this madhouse!" He actually smiled. Butterflies fluttered away in my stomach, convinced that we were about to witness an utter failure.

The auditorium chaos ensued until...the lights dimmed and, as if by magic, a veil of awe descended upon the children. All movement stopped, all eyes trained forward, all breathing began as if in unison. The anticipation was palpable. A group of three actors costumed as fairies entered from the back of the auditorium and wandered through the audience, asking the children if they knew the direction to the castle. The fairies explained that they were late for Princess Beauty's first birthday party, and it was crucial they arrive to the castle on time. This direct interaction not only delighted the children, but they took the situation's urgency very seriously.

At the same time as this fairy conversation was going on, the onstage curtain slowly drew open, revealing a castle interior. Without any instruction, the children in the audience pointed to the stage, directing the fairies to their destination. The fairies made several silly false starts, going through rows of seats or up the center aisle the wrong way, allowing the children to correct their movements and guide them toward the stage. Before reaching the stage/castle, the fairies turned to the audience, thanking them for their assistance, and asking them to be on hand in the future. They showed them a special hand signal they would use when they needed the children's help.

During intermission, Doug poked me. "Did you get your answer? Did you see how the 'poor actors' were able to manage the 'madhouse'?"

"Absolutely. How clever. The fairies used a hand signal – a control device! You don't want the kids blurting out things all over the place. And the playwright gave the child audience a special and important job to move the plot forward. The director helped by having the fairies enter through the audience at the top of the show. I think I'm catching on! I can do this!"

Watching that production of *Sleeping Beauty* at SoHo Playhouse won me over. The way the kids were mesmerized by the theatrical effects, the actors, the story, and their special part in the production psyched me up. Writing for Children's Theater may not solve all the world's global issues, but I could weave in positive morals and important messages. Wouldn't emcouraging young people to think about values and integrity be a good place to begin bringing awareness about the world's issues? The excitement about writing a Children's Theater script swelled inside me to the point that I absolutely had to get started. Maybe Miguel *was* right about this New York energy thing. I felt it driving me.

****

With a little prodding from Doug and Gordo, my writing purpose became clearer. I wrote plays with a child audience in mind. And I had a blast. While worries about Dad's reaction to my shift in creative focus lingered, I shoved them to the back of my mind and wrote with enthusiasm. Meanwhile, as the late summer months signaled a transition to fall, August and September also set the stage for changes among my New York family. Crystal floundered further in her direction-less haze. And Gordo became obsessed with concern about Doug's health since returning from summer stock.

As per our normal routine, Gordo and I took the subway home from our writing group on the last Saturday in September. I noticed he sat quietly. Usually, our rides home consisted of dissecting our current writing assignment or gossiping about Gwendolen's latest self-aggrandizing rant. After a bit of probing, he revealed what was distracting him.

"It's not like Doug to be lazing around all the time," Gordo said. "I'm worried, but he keeps brushing me off. He calls me overly protective."

"It does sound like this summer season was especially hectic, what with that Playwright-in-Residence guy being a flake. That may have caused him more stress than he realized. Maybe he needs a bit longer to recover."

"It's not only that." Gordo stared out the subway car window as another train whizzed by on the next track.

"Gordo, what is it? Is anything else going on with Doug?"

"I figure he'll kill me for saying anything but…well, he's got this swelling in his neck." I didn't know what that meant or how to respond. I simply reached out and touched his arm. "He keeps saying it's probably nothing, but I'm hearing stories of others who have similar symptoms – fatigue, lumps, lesions…

"I don't get it. Can't you take him to the doctor to have it checked out? Wait, you think…"

"It's possible it could be A.I.D.S.-related. But he's in denial. He doesn't want to face it."

"What's A.I.D.S.?"

"The CDC's new article yesterday is now using A.I.D.S. – Acquired Immune Deficiency Syndrome – to refer to the disease. Much better than GRID. I sure hope it catches on."

"Oh. I didn't know." I felt guilty not keeping up with the latest information about the disease, but frankly, the news and the government continued to move sluggishly since the April congressional hearing where the Center for Disease Control estimated that tens of thousands of people may already be affected by the disease. It's been frustrating. "This swelling thing…Do you think Doug should go to the doctor and at least be checked out?"

"Margie, the doctors might be trying real hard, but they're still only stabbing in the dark, and even if they figure out what the hell this sickness is, they still don't know how to fix it."

"Gosh, it feels hopeless. I wish I could do something to help, Gordo."

"You and me both, darlin'." After a long pause, he uttered

quietly, "God. I'm scared." I reached over and held his hand for the rest of our subway ride to our Lexington and 68th Street stop.

****

A seemingly high Crystal informed me that she dropped out of Parsons School of Design in mid-September. "I'm not into the school scene anymore, *mon amie*" was how she explained it. Then the rambling, paranoid logic set in.

"I think the staff is going through my fabric storage cupboard when I'm not at school. I'm sure they are. They're watching me all the time."

"Crystal, why on earth would your teachers be watching you at school?" I did wonder if she was behaving strangely in class or if they simply recognized that Crystal was high.

In a way, it made sense. Lately, Crystal stopped caring about how she dressed. No coordinated accessories, no upgrades to her wardrobe. Basically, she'd been a slob. Also, she had missed more classes than she attended this fall semester – and it was only the end of September! *I wonder if the administration asked her to leave. Yikes!*

"What will you be doing instead?" I asked. "Picking up more waitressing shifts at the diner?"

Crystal rambled. "Right, right. Well, daddy will still pay rent until he realizes I've dropped out of school. I'll keep waitressing one day a week for now. You know, until I figure things out. That way I can spend more time with Girard. Hey, maybe I'll even go to Amsterdam with him next time. That'd be totally rad!"

Crystal's plan seemed completely wigged out. Not planning on telling her parents that she dropped out of Parsons? Not creating a backup career plan? Basing her entire future on "hanging out" with sleazebag Girard? *She's a mess.*

There was no point in using logic and reasoning with her when she was flying high. Since she had caught me completely by surprise with her news, I had no idea what to say or do to convince her of any rational alternative anyway. And I was late for work. *Typical Crystal...she springs monumental news on me at the worst time, like "Oh, you're using the bathroom? We're out of toilet paper."*

# 18

# The Past Visits

*October, 1982*

I shook out my umbrella in the vestibule at the Silver Star Diner on a gusty, drizzly October evening, hungry for my favorite meal: spanakopita and hot tea with lemon. Alissa rushed past me with an order for another table as I made my way to an empty window booth. I whispered, "The usual," as she scooted by.

Setting down an empty cup and saucer with a slice of lemon on the side and an aluminum container of steaming water, Alissa asked what was going on.

"I've got exciting news," I started. "Amy, a singer friend from touring days, is coming to the city. I hope you have a chance to meet her – she's bubbly and funny and cute as a Cabbage Patch Doll."

"You're not selling me on her, but if she's a friend of yours, I'm in." I looked at Alissa's latest spiky hairstyle, dark roots with tips dyed orange, and her multicolored eye shadow. None of that phased me anymore. I loved the person she was, despite her gruff demeanor at times. Alissa had become a sister to me.

"Help me think of a cool place to take Amy to dinner on Sunday."

"I know the perfect place!" Alissa always knew "The perfect place!" The best music venues, the funkiest thrift shops, the cheapest markets for fresh vegetables. *The "I Love New York" campaign should scoop up that girl.*

"Great, I'll hold you to that," I said.

"By the way, how is Crystal doing?" she asked. "She never waits tables here anymore." *That's news to me.*

I thought about Alissa's question for a moment. "She has been spending most of her time, day and night, at Girard's apartment. I'm trying not to wig out cause she's a big girl, but I'm worried about her."

"We could come up with a plan to confront her. I've heard of people doing this with drug addicts and alcoholics. We could ask Doug and Gordo to help. It might work."

"I don't know. It seems harsh. I mean, Crystal…a drug addict?"

"Look, Margie. She's blinded by that asshole, Girard, you get me? She thinks he cares about her, but he doesn't. He keeps her dependent on him so she's there whenever he needs her. It's how he operates. He's crafty that way."

Alissa was right about that. Crystal gobbled up his cool looks and smooth talk the way a teeny bopper ogled a pop star at a concert – getting all bug-eyed and giggly anytime Girard entered a room. "Let's think about it. Crystal's not stupid. Maybe she'll come around." Alissa shook her head and trudged back toward the kitchen to pick up an order.

As I drained my teabag against the spoon and poured the steeped brew into the porcelain cup, I considered Alissa's idea about confronting Crystal. It was hard to believe that she was a cocaine addict. I mean, she wasn't that hooked, was she? It wasn't like she was a junkie on the street. A confrontation seemed harsh. But Alissa assured me a group showdown may be the only way to get Crystal to snap back to reality. Alissa's been through this...maybe she knows best. *And what if we're doing more harm by not confronting Crystal?*

****

Alissa suggested a trendy restaurant on the West Side for my dinner with Amy. "Not my kinda place, but your Cabbage Patch friend might like it." I entered the cozy, wood-paneled bistro near the corner of Broadway and West 72nd Street and pulled off my sweater coat. A hostess escorted me to a table covered with white craft paper. Crayons of various colors in an empty orange juice can served as a centerpiece, inviting patrons to become amateur artists while waiting for their meals. *Cute idea.*

I waited for Amy to arrive, reflecting on my many attempts to reach her since Chaz gave me her phone number several months ago. I'd left a ton of messages, but she never returned my calls. Chaz and Jimmy hadn't given me an update about Amy, simply saying, "Kinda sounded like Amy wanted to fill you in herself." *Seems like an odd statement.*

Pleased and a bit shocked that she had agreed to meet me for dinner, I reflected on our summer together and Amy's story. Despite being the band's youngest member at only nineteen years old when she joined, Amy and I became fast friends. She fell in love with the guitar player in King Vido's Swing Band, although he was already involved with the bandleader's daughter. Amy was sure Ted planned to break it off with Connie, but that never happened. I tried to help her when Amy confided to me that she was pregnant – arranged to take her to Planned Parenthood for a consultation while on break from the tour, brought her to my parent's home in Church Creek to let her figure things out, and became her confidante. But after the guitar player made it clear he wasn't going to step up, she freaked out. During a recording session in Pittsburgh, she disappeared, leaving a note on the hotel room pillow. I never heard from her again or found out what she decided to do about the baby. She knew I'd support her decision – have the baby, give it up for adoption, or get an abortion. The choice was hers. But she left without a word. No contact in four years.

*How strange that she chose to contact Chaz rather than me. I'm sure she had my phone number in Church Creek. Oh well…Push all that aside now, Margie. You finally get a chance to see your perky friend again from King Vido Swing Band days.*

Amy appeared at the restaurant's doorway and I eagerly waved her over to our table. Short in stature, she was much thinner than I recalled. Her red hair hung below her shoulders, lackluster and straight. I immediately noticed that her "bubbly" exuberance had also disappeared – no bounce in her step, no energy in her smile. *Is she depressed? Maybe tired?*

I rose to greet her with a hug. She half-hugged me in return. *Okay, not the warmest of greetings but we haven't seen each other in a long time.*

Amy draped her jacket over the back of her chair and plopped down, slinging her large purse over the arm. I waited until she was settled before I spoke. Not wanting to appear to jump down her throat, I positioned my attempts to connect with her as my fault. "I must have called at bad times" and "Perhaps you were away, maybe on vacation."

To that she muttered under her breath, "Not a chance." I wasn't sure what she was driving at or how to respond. I remained quiet.

The waiter broke the tension at our table by taking our drink orders. I requested a glass of white wine. Amy began to ask for a martini; then, as if catching herself, she changed her order. "No, a club soda with a slice of lime."

Once the waiter left, I asked the inevitable. "Amy, please bring me up to date. Chaz and Jimmy said that you'd contacted them, but they didn't have any details about what's been going on with you. Only that you're living in upstate New York. The last information I had was the note you left in the hotel."

Amy grabbed a red crayon from the orange juice container and began to doodle. Silence. Her face flushed. I didn't want to push. I waited. The waiter returned with our drinks. We both took long swallows – more like gulps. *Why is this awkward? What's going on?*

I couldn't stand it anymore. "Did something happen with the baby, Amy?"

At last she looked up. But instead of sadness or thoughtfulness, her eyes were full of rage and anger, which seemed to be directed at ME! I was confused.

"Yes, Margie. And it's a huge mess. My life is a huge mess."

Amy became silent. I waited for her to continue but she went back to doodling. *Do I ask her more questions or wait until she's ready to talk? She's so angry.* Excruciating silence continued for what seemed an eternity. I needed to help move the conversation forward.

"Can you explain to me how things are a huge mess, Amy? Maybe I can help."

Again, she lifted her head with a fire behind her eyes. "You help? Thanks for nothing. Look at you. Chaz told me all about your great life as a writer in New York. Meanwhile, my life is in the dumpster."

"What? Wait! Let's focus on you and start at the beginning."

Between sobs and gasps for air, Amy blurted out, "You were my best friend in the world; instead of telling me to get an abortion and continue with my life, you took me to Planned

Parenthood, where they offered all those options about what to do. And you sat back while I went on and on about how I was sure Ted would marry me. What an idiot I was! Why didn't you stop me? Why didn't you slap me across the face and tell me to take a chill pill? When Ted rejected me, I was freakin' confused. All I could do was go home."

It was true that I didn't tell her what to do during her crisis. That wasn't my style. I didn't like to confront people and tell them what to do with their lives, as evidenced by the whole Crystal situation. As a friend, I thought it best to be a shoulder for her to cry on and support her in whatever she decided to do. *But now she's blaming me for whatever happened.*

I didn't attempt to defend myself. "What happened when you told your parents that you were pregnant?"

"My parents – my 'loving, non-judgmental' parents – were humiliated. They said I brought shame to them. More like to their standing in the Baltimore country club world. 'What will the neighbors think?' and 'What will my boss think?' and 'What will the church members think?' I wanted to talk about the options that the Planned Parenthood people had given me."

"And what did your parents say about those?"

"Hah! They said, 'You don't know what you're talking about, Amy. You're only nineteen.' They didn't pay attention to anything I wanted."

My heart ached for her. "How sad for you, Amy?" I knew Amy as a bubbly, happy young woman; she looked defeated and in pain. "So, what did your parents decide?"

Amy broke down, crying openly. The waiter approached the table to take our orders, but I waved him away. He gave a knowing nod and retreated.

After a long silence and a deep breath, Amy continued. "My

parents shipped me off to Aunt Laura's place in upstate New York where I was told: 'You will have the baby and immediately give it up for adoption.'" She fought back more tears, but the anger returned, replacing the pain in her eyes. "I didn't want that. I wanted to have the baby and raise it on my own. I knew it would be hard. I hoped my parents would be willing to help me until I could get on my feet. But no…that would be a bad look for them."

My heart broke for her. No wonder she looked beaten down. At twenty-three-years old, she radiated defeat. "I'm sorry, Amy. What are you doing now?

"That's the kicker, Margie," she said, oozing bitterness. "Even though I did exactly as my parents wanted, they've disowned me. I'm stuck in that tiny town upstate, waiting tables, barely getting by, full of regrets. I regret that I listened to my parents, and there are even days I regret that I didn't get an abortion in the first place. My life is a huge mess."

"Oh Amy." I reached out to touch her hand. She pulled it away. *She's consumed with bitterness.* "But you can turn things around. I know you—"

"It's a little late for *you* to offer me advice, Margie."

"Hold on. I understand that you're angry about what's happened, but blaming me doesn't make any sense. Friends are there for support. That's what I tried to do. I couldn't make decisions for you."

Amy stood up and roughly pulled on her jacket. She dug into her purse for a twenty-dollar bill and tossed it on the table. *Had she said what she had wanted to say? Something still seemed off.*

I jumped up and caught her before she rushed out the door. "Hey, why did you really come all the way into the city to meet with me tonight?"

She wouldn't look me in the eye. "Part of my Twelve Step program. Number nine. Make direct amends to such people you have harmed wherever possible. I wanted to let go of the pissed off feeling I have toward you but....well, I guess I still have a lot of work to do."

She turned and walked out of the restaurant without a goodbye, disappearing from my life...again.

On the cross-town bus through Central Park from the West Side, I looked out the window, vision blurred as I fended off tears. I attempted to make sense of this bizarre encounter with Amy. I had hoped for a pleasant reunion; instead, I became the target of her rage. My emotions swirled. Betrayal, anger, confusion, sadness, pity. I had tried to help her when she came to me with news of her pregnancy, and now she blamed me for the way her life turned out? *That's too loco, as Miguel would say.*

My cheeks grew hot as I thought about Amy calling Chaz and complaining about her life. She probably blamed me during those phone calls too, although Chaz would never fall for that. He was much too sweet and a good friend. No wonder he didn't want to explain her situation when I saw him last December. He'd want us to work it out directly.

The bus edged closer to my stop and my harsher feelings softened. I put myself in Amy's shoes. Thinking back to a time right out of college, I remembered my own feeling of desperation after I caught my boyfriend David cheating. I had begun to slip into a downward spiral of depression, even having thoughts of harming myself. I had to snap out of it. For me, going on the road as a singer with the band was the answer. I ached for Amy. *Maybe, along with A.A., Amy needs a counselor to help show her the way. Blaming other people for your own life's problems is never the answer.*

****

After a terrible night's sleep, my morning at Radio City proved to be disastrous. Between typing errors and envelope sorting mix-ups, Miss Chambers suggested I take an early lunch. I spent my break sitting quietly in St. Patrick's Cathedral, decompressing. I dragged myself up the concrete steps and opened the massive cathedral door. As usual, I wandered to a pew toward the front of the sanctuary, away from noisy tourists. Settling into an isolated pew, the calm and quiet washed over me immediately, blocking out the excessive traffic noise outside the cathedral's thick walls and the negative chatter inside my mind.

A sense of peace swept over me. My body reacted accordingly – shoulders dropped, tension melted away, breathing restored to rhythmic inhales and exhales, and a gentle smile spread across my face. I flashed back to my practices of several years ago – of meditation, of positive thinking, of yogic breathing – skills I had learned while reading and studying different Eastern philosophies. Sitting in that serene cathedral pew, I reflected on my encounter with Amy from a new perspective. I wanted to release any defensiveness or anger I carried toward her. *What positive energy can I send her way? She's seeking help through A.A. She's got a job as a waitress. She's navigating her way, however slowly.*

While Amy blamed me for the unfortunate things that had happened in her life, I couldn't control her response. I breathed in the word "forgiveness." As I considered any defensiveness I had about Amy, I breathed out the word "release." In the tranquil setting of St. Patrick's sanctuary, I cleared away the heaviness of my visit with Amy from my mind and soul – at least for that day.

Just as Amy stated that she still had work to do to resolve her Twelve Step program, I knew my positivity plan would be ongoing. Dark feelings toward Amy's treatment of me would flare up from time to time. And I still held on to fears and worries about my career choices, and Dad's pressure, and other decisions I needed to make, and…well, you name it. *One step at a time.*

# 19

# Career Confusion

*November, 1982*

November proved to be a totally weird month for me. Even though Crystal spent much of her time at Girard's place, I missed her unannounced pop-ins to grab a couple beers from the fridge or a box of crackers off the shelf. I caught myself talking aloud to my window sparrows each morning. Their daily portion of breadcrumbs kept them returning, soon bringing friends and family members. *Word travels fast in NYC, even among the bird community.*

While my freelance writing job at *The Village Voice* stretched my patience, I was driven by my promise to Doug to develop Children's Theater scripts for Mr. Tarkington before the year's end. As Doug suggested, I chose to modernize a folk tale and a fable. Using the story of "The Emperor's New Clothes" as a base, I wrote the play by injecting moments of audience interaction and comic bits. I also incorporated a lot of recorded contemporary rock music as well as regal classical music. Each character had a theme or motif – similar to "Peter and the Wolf" – only more contemporary. The second script retold the "Tortoise and the Hare" fable. I suggested the actors be costumed in modern clothes with the addition of simple animal noses, ears, and tails. I included other woodland animals to watch and cheer on the two racers. To add audience participation, the race wove through the aisles and theater rows with lots of opportunities for fun interaction and silliness, while still highlighting the fable's moral throughout.

Once the two scripts were completed, I used a solid week to edit, polish, and agonize over every single word. Supplying pizza and soft drinks as a bribe, I planned an informal play reading night at my apartment with Doug, Gordo, Alissa, and Miguel assuming all the roles.

After the reading, Doug gushed. "This is exactly what I was talking about, Margie. The interaction, the funny bits. By using a fable and folk story, Mr. Tarkington will love these."

"Do you think so? I've got to tell you…I had a lot of fun writing them."

"I'm meeting him early next week. If Mr. Tarkington's interested in using these scripts and offering you a job as Playwright-in-Residence next summer, I'm sure he'll call you within the week. That's how he operates. He'll probably want even more scripts."

"Thanks, Doug. I appreciate you going to bat for me."

After the gang left the play reading, Miguel stuck around to help me clean up, as usual. I appreciated his thoughtfulness. Strangely, he hadn't offered much feedback about the plays throughout the evening. As he gathered drink glasses and handed them to me to soak in the kitchen sink, he seemed especially quiet.

"What's on your mind, Miguel. Wanna talk about it?"

"I am not sure…"

I put down the sponge, dried my hands, and faced him. "Miguel, what is it? We can talk about anything. You know that." Surprised by his reluctance to share his feedback, I worried. *Bad news? Is he ill? Is he angry with me?*

"I think your children's play are *guay*…cool, yes, but…"

"My plays? Okay. What about my plays? You don't like them?"

"It is not that exactly. It is…well, the first plays you shared in the writing group…the one about the wealthy and the poor, or the peace play. Those had a message; they spoke about society."

"Okay..."

"These children's plays – with the animals and the silly Emperor – what I mean is…Margie, you have talent as a writer. You should be writing plays with greater meaning, yes?"

Miguel caught me off guard. I wasn't sure how I felt about his comments. Sure, he wrote literary short stories deeply connected to his Puerto Rican community. I understood his purpose and the greater good he served with his writing. But I was excited about these children's plays, the creativity and theatrical devices I explored in writing them as well as the good I could also serve. I took a moment to collect my thoughts.

"What about the moral of each play? Isn't that sending a strong message, even though the message is for younger people?"

"Maybe…but the stories. They seem so…*loco*, no? Silly. Not serious."

My face became warm. "Well, I like to think that through a fun theater experience the children will also be touched by the story's moral and strive to be better people."

"But the characters are animals or ridiculous people…"

*Isn't he listening to me?* I released an exasperated breath. "That is true, Miguel. In Children's Theater, many stories do use animals and funny situations to keep the kids' attention. It's up to the playwright to weave the important messages into the characters' actions and words. It's not as easy as it looks."

"I still think your writing talent is great, meant for bigger things. But you are wasting your time and talent with these kiddie plays."

I flashed to conversations with my Dad, where he'd plow through with his viewpoint – not considering what I had to say. I raised my voice in an effort to be heard.

"Miguel, can you please…." But I caught myself. I paused, deciding on a different approach. "Remember when you told me about New York's special energy, that creative pulse. Don't you think it can resonate differently in each writer?"

"Yes. You like plays now; I like to write short stories. We are both inspired by the energy we feel here, but if you are pulled to writing plays, should you not be focusing on serious topics, like your peace play?"

"Miguel…ugh!" I couldn't hold back. "There's value in both types of dramatic work. You seem to refuse to see it." Certain my arguments weren't getting through to him, I finally said, "Maybe you should go. I can finish straightening up by myself."

Miguel's eyebrows shot up in shock. "I suppose you are right. We can talk later."

He grabbed his wool coat and knitted scarf from the rack in the kitchen. After a quick kiss on my cheek, he left. I needed time to think about the direction I was taking my writing.

*Miguel's candid assessment shook my confidence. He's a serious writer whose opinion I admire. What if he's right? What if I am going backward?*

****

I arrived at *The Village Voice* office on Monday, November 15th to check the assignment board. Since the pickings had been slim recently, I refused to get my hopes up. Much to my surprise, I pulled the assignment details under my name and read: The

Beastie Boys at CBGB's.

"Crap," I said under my breath – and not in a positive way.

Most other reviewers would be thrilled. CBGB was a primo venue assignment. The original country, bluegrass, blues club opened in 1973, although punk and new wave had taken over as its primary focus. Its recent history included hosting talent like Patti Smith, Talking Heads, The Heartbreakers, Elvis Costello, the B-52's, and Blondie, among others. I knew the place was legendary, but for my second assignment with *The Village Voice*, I had my heart set on a music genre more in my comfort zone. *Maybe if I mention this to Joe?*

"Gosh, Joe. Another punk band? When I interviewed, I described my musical interests and strengths. I was hoping you'd throw me a gig at the Blue Note, like a jazz or funk quartet for my next assignment. That would be more up my writing alley."

"Hey look," he said. "I sent you to My Father's Place for your first assignment – a top venue for original talent and a premier tour stop for national acts like The Ramones. A peach of an assignment, even though it was a trial and we had a regular *Village Voice* reporter covering it. But now I'm sending you to freakin' CBGB. Are you kidding me? You should be thanking me from here to Broadway for throwing CBGB and The Beastie Boys your way. But if you're disgruntled, I can always give it to another freelancer who needs to pay the rent."

Joe Reedy had a way of making me feel ungrateful.

I took the assignment.

****

Walking into the CBGB venue, the length of the space surprised me. I'd only seen pictures of bands set up on the stage and never considered the rest of the club. A quick scan of the room had me imagining how claustrophobic bands must feel performing on that postage stamp-sized stage with its raised platform and low ceiling. Throwing in the hanging stage lights, the clutter of posters and playbills randomly plastered over any available wall space, and the packed house full of fans crushing against the stage area, I didn't know how the musicians could even breathe while they performed. That "post-modern clutter" décor extended through the entire venue. Playbills, photographs, graffiti, and advertisements covered columns, nooks, and crannies throughout the joint. Perhaps people thought of it as a living canvas.

The crowd went wild for the Beastie Boys' punk music. The group consisted of vocalist Michael Diamond, bassist Adam Yauch, drummer Kate Schellenbach, and guitarist John Berry. The set list included "Beastie Boys," "Transit Cop," "Jimi," "Holy Snappers," "Improvisation," "I Don't Want to Fight," a cover of "House of the Rising Sun," "Michelle's Farm," "Sampson Is King," "Riot Fight," and "Egg Raid on Mojo." I may have missed one or two songs because they were all super short, a few only lasting a minute or so. It became hard to distinguish if the band played an actual number or jammed on the spot. In true punk style, Beastie Boys favored heavy electric guitar in all its feedback glory over vocals. The crowd ate it up. My favorite number of the night was their cover of "House of the Rising Sun," probably because I recognized it. *I'm such an old soul when it comes to music and completely out of my element at a club like CBGB.* I did my best to keep an open mind while listening to the Beastie Boys perform. I wanted to write a fair review for *The Village Voice* and for the band.

The following day, while sitting in the living room in front of my manual typewriter hammering out a first draft of my review, I tried to capture the essence of what I experienced, and the irony did not escape me. *Here I am a classically trained vocalist with experience touring with a swing band writing about the Beastie Boys.* I wanted to be a professional journalist, even though punk wasn't exactly my favorite genre of music. I recalled the crowd and put myself in their headspace. *What is it about the Beastie Boys and those ultra short pieces that revs the fans up?* I had to admit the band released a magical and musically interesting show at CBGB that night. Those young men – boys really, barely eighteen – had tapped into unique rhythms, beats, and sounds without fear of experimenting on the spot and letting the crowd be part of the formula. I wondered if the Beastie Boys were searching for their authentic voice and using their instruments as the only way they understood to express emotions like frustration, love, hurt, anger, hopelessness? My review laid out that premise as I described what I saw at the club throughout the Beastie Boy's gig.

The minute I put the finishing touches on the review; I pivoted my focus to Mr. Tarkington. Was Mr. Tarkington reading my Children's Theater scripts that very moment? Did he like them? Did he think he could use them next summer? *Relax, Margie! What happened to your "Be Here Now" philosophy?*

Four days after the Beastie Boys concert – *I remember the date clearly: November 24th, a few days before Thanksgiving* – Mr. Tarkington called. My hands shook as I held the receiver. He told me he liked both plays. *Did I hear that right? Validation is sweet; I don't care who says otherwise.*

> Mr. T.: These plays are exactly what The Red Barn Summer Theater audience needs – funny, fast paced, and interactive.
>
> Me: Thank you. This is great feedback.

Mr. T.: And I'm feeling your creativity matched with Doug's directing skills, well…I think you two would make an excellent team. Would you like the job of Playwright-in-Resident for the 1983 season, Margie? We'd love to have you.

I nearly dropped the phone.

Me: I'm immensely grateful, Mr. Tarkington. I'd like to look over the contract, but I'll tell you right now, I'm interested.

Mr. T.: Yes, yes. Absolutely. I'm meeting with Doug this Friday, the day after Thanksgiving. Would it be alright if I gave him the packet of information to deliver to you? I understand you and he live in the same apartment building.

Me: That would work great. And thank you again.

Hanging up the phone, I wanted to jump up and down, shout to the world. I reconsidered, knowing that Broom Man would have a conniption. *No need to create a national incident!* Amazing how Miguel's reservations about me writing children's plays instantly vanished when a producer was offering me a contract for my writing!

I went to the refrigerator, grabbed a can of root beer, and pulled off the tab. Taking a long sip, I stood in the kitchen and visualized how great it would be to go to the summer theater with a person I already knew and who understood my plays, to work directly with Doug.

Was it weird that I felt more excited about the opportunity

to write plays for kids than to review more music in the city? It probably didn't help that Joe decided not to print my Beastie Boys review in *The Village Voice* after all. At least he didn't shred it.

"Your reviews are showing promise," he said. "You're starting to feel it, Margie. Keep digging."

Good advice that I also applied to the way I'd been exploring my writing options. I recorded these ideas in my journal.

> *New writing goals*
>
> *Be less concerned whether people "like" what I'm writing. Instead, start asking myself: What is the best way to connect to my heart and soul and express what's there? What is the best vehicle? Journalism? Short stories? Plays?*

*Isn't that why I moved to New York in the first place...to figure this out?*

While I'd like to say that my ego was in check and it didn't matter whether I got paid or not, it sure felt great that Mr. Tarkington offered me a contract for my written work. *Validation is a wonderful motivator!*

# 20

# Promoted and a Christmas Directive

*December, 1982*

On a Monday morning in early December, Miss Chambers called me into her office and handed me an interoffice memo. It instructed me to report to Vice President Mason's office at eleven o'clock for a meeting. I asked Miss Chambers if she knew what the meeting could be about, but she shrugged. *I hope I won't be fired on the spot. I need this job at least until the summer.*

At the appointed hour, I knocked on Mr. Mason's door and entered. Although nicely decorated, his office lacked the beautiful Art Deco furnishings featured in the other administrative offices. It reeked "corporate." *How sad for him.* I took a seat across from his beige metal desk. My breathing had become quick and shallow.

Mr. Mason leaned back in his chair. "Margie, we've been extremely impressed with your work these past eighteen months. You've shown great initiative, stepping up without being asked and always making yourself available for extra duty."

"Thanks, Mr. Mason. Doing my job, is all." *Still not sure if there's a "But" coming…*

"There are going to be several changes at Radio City Music Hall in the next few months – mostly involving the executives."

He paused to allow me to consider what he had said. *Crap, they're going to cut me!*

"I'm being promoted to the role of Chief Executive Officer."

"How wonderful. Congratulations!" I knew that meant he'd be moving upstairs to a lovely office in the Executive Suites. I'd only been there once to deliver a package, but it was exquisite. *Good for Mr. Mason!*

"I plan to keep the current Executive Secretary in the CEO's office, but would like to add a support secretary. I believe you would be a great addition to our team. How do you feel about moving upstairs beginning early January?"

Dumbfounded, I sat like a ventriloquist's dummy waiting for someone to operate my mouth. Mr. Mason continued. "Now, the position will come with a pay raise and benefits. I understand from Miss Chambers that you have an interest in writing. Playwriting, is it? We can be flexible with scheduling around those commitments, since we'll have two staff to work with."

"Wow, this sounds amazing. Thanks a lot."

I got up to leave the office, but Mr. Mason stopped me. "And Margie. If you keep up the good work, this is only the beginning of potential promotions for you here at Radio City Music Hall."

I floated back to my receptionist's desk and happily sorted through a stack of typing assignments that would fill the rest of my Monday – accounting reports, labels for marketing, a pile of letters for Miss Chambers, and a document for Legal. *Ugh. These legal documents are the worst! But never mind...I got a promotion!*

As I worked I began to wonder: What other possibilities could Mr. Mason be talking about? Did I even want to be anything more than a secretary? Was this the beginning of climbing the corporate ladder at Radio City Music Hall? *Who cares? I got a promotion!*

As I walked the nearly twenty blocks from Rockefeller Center to my apartment in the December dusk, hovering near buildings to avoid the whipping wind, I thought about what would happen to Miss Chambers in this upcoming transition. *Hm...passed over to become Mr. Mason's Executive Secretary but too much seniority to become a support secretary.* I supposed she would keep her current position for the next appointed V.P. of Finance. *The corporate world is odd.* There I was looking for a "pay the rent" sort of job and I ended up getting a promotion. But the promotion also caused me some guilt: Was it fair to only stick around Radio City for five months until the summer theater position started? *Now I'm not sure what to do or what the future holds. Focus, Margie!*

When I got home, I brewed a cup of tea, snuggled on the sofa, and opened my journal to jot down my reflections as the reality about this latest Radio City Music Hall development set in.

*Career Developments and Doubts*

*The biggest surprise happened today: Mr. Mason promoted me to full secretary in the Office of the CEO! I know I should be thrilled. I mean, secretary in the CEO's office sounds impressive. The executive secretary I'll be working with is super nice, and the office is lovely. But I'm toying with several gigantic personal issues. First, the tiny successes I've had lately with playwriting has whet my appetite for wanting to explore this genre even more. And this makes me want to move away from writing music reviews, which is surprising and crazy. Plus, I'm starting to question if the negatives of living in New York City outweigh the positives. I am inspired by the city's creative energy that Miguel talks about, but is that enough to make it worth living in Manhattan? I do know I want my chosen career to make an impact in a way that being a secretary never will. So, while the extra money that comes with being a secretary for the CEO at Radio City Music Hall will be a benefit, the whole "promotion" thing may not be the big deal I first thought it was. And as much as I love working at Radio City, do I want it to be my career? On top of all of this, what will Dad and Mom think? Dad will probably have a fit because in his mind, a promotion makes it more enticing for me to stay in New York - not in his game plan for me. I wish I could discuss these life decisions with him, like other fathers and daughters do, but we don't communicate well. Lots to consider.*

****

Arriving at Baltimore's Penn Station a few days before Christmas,

I walked out the tall front doors and immediately spotted our beat-up truck. Surprisingly, there sat Mom in the driver's seat. *Why would Mom pick me up, a task always assigned to Dad in the past?*

Tossing my duffle bag into the back of the pickup, I searched for clues to reveal the reason behind this disruption of routine. I came up empty. As I hopped into the passenger seat, I asked Mom directly, "What's going on? Is Dad okay?"

"Things at the general store have got him a bit worried, is all. I told him I'd come pick you up this time." *Seems reasonable.* She reached over and patted my arm. "It's good to have you home. We missed you at Thanksgiving again this year."

"Aw Mom. You know I've been busy writing plays and free-lancing at *The Village Voice*. Super busy."

"What happened to your hair, Margaret?"

I laughed, deciding to keep that Alissa story to myself. "Trying out a new look.

As we drove through Baltimore and the suburbs toward the Bay Bridge, memories of my band friends, Jimmy and Chaz, and even Amy, flooded my mind. A wave of sadness swept over me as I thought of Amy struggling to find her way. On the other hand, I felt relieved that Jimmy and Chaz had landed a new gig after the disastrous end of King Vido's Swing Band. And what about me? *Look at my journey…how far I'd come navigating my life from tiny Church Creek to Baltimore's Little Italy, around the country, and now to New York City. And who knows where my career may take me?*

"Where are you, Margie? You seem far away"

"Sorry, Mom. Thinking about the past few years…and wondering what might be next."

"Yes, well…your Dad has ideas about that. I wanted to give

you a heads up."

Crap! My pleasant daydream suddenly exploded as if she'd taken a pin and popped a glorious bubble.

Driving over the Chesapeake Bay via the Bay Bridge, my anxiety level increased, and my mood felt as gray as the choppy waters below. *This is shaping up to be another "pleasant" visit.* I could already hear Dad hounding me about moving home, settling down, getting serious, blah, blah, blah!

By the time we crossed the Choptank River and cruised through Cambridge, I had resigned myself to being miserable for the holiday. I only had to endure Dad's harassment for a few days, and then I'd be back in the city before New Year's Eve. Grasping for positives, I asked, "What do we have planned for Christmas, Mom?"

"Oh, nothing much this year. Your Dad's not been in the holiday spirit."

That sounded depressing. What about hanging the lights? Searching for the perfect tree? All the seasonal rigamarole?

"At least you and I can make Christmas cookies, right?" I asked. Although she looked ahead without a smile, she nodded, though not enthusiastically.

We pulled into the driveway at our Church Creek home, where everything looked exactly the same as the last time I visited – the window trim could use a coat of paint, the tiny front porch railing still missed a stile here and there, and the driveway gravel was thin. But otherwise, the house stood in a neatly tended yard, thanks to Mom. Dad's focus had always been on his general store, not on keeping up the house. Mom and I couldn't fault him for that – he worked hard keeping that general store afloat.

I hopped out and grabbed my duffle bag from the back of

the truck. Mom started toward the front door, but to our surprise Dad appeared.

"The wayward daughter has come home at last," he said in a loud voice.

*Oh great. He started drinking early today.* I thought for sure he'd be at the store. Even Mom took a few steps back in shock to see him in the doorway.

"Hi Dad. Good to see you." He made a weird face – a cross between wrinkling his nose and a big fake smile. I had no idea what he was attempting to convey, but then I never did when he'd been drinking.

Thankfully, Mom suggested we get in from the cold.

We all moved into the house where Mom had done her best to place a few decorations, probably those she could reach in the attic without Dad's help. The true picture was coming into focus: Dad's drinking had increased, and he was basically useless. What a sad family portrait!

Despite the lack of a tree, Mom had managed to make the wood paneled living room exude warmth by positioning candles on the mantle and the side tables. She tucked fir boughs and berries she'd cut from our property around each surface, filling the room with a seasonal evergreen scent. Tossing her crocheted red and green throws over the Early American slipcovered sofa and chairs added cheerful holiday color. Truthfully, we didn't need any more decorations than that, although I knew Mom loved those colored outside lights around the windows and on the bushes each year. That was Dad's one major Christmas chore. That and bringing home the tree.

"The living room looks totally rad. Super Christmas-y, Mom," I said as I gave her a hug. She turned her head away. *Is she sobbing ?*

Mom wiped her eyes. "I've got chili on the stove. And I'm mixing up cornbread. Nothing special for dinner."

"Sounds great. I'll take my duffle up to my room and come down to help set the table."

I took the steps two-by-two. Once in my bedroom, I overheard Dad and Mom going at it. With Dad's slurred words, I couldn't make out his initial beef, but Mom said clear as a bell, "Give it time. She just got here." *They are obviously arguing about me. Brace yourself, Margie.*

At dinner around the kitchen table, Dad barely ate his chili, picking at a piece of cornbread instead. He stared at me while Mom and I made small talk. Her questions came at me like buck shot during deer season.

"How has the weather been in the city? Getting much snow this year? How are your boots holding out?"

I suppose Dad couldn't contain himself despite Mom's directive, because at last he burst into the conversation. "Been curious to know how this whole writin' career is goin' for ya, Margaret. Last time ya came home ya told us ya lost your internship. Then ya called about another internship of some sort. Now you're writin' plays." His vocal volume increased as he continued. "I don't understand what you're up to in New York City after a year and a half with little to show for it. All I see is a girl hoppin' from one thing to the next like a damned jackrabbit."

I shouldn't have felt blindsided. I mean, Mom did warn me, but geez. I thought Dad had *some* understanding of what I was trying to do with my career. I looked at Mom. All I saw was desperation and exhaustion in her eyes. Why wasn't she speaking up? She always had in the past. *No, Margie. You're on your own.*

"Dad, I'll try to explain…again. I moved to New York to explore my options for a career in writing. Yes, I have a freelance job at *The Village Voice* – it's like a paid internship, even better, right? And yes, I have a great writing group where I'm learning about other forms of writing, including plays. These are all good things, Dad."

"Accordin' to you."

I took a breath and tried again. "And, in case you forgot, I still have a job at Radio City Music Hall, where last week I found out I will be promoted to a new position with more money come January." I chose not to bring up the summer theater opportunity at that point. I had no idea how to approach the idea with either parent. *Best to layer in these things in small doses.*

"A promotion sounds wonderful, dear," Mom said. Dad remained silent, poking at his chili. A long awkward pause in the conversation ensued. Mom continued to eat her dinner while Dad glared.

I rubbed my temples to release the tension building behind my eyes. Finally, I broke the silence. "I see that's not what you were hoping to hear, Dad. What is it that you want from me? I don't understand."

Dad pulled his flask from his jeans back pocket, took a long swig, and wiped his mouth with the back of his hand. "I'll tell ya what I want. Ya been in that damned city for close to two years and I'm not seein' anything published. I think it'd be better if ya came home and helped me with the general store, like the old days, Margaret. Now there...ya asked what I want. Well, that's exactly what I want."

The same conversation I'd heard many times before, aside from the painful writing jab. With words occasionally slurred and sounding much more desperate than logical, my heart filled with sadness and even empathy for him. I didn't argue anymore because...well, there was no point trying to speak logic to a drunk.

****

The following day Dad went off to the general store, leaving Mom and me to our Christmas cookie task. A favorite tradition, she was up early and already had the large balls of dough chilling in the refrigerator by the time I came downstairs in search of my morning caffeine. After warming up the coffee in the aluminum pot on the stove, Mom poured us each a steaming cup, adding a slight teaspoon of sugar – exactly how I liked it. We settled at the kitchen table.

Mom probed to see how upset I was about the previous evening's conversation. "It sounds like things are going well in New York for you with your promotion and all." I took a long sip of coffee and merely nodded. "Look, I know your father sounded stern last night, but he does worry about you living in New York." I took another long sip with a nod.

She sighed and tried a new approach. "I know you hate it when I ask, but are you seeing anyone special? What about that one boy…Miguel is it?"

"Okay Mom, you win. Yes, if you must know, Miguel and I are dating. In fact, we're planning to elope and honeymoon in Puerto Rico. How's that?"

"What? Oh, Sweet Jesus!" The color drained from Mom's face. I had to come clean.

"I'm kidding. Miguel is genuinely nice. We're dating, that's all. Don't worry, Mom. I wouldn't do anything stupid like elope with someone you never met just to spite Dad." I expected her to be smiling, but Mom still looked concerned.

"Why the worried look, Mom?"

"I'm thinking about your Dad, wondering how he'll…. You know your Dad means well. I hope you don't think poorly of him because he was born in a different era."

A light bulb suddenly lit in my brain, as an angry heat rose from my neck to my cheeks. "Wait a minute. Am I getting this right? You're worried about Dad finding out that I'm dating a man with Puerto Rican roots, aren't you? Please tell me that you don't have a problem with this, Mom. For as long I can remember, you've never shown any kind of prejudice toward anyone."

"Of course not, Margaret. I feel the same as always. It's just that your Dad…lately he's been…well, he's under a lot of stress with the store. And when he's stressed, he can become a bit…unrealistic in his expectations. Maybe we don't mention that you're involved with, well…anyone for the time being."

Mom's excuse-making and sneaky tactics annoyed me, but at least it put off another confrontation with Dad…for a while. I still had to deal with his current "Holiday Pressure Campaign." I hoped to get Mom's assistance to get him to back off.

"Any chance you can get Dad to lay off while I'm home? It's always the same. He doesn't listen to me or even try to understand what I'm doing with my life. It's always 'Come home, get married, have kids!'"

"His values are all about hearth and home…that's also how he was raised."

"And that's fine but…geez, Mom. It's 1982. It doesn't mean I plan to live my life like that."

Mom sighed as she took a single dough ball from the refrigerator, kneading it on the floured cutting board. I pulled out three large cookie sheets from the cupboard and greased them with shortening.

"I need to bring you current on your Dad, Margaret. I should have told you on the ride from the train station, but I was hopeful…." Her voice trailed off and she looked away. I could tell this was painful. "It started with things going south at the general store. New grocery stores are coming to Cambridge, and people are less inclined to use Dad's general store. The prices are better in Cambridge and…"

"Well, come on, Mom. He's been price gouging for years. People are getting smarter, that's all."

"You're probably right. The problem is that instead of facing the issue, Dad's been drinking more, blaming anyone but himself."

"Including me!"

"I know it's ridiculous. He's got it in his head that if you come back and help with the store things will magically return to how they were a few years ago."

"Mom, first of all, that's crazy. Second of all, it's not fair. Have you told him that?"

"I've tried but he won't listen. Look, I don't want you to give up on your dreams or your life in New York, even though I am worried sick about you living in that city. Maybe if you came home more regularly, he'd stop drinking as much…oh, I don't know. He's unreasonable."

We continued our cookie making process in silence, but I was consumed with sadness for my Mom…and even for Dad. He worked for years building the store into a business that could support this family. And he succeeded. It must have been hard to watch it slip away. I hoped he would realize that misplaced anger, blaming others, and excess drinking only made his problems worse.

****

On Christmas Eve morning I drove Dad's truck into Cambridge to walk along the Choptank River banks – a place that always brought me calm and peace. I sought refuge from the tension of

Dad's irrational thinking and his drinking and Mom's defeated attitude. A knot in my stomach and pressure in my forehead developed whenever Dad came around. Not the holiday visit I had envisioned.

The Choptank River flowed easily that day. Patches of pale blue and pink sky peeked through the otherwise overcast gray clouds. I breathed in the crisp air, releasing vaporous mist from my pursed lips. I loved the smell of this river, fresh and bold. Manhattan provided wonderful energy for inspiring creativity, but my Choptank River was the perfect salve for restoring peace to the soul. *Maybe I need to have both places in my life...*

Refreshed and centered, I returned to the house and was greeted by the delicious odor of cinnamon rolls baking and sizzling bacon cooking on the stove. Mom had already placed three bowls on the table of her traditional "Christmas Fruit" – a combination of chopped apples, juicy pink grapefruit sections, and sweet syrupy strawberries. Dad came in the front door a few minutes later with an armful of logs for the fireplace. *Okay, this all looks pleasant enough...so far.* I only needed to get through the rest of today, Mass tomorrow morning, and Christmas dinner. Then I'd be on the train the following day! *You can do this, Margie.*

After an incident-free Christmas Eve breakfast, the three of us retreated to the treeless living room to exchange gifts, a family tradition. Dad built a roaring fire; Mom played holiday albums on the Hi-Fi. She played those same albums for twenty years – Frank Sinatra, Andy Williams, The Glenn Miller Orchestra, even Rudolph the Red Nosed Reindeer! *I should have bought her a new Christmas album as a surprise.*

On Christmas morning, Dad insisted that we attend Mass at dawn. It snowed the night before and the temperature had dropped, but Dad was undeterred. Mom and I bundled up in our boots, wool coats, knitted scarves, hats, and gloves, and huddled together in the truck's front seat. Dad drove in the predawn darkness along unplowed roads to the church, where only a handful of cars sat in the parking lot. *Maybe that's why he prefers the earliest Mass. Is he afraid to face people he knows?*

The Christmas Mass was surprisingly moving. I had long ago moved away from my Catholic roots, searching elsewhere for spiritual answers. I never could align the example my Dad provided with the Church's teachings – the guy who attended church regularly, claimed to follow its teachings, then turned around and berated Black people, overcharged folks in his general store, and was prejudiced toward anyone who was different. And he used the Catholic Church to support his actions. But the more I explored other options, like Eastern philosophies and religions, I learned that anyone could bend a religion to work in their favor. That Christmas morning, I tapped into a calm and quiet spot in my heart and focused on Goodwill Toward All People – Miguel, Mom, Dad, Gordo, Doug, Crystal, Alissa, Dr. R., Gwendolen, Miss Chambers, Mr. Mason, Jimmy, Chaz, Amy, and even that sleazebag, Girard. *Hey, it's Christmas.*

****

The morning after Christmas, Mom drove me to the train station in Baltimore. We chatted along the way, recapping the visit. As always, she pressed me about when I planned to visit again.

"I'll make an effort to come home over Easter, Mom. Not promising, though."

"That would be wonderful."

An awkward pause lingered between us as we knew we needed to acknowledge the Dad situation. I broke the ice first.

"I wondered if you spoke to Dad about maybe laying off me

for the rest of this visit, since he hadn't said anything else to me about moving back to Church Creek."

"Well, I wanted you to have a nice Christmas, is all."

"Sure, I get that." I drew in a breath before broaching what needed to be said. "Mom, I hope you understand that I need to be in New York right now doing my thing. But I'm worried about you, too. I feel bad that I'm not home to help you with this Dad situation, although I'm not sure what I can do."

Mom slowed down and suddenly pulled the truck off to the side of the road. Traffic continued to whiz by.

"Mom…what are you…"

She repositioned herself in the driver's seat to face me as best as she could. "Now you look, Margaret. I know I wasn't too thrilled with you changing your mind about graduate school, but I completely understand that you are making a life for yourself in New York. I support that you're exploring a new direction for your writing and that you are meeting people and making friends and dating a special person. That's what a young woman in her twenties is supposed to be doing. I will not have you thinking that you need to come home to fix your parent's problems. Now, stop worrying about me or what's going on at home or what your Dad is ranting about. We'll figure it out. Right now, I want you to live your life."

*Wow, Mom rarely lets loose but when she does…Okay, I have my directive. Back to the Big Apple it is to see what unfolds.*

21

# A Shakey Beginning

*January, 1983*

What a difference three hundred sixty-five days made when it came to deciding how to ring in the New Year. No trekking to Times Square. No big fancy dinner celebration. A simple bottle of champagne and soft drinks with a few friends fit the bill. Due to health issues and loyalty to boyfriends, our little band of merrymakers was reduced to me, Alissa, and Miguel. Doug was home with the flu…again…so Gordo stayed close by. And Crystal? Well, Crystal was with her man. Wherever that may be. She rarely spent time with us anymore. And when she did, her manic personality reigned.

With the Times Square festivities quietly humming in the background on the television, Miguel and I sipped champagne from juice glasses while Alissa drank a root beer. We reflected on our hopes for the upcoming year. I blabbed about my potential summer Playwright-in-Residence position at the Red Barn Theater in Massachusetts.

"How will that work out with your Radio City Music Hall job?" Alissa asked.

"Good question. I haven't figured that out yet. It's one reason why I haven't signed the Red Barn contract, as much as I want this Playwright-in-Residence opportunity."

"The producer would need to know by now, yes?" Miguel asked.

Alissa nodded. "Yeah, don't you have to decide soon? I mean, if you decide not to go, that producer guy would need to find a replacement, you get me?"

Alissa and Miguel were right. But with the Dad crap going on at home and Doug being sick on and off, I had been worried. And then there were new doubts creeping into my psyche. *What if Radio City Music Hall is where I'm meant to be? What if I give up my new secretarial position to go to the summer stock and when I come back to New York in the fall, I can't find a job as wonderful? What if I'm forced to move back home? What if I never write again? What if... ugh!* That negative chatterbox was at it again, tearing down my confidence and rendering me immobile. I had to figure out my next steps and fast!

Alissa shared her vision for 1983 next. While she always seemed content to wait tables and flow like a feather in the wind, apparently, she'd been feeling stuck. While Miguel and I knew how much she loved to listen to music of all kinds, from punk to folk to blues, we had no idea that she played guitar! With a raise of her root beer, Alissa announced, "Since mid-December, I have secretly enrolled in guitar lessons."

"Why keep it secret, Alissa?" I asked.

"Because I was sure I'd fall on my ass."

"You dork. That's wonderful."

Miguel asked, "What type of music are you learning?

"Well, I already knew the basics – I'd played guitar since I was a kid. But while I was in rehab, music became my salvation. Oh crap...that sounds stupid. It's why I never talk about it."

"No, Alissa. It's not stupid at all. Tell us." I wanted to encourage her to open up.

"It's nothing. In rehab...the last time...I rediscovered the guitar and...well, I connected to the music and practicing and learning new chords. When I went home, I told my parents I wanted to take lessons and maybe become a musician. That's when they totally wigged out. 'You want to live like a druggie rock-and-roll musician. Sex, drugs, and rock and roll.' I mean, I get it. They were terrified I'd slip. But they didn't understand how the music had saved me. That's when I realized they were never going to let me be me. If a simple thing like playing the guitar was too threatening for them...well....ugh. So, I bolted, and here I am. But once I moved to New York, I couldn't afford a therapist anymore. I used my music instead. I started grooving on the blues. Hey, I'm still here and I'm clean."

*Good for her.* I loved that she finally felt safe enough with us to share her story. And it explained a lot about her gruff outer personality...until you really got to know her.

Miguel announced that he had news. Alissa and I were super curious.

"Great, Miguel," I said. "We're all ears."

A huge smile spread across his face. "The Iowa Writers' Workshop has accepted my application into the program."

At first, Alissa and I were speechless. She could tell from the blank expression on my face that shock had crept in. She jumped in to cover for me. "Wow, Miguel. That's huge."

"Yes, they will provide a scholarship for the three year program," Miguel continued. "Not only that, but my *Titi*, my aunt in Puerto Rico, has given me money to attend the summer program. She has always believed in my dream of writing since I was a young boy. She wanted me to get a good start by getting to know the faculty before the creative writing program begins in the fall."

Caught off guard, I could barely squeak out, "How did this come about, Miguel?"

"Ah...Dr. R. first told me about this school," he explained. "She said it would be an excellent program for me and helped me with the aid forms. She even helped to explain things to my parents, who were very reluctant at first."

Alissa looked at me, but I was still too shocked to speak. She took up the slack. "Uh, Miguel, when will you be leaving?"

"In May, to find an apartment and get settled before the summer classes start. My cousin has a station wagon. He will be driving me." He glanced over at me. "There is still much planning to do."

Silently gasping as if I'd been punched in my gut, Miguel's news floored me. He and I hadn't talked too much about how my leaving for the summer would affect our relationship. I guess I selfishly thought a couple months wasn't a huge hurdle. But now, he planned to go away for a three-year-long program. *And this is the first I'm hearing of it?* I made a flimsy excuse to exit to the kitchen, throwing crackers onto a plate while suppressing my hurt and anger. Alissa followed me, zeroing in on the tension.

"I'm sensing Miguel's news wasn't only a surprise to me," she said.

I shook my head, perturbed.

"I think I'll stop over at Gordo and Doug's place and watch the New Year roll in with the sicko," she said in a voice loud enough for Miguel to hear. Then she whispered, "You two might have things to talk about, you get me?" I hugged her, pulled down her coat and scarf from the peg on the kitchen wall, and watched her leave the apartment.

I returned to the living room where Miguel was glued to Dick Clark on the TV, talking about the record crowds cramming into Times Square. "This crowd…*loco*, yes? I'm glad we are not there."

"Me too." I sat down on the sofa next to him and took his hand. "Miguel, I want to talk to you about your news, about you going away to Iowa."

"Yes, I have wanted to talk to you too, but I wanted to make sure I had been accepted first. And we have both been busy. But now that I am sure I am accepted, I have a great idea." Before I could express how hurt I felt that he hadn't shared any of these plans with me earlier, he launched in. "I have it all figured out. I want you to come to Iowa with me. We can find a small apartment together – I can attend classes; you can keep writing. This will be wonderful, right?"

"Um…I'm not sure. Miguel, you'll be busy day and night with your program and your writing assignments. What would be the point of having me there?"

He pulled his hand away from mine. "But we are together. We should be together."

"Of course, we care for each other. And you have been amazing to me – helpful and understanding. We love spending time together and supporting each other's work but…" He closed his body off to me, crossing his arms over his chest and stared straight ahead. *What can I say to make him understand?* "Miguel, what about my plans to go to the summer theater?

"Again, the summer theater. Since you did not sign the contract yet I…Are you planning to go? You still want to write the plays for the children?"

"Yes, Miguel. I do enjoy writing the children's plays. We talked about this before—"

"We did, and I told you then…You are better than this. Your writing talent is—"

I held up my hand to stop him. My face flushed and for the first time, anger rose in me, directed at Miguel. "I get it, Miguel. You think I should be writing other stuff. But I don't like this pressure from you. I can make my own decisions."

"But I see you wasting your talent and I want to help you make a better decision…"

*That's it!* "Wait a minute," I said, raising my voice. "So, you're deciding how I should manage my life…like my Dad wants to decide how I should manage my life. Hmm…what's the better way? Miguel's way – only write the type of plays Miguel says I should write, or Dad's way – leave New York, get married, start a family, and forget this crazy writing dream. Certainly not Margie's way. Oh no!" I paused to catch my breath. "Well, I'm nearly twenty-eight-years old and you can't decide what I will or won't write. That's not fair. And you can't decide if I will or won't go to the Red Barn Theater this summer."

Miguel opened his mouth as if to speak but merely sucked in air. He rose abruptly. "Yes, okay, fine. You do what you want. And I will too." He rushed into the kitchen, grabbed his coat, and stomped out of the apartment.

Sitting alone in my apartment with the Times Square New Year's Eve celebration noise playing on the television, I failed miserably at stifling a sob. I may have sounded strong in my admonishments toward Miguel, but I shook inside. It bothered me that he started dictating how my career should be handled. Or was he genuinely concerned? *I'm confused about his motives.* I cared about him deeply, but he was leaving me and it hurt. *This is a hell of a way to start the new year, that's for sure.*

# 22

# New York Family Faltering

*January-February, 1983*

While I settled into the new secretarial job at Radio City Music Hall during the month of January, things grew troublesome among my New York family. Doug's health had been on a roller coaster trajectory – one week good; one week not good. Crystal continued to spin out of control, spending *beaucoup* amounts of time with the sleazebag when he was in town. Miguel and I remained on the outs after our argument. The January chill permeated.

Doug's flu-like symptoms continued off and on through February. Gordo had read about a specialist on 54th Street near Fifth Avenue and insisted Doug go there to be checked out. I agreed to go along for moral support. Gordo wanted to take a cab, but Doug preferred to walk. We split the difference, exiting the cab near the Plaza Hotel on Fifth and 59th Street. Doug liked walking down Fifth Avenue to gaze at all the high-end window dressings. *Always fun to dream.*

Two blocks into our walk, Doug exclaimed, "There it is! We have to go in!" He acted like a teeny bopper seeing the Beatles getting off the airplane on U.S. soil for the first time. *What in the world was he wigging out about!*

As we approached 57th Street, a gleaming glass façade rose

straight up into the sky. The tall, deep entrance framed in lights and gold lettering announced that we had arrived at TRUMP TOWER.

The building had opened less than a week prior on February 14th. Doug was desperate to go inside and see what the media hoopla had been all about. *The New York Times* had published a slew of articles about Donald Trump, the thirty-seven-year-old whiz kid real estate developer, who had purchased the original building in 1977 and boasted about his vision for premium condos and exclusive shopping for the wealthy right in Manhattan's mid-town.

"I read in the *Times* that this Trump fellow and the city are in a legal battle about the building," Gordo said. "Mr. Trump thinks he should be getting like fifty million dollars in a tax abatement 'cuz Trump Tower benefits the city, according to him. The New York Housing Commission doesn't quite see it like that!"

"I'm surprised you're impressed with this Trump guy, Doug," I said. "I'd read that a lot of New Yorkers are upset by his decision to smash the Art Deco friezes that sat on top of the original building he razed to build his 'Trump Tower.'"

"It's not the guy; it's the building." Convinced that was why he insisted on walking down Fifth Avenue, Gordo and I indulged him and entered Trump Tower.

"But only for five minutes!" Gordo warned. "We still have a doctor's appointment to get to!"

We could not take in all five levels of retail, galleries, and restaurants filling Trump Tower in five minutes. Billed as "a midtown shopping destination for the elite," our motley little trio was completely out of place. We gawked at the five-story atrium, the amazing sixty-foot waterfall, and the suspended golden escalator. I especially liked the huge planters and greenery surrounding the terraces. *I do admit the building is gorgeous, but it further verifies my theory of excess in New York. The Haves versus the Have Nots.*

Despite the side trip, we got Doug to the specialist's office on time. Gordo wanted to go into the exam room with him but was told that, unless he was family, he couldn't. *Geez!* Gordo tried to act brave, but I knew he had been worried ever since Doug came back from summer stock with extreme lethargy and constant flu-symptoms.

When Doug left the doctor's office, he looked somber. The specialist confirmed the swelling in his neck was not normal but was stumped as to what the exact cause could be. The scary news showed up in the blood test results Doug had taken earlier. Something about deficient T cells and B cells that help the immune system function. The plan was to repeat the bloodwork and run a series of additional tests. Doug had an antibiotic prescription to fill for bacterial infection.

"So, this is good news, right? They think you have an infection, and the antibiotic will fix you right up." I tried to put a positive spin on the whole ordeal to calm myself as much as Doug and Gordo.

The expressions on Gordo and Doug's faces told a different story.

****

While snowfall had been minimal in February, the bitter cold temps turned sidewalks icy and treacherous. One Saturday in late February, I arranged with Crystal to do our least favorite task: the laundry. This involved lugging two rolling baskets as well as knapsacks full of clothing, linens, and detergent several blocks over to the 1st Avenue self-serve laundromat, washing and drying multiple loads, packing up the clean laundry, and lugging it back to the apartment. *New York City living can be difficult for the lower classes!*

The deal with Crystal was that she would help me with the lugging to and fro, if I would do the actual washing, drying, and folding at the laundromat. She helped me get the laundry to the laundromat and then flew out the door – as expected.

I shouted down the street, "Don't forget to be back here at two o'clock, Crystal. On the dot!"

I finished drying, folding, and packing the clothing and linens by two, and waited for Crystal for over an hour. There was no way I could maneuver two baskets and two stuffed duffels on those icy sidewalks without killing myself. *Speaking of killing...I'm ready to strangle Crystal!*

I waited another thirty minutes and ended up going to a corner phone booth to call Doug and Gordo, who weren't home. *Crap!* As a last resort I called Alissa who lived over twenty blocks uptown. What a saint! She took a cab and came to my rescue about twenty minutes later – and on her day off, too! As we lugged the two rolling baskets plus two duffle bags full of laundry over treacherous sidewalks, dodging Sunday pedestrians and avenue traffic, I gave poor Alissa an earful.

"Crysal's never been the most responsible person on earth, but what the hell! I don't know what I would have done if I couldn't reach you, Alissa. I mean, crap. I told her a hundred times to meet me at two o'clock. I even left a freakin' note. What is wrong with her?" I stopped to catch my breath, sweat dripping down my back, despite the brisk February temps. Redistributing our heavy loads, we continued down First Avenue toward East 65th Street.

"You know damn well what's wrong with Crystal," Alissa said. "She's addicted to cocaine and has no control. Can't depend on someone like that. You don't want to admit it, Margie. She's dropped out of school, looks like hell, only lives for her next hit. Damn, she was so desperate the last time Girard left town, she actually asked me if I had any blow."

"Any what?"

"Blow…coke…cocaine. God, Margie. I love how naïve you are. But the point is, she asked me! She's too scared to ask on the street, and Girard keeps her pretty isolated. She's spiraling, you get me? And as long as that guy's in the picture…."

Alissa was right. Like one of those stupid cartoons, the lightbulb turned on in my brain. "I get it…finally. She's not going to snap out of this. It's time we all sit her down and have a talk. Let's figure out when to gather the gang and approach Crystal."

****

I returned to my apartment building after work the following Monday and found Miguel sitting on the stairway in the foyer. When I didn't hear from him for a couple weeks after he walked out on New Year's Eve, I tried leaving messages on his answer machine. He didn't return them. I figured he needed more time. But after nearly two months, I assumed our relationship was over. Yet, there he sat – looking distraught with shoulders slumped and head bowed. He looked up as I entered the lobby, a flicker of hope in his eyes. *Do I dare feel hopeful too?*

"Miguel, I'm surprised to see you here."

"I think we should talk…if that is okay with you."

We climbed the stairs in silence, and I unlocked the apartment door. I immediately started the tea kettle even before hanging our coats on the wall hooks. Avoiding eye contact, I busied myself by placing cups and spoons on the kitchen table while Miguel found the teabags and sugar bowl in the cupboard. The whistling tea kettle broke our awkward silence. After pouring boiling water into our cups, I planted myself in the chair across from Miguel.

"I missed you," we said simultaneously, defusing an inkling of tension.

"I'm sorry I was angry with you, Miguel. I appreciate that you think I have talent as a writer. But please understand that I have to find my own way. If I believe that writing plays…even children's plays…is the best way to express myself, then you have to let me explore this kind of writing."

"Yes. You are right. I only wanted what was best for you." Miguel continued, "Was it wrong that I wanted you to come with me to Iowa?" Miguel's arms were crossed and his shoulders still resonated defensiveness as he spoke.

I needed to make him understand. I searched my mind for an example that would speak to him. "Look, would it make sense if I said, 'Miguel, I want you to come to the Red Barn Theater this summer, where you can sit in my assigned room and write all day and night, even though I'll be required to be at rehearsals or doing rewrites on scripts by myself?"

Miguel's body softened, his arms unfolded, and he turned his face to look at me directly. "I understand what you are saying. I am thinking we are at different places in our careers." He took my hand again, caressing it.

"That doesn't mean we don't care for each other, Miguel. I do care…so much. But I don't want to hold you back, and I don't want you to hold me back either. That's not a thoughtful relationship, is it?"

Miguel leaned into me. "You are right." He kissed me softly. "I guess all we can do now is enjoy the time we have together, yes?" Though I nodded in agreement, my heart broke. In less than three months, Miguel would be packed up and moving to Iowa, slipping out of my life.

While talking about how difficult it was for two writers whose careers seemed to be pulling them in opposite directions, we came to an understanding: to make the most of the precious months ahead of us. But listening to this beautiful, intelligent, gentle man sitting close to me created an urgent longing in my heart and body. *What's come over me? Is the thought of Miguel walking out of my life in three months creating this intense physical desire?* All I knew was that in the urgency of the moment, I wanted him more than ever.

I moved closer to Miguel and turned his face toward me, kissing him passionately. He responded in kind, wrapping his arm around my waist and pulling me into his body.

"Miguel, I want you to stay with me tonight. I want you to make love to me." With a questioning look, he started to speak, but I cut him off. "Yes, Miguel. I'm sure."

We retired to my tiny bedroom, undressed, and climbed into the bed. Miguel knew exactly what to do to make me feel secure in his naked embrace – soft kisses, gentle touches, slow movements. He stayed connected to me through eye contact and smiles and sweet murmurs. Never once feeling my past trauma creeping in like an unwanted guest, I seized the moment and focused solely on Miguel and our united bodies.

I knew Miguel and I had limited time together. Maybe becoming physically closer was only setting myself up for more pain. But in this case the heart won the battle over the mind!

# 23

# Stark Reality

*February, 1983*

While Miguel and I moved in a positive though finite direction, Crystal continued to slide further down her path of dependency on both Girard and her next hit. Alissa and I looked for an opportunity to approach her. The stars and planets aligned perfectly a week after the laundry incident.

Doug, Gordo, Alissa, and I were sitting in my apartment listening to a Pointer Sisters' album when we were interrupted by a loud commotion on the landing. Sounds of pounding and shouting caused Doug and me to rush through the kitchen and peek out the door.

"Is that the F.B.I. at Girard's apartment?" Doug asked. Through the cracked opening of the door, we could see two officers with F.B.I. insignias on their jackets entering Girard's door. "That's not good."

"Crap. I'm sure Crystal's over there," I said as I yanked Doug back into the apartment.

About forty-five minutes later, my front door opened. Crystal bolted into living room, half-sobbing and half-ranting out of control.

"The stupid F.B.I. are doing a crackdown. They raided Girard's apartment! Can you believe it? They took him away.

They wouldn't let me go with him. I was right there in his apartment when it happened. It totally freaked me out. Why would they raid Girard's apartment? Okay, he might have had a little bit of coke on him, but come on…the F.B.I?"

Doug, Gordo, Alissa, and I decided enough was enough. A few quick glances between us confirmed the time had come to confront Crystal.

Alissa approached her first. "This isn't the first or last time Girard's been arrested. Before you bailed him out in April, his last girlfriend did the same thing…and his girlfriend before that. That is, until those girls wised up and got a life!" *Typical Alissa. Right to the point.*

Crystal's shoulders tensed, fists balled up, and eyes narrowed. "No, you're wrong. This time it's different. Girard loves me."

"Honey, Alissa's right," Doug said. "Girard has a pattern, but you're too close to him to see it. And, well…you're kinda messed up."

My heart went out to her. In less than a year and a half, Crystal, our impeccable fashion plate, had spiraled into a directionless heap of desperation. She sat before us with greasy hair in dirty sweatpants and a torn tee shirt, mascara streaming down her face, lethargic yet restless. Having completely withdrawn from Parsons School of Design, Girard had become her sole focus. Well, that and her next high. Doug interrupted my thoughts.

"Girard uses his women as cover until either they get smart and leave him or, if they end up using too much of his 'product,' he kicks them to the curb," Doug said. "We've seen it over and over during the five years before you moved into this apartment. Why do you think Girard avoids me and Gordo? Well, that and he abhors gay men." Doug said the last part under his breath, but we all knew it was true.

Gordo nodded. "Doug and I are surprised he hasn't been arrested by the Feds before today. We always kinda figured he'd been bringing in cocaine from Amsterdam for his own use. We wondered if he'd found a way to smuggle in enough to distribute."

"What?...No, Gordo. Girard wouldn't be doing that. He-he's got friends there. That's why he goes," Crystal said, unable to believe Girard could be dealing drugs. *Not her upstanding Girard!*

"Aw, darlin'. I'm sure he has plenty of friends there, but you know that's probably not why he goes to Amsterdam," Gordo said.

Crystal dropped her head into her hands.

"They're telling you the truth. The guy's manipulating you," Alissa added.

As if hit by a tsunami of stark reality, Crystal broke down, "Oh God." Crying and wailing and rocking in her chair, she took us by surprise.

"What is it, Crystal? Is there something else?" I asked.

"Oh God, oh no…I-I-I can't believe how stupid I've been. Oh shit…they're gonna be after me next." Crystal jerked her head up. "Did you hear that? Was it a knock? Are the Feds here?"

"No one knocked, girl. Calm down. What are you freakin' out about?" Alissa asked.

"Shh. They'll hear you." Crystal's frightened eyes darted around the room, searching for the imagined sound.

Resting my hand on her shoulder, I tried to reassure her in a hushed voice. "It's alright, Crystal, I promise. What were you about to tell us?"

Crystal stood abruptly. She raced into the bedroom, waving for us to follow her. Alissa, Doug, Gordo, and I squished into the tiny bedroom and watched Crystal drag her large suitcase out from under the bed. We were confused but gave her time to connect her actions to her thoughts.

She spoke in a whisper, looking around as if being watched. "Girard asked to borrow my suitcase the first time he went to Amsterdam – when was that? – a year or more ago. He always used it whenever he traveled overseas. I didn't think much of it. He always returned it to me…" She paused. We weren't sure where she was heading.

"Go on, Crystal." Gordo placed a hand on her arm.

"Right. A week ago, I wanted to pack my thick winter sweaters in the suitcase to store under my bed. I opened it and…" Crystal opened the suitcase and showed us what she had found. She pulled up a section at the bottom of the suitcase, which looked as if someone had built a lightweight false compartment and covered it with matching fabric. "I found this loose piece fitted into the bottom section of my suitcase."

"Shit, Crystal. That section is large enough to sneak several pounds of cocaine through Customs," Alissa said.

"Did you ask Girard about it?" I asked. "I mean, it's clear he did this to your suitcase."

A tear trickled down Crystal's face as she attempted to hold back her sobs. "I was afraid. Whenever I asked him about his trips, he got angry and told me to mind my own business. He started to scare me."

"Always felt that guy was a sleazebag," Alissa said.

"Crystal, didn't you wonder how Girard always had cocaine when he got back from his trips? Didn't you put two and two together?" I asked.

"No, no. I figured he scored it here in the States when he got home…I focused on him and partying. I didn't think…he told me he visited friends…I believed that's what he…."

Alissa, in her not-at-all subtle way, reminded Crystal about the impact of the whole suitcase business. "You do understand that the sleazebag was using you, don't you? By returning the suitcase to you after each overseas trip, he got rid of any evidence from his own apartment, you get me? What do you think he's going to be telling the Feds right now?"

Crystal dropped her head in both her hands, rocking back and forth.

Wanting to assure her, I searched for calming words that might make an impact. "Crystal, we're not ganging up on you. We're all concerned because we love you." She looked up, apparently shocked to hear this. "It's true. We all care about you. And we're worried about what you're doing to yourself."

"Whaddaya mean?" she mumbled.

"Come on, Crystal," Alissa said. "We all know you're using. And we all know it's more than a hit here and there for fun, you get me? You're dependent on cocaine and Girard's made it easy for you to be well supplied."

"But..." Crystal started to argue, but she got shut down immediately.

"Remember, it's what Girard does," Doug said. "Before you arrived, he always made sure he had a girl on the side to cover his tracks – bail him out if he got caught with his restaurant scam, hang around on the promise of more drugs during his long absences – he's a master manipulator."

"I figure he's in pretty deep this time. The F.B.I. doesn't cozy up to pretty boys who rely on their charm to get out of trouble," Gordo added.

I watched Crystal take in all this information, processing a different perspective about Girard than she had ever considered. *Should we have had this talk sooner? Who knows if she would have been ready to hear us? Who knows if she's even hearing us now? But we have to try…*

I wanted to continue to let Crystal know we were there for her. "We don't want to see you get dragged down by Girard's legal troubles this time. And we want to do whatever we can to help you get healthy again."

At that point Crystal completely broke down, her entire body convulsing as she bawled in agony. We all rallied around her like a fluffy warm quilt and let her cry it out. In fact, we all sobbed. Once composed, Crystal agreed that she needed help.

"The first step is to call to your parents, Crystal," I said. "Your father's an attorney and has plenty of legal connections in Baltimore. They can help you navigate the F.B.I. and clear yourself, if necessary. And then I'm sure your parents will want to help you get clean. We'll be right here if you want."

Sobbing, Crystal walked into the living room, picked up the receiver, and dialed.

# 24

# World Shattered

*March, 1983*

What a surreal scene! Crystal's parents arrived from the Eastern Shore to pack up her belongings and whisk her away to Mountain Manor Treatment Center in Baltimore. Like a pair of whirling dervishes, they twisted and raced through the apartment, tossing clothing and linens into cardboard boxes, canvas bags, and suitcases. Rendering herself completely useless, Crystal plopped her afghan-wrapped self on the sofa and sobbed uncontrollably, uttering the occasional wail and gasp for air. I assisted with the packing process, mostly to make sure none of my precious few items accidentally got heaved into the mix. Crystal's parents were definitely on a mission: Pack up and get out!

After that March morning of utter chaos, the sudden silence hit me harder than I expected. It wasn't like Crystal inhabited the apartment that much recently. Maybe the idea of Crystal *never* being around took me by surprise. The important thing was that now Crystal would get the help that she needed: rehab and therapy if that's what it took to get over that creep Girard. Still…I couldn't deny the changes confronting me: Crystal gone, the apartment half empty, and our New York family beginning to unravel.

Shaking off the quiet, I had decisions to make. I shoved in

George Benson's "Give Me The Night" cassette, hoping a little soulful jazz would be the perfect background to ease me into a reflecting frame of mind. Lots to consider, lots of uncertainty, lots at risk. Every time I sat down to unscramble this mess, my heart raced and head pounded. The stress became unbearable.

Rent had been paid through March but that was the end of our sublet. Two years in New York City had flown by! But looking ahead, should I think about Crystal returning to New York? If Crystal got her act together, would she even want to go back to the fashion program? Who knew? *No, I can't depend on her.* And if I do the summer theater job, can I afford to keep the apartment while I'm in Massachusetts. I still hadn't discussed the summer stock position with my parents, another source of self-imposed pressure. I had the perfect opportunity to tell them during my birthday phone call, but I chickened out. I could imagine how that conversation would have panned out:

> Me: So, Mom and Dad, I've been offered a great summer job in Massachusetts as a Playwright-in-Residence.
>
> Dad: Now ya wanna to go to Massachusetts to write plays? Jesus, Mary, and Joseph!
>
> Me: But hear me out…
>
> Dad: Come on home, Margaret. Ya aren't thinking straight. Come home, work in the store, and blah, blah, blah.

*Nope. That would never work.* I took the coward's road and avoided that confrontational phone call altogether. But I knew I'd have to make a decision soon and face the consequences.

My floundering about the summer theater was due in part to my constant concern about Doug's health. Even though Gordo shared very little, I could tell from the strain on his face that he was worried. I told myself that Doug would rally, that the medications the doctors provided were helping, that the CDC knew what the hell they were doing. *Was I being selfish because I needed Doug to be well enough to travel with me to the summer theater in June?* We had it all planned out – he'd direct my plays, I'd collaborate with a director I knew, and all would be perfect. I refused to admit my fear of the unknown.

And then there was Miguel…I avoided the reality of Miguel leaving for Iowa in May. *If I shove it down, maybe I can stop that world from crashing.* Of course, I knew that packing emotions away never worked. Reality will catch up with you and smack you upside the head with a two-by-four, bringing those painful feelings right up to the surface. My attraction to Miguel grew deeper whenever we spent time together, in part because of his understanding about the direction our careers were taking us. He considered my hopes and dreams unlike previous boyfriends and especially my Dad. Miguel deserved a medal in relationship patience the way he approached my past assault trauma, always making sure I felt secure and protected. When I considered how he helped me overcome my intimacy anxiety, I wondered if I was crazy not to follow him to Iowa. *You may never find another guy as great as this one, Margie!*

Crystal gone, Miguel leaving, Doug sick, my New York family falling apart in front of me – this was the support system I had come to depend upon. Frankly, I felt myself backtracking, losing the battle to my fears and self-doubts, becoming a huge coward when facing new situations alone. *Heck I could barely get out of the car when Crystal and I arrived in New York two years ago. If not for her, I'd probably be a shriveled corpse in the passenger seat right now!*

****

Finally breaking through the logjam that had been consuming my life, I made a decision, an actual decision. I planned to sign Mr. Tarkington's contract for the Playwright-in-Residence position at Red Barn Theater. It took major scolding by Doug for me to come around.

"You mean you haven't returned the contract yet? What are you thinking? This is the perfect opportunity for you, Margie." Doug and Gordo sat in my kitchen, watching me whip together the only meal beside spaghetti I had mastered: boxed macaroni and cheese with sliced hot dogs for a "gourmet" treatment. Saints for putting up with my cooking, I was thrilled that Doug even had the energy to come to dinner. He'd been turning down a lot of invitations lately.

"I know, I know. I'm a wimp who's terrified of taking risks. Did I ever tell you about when Crystal and I first moved to New York and how I could barely get out of the car?"

They chuckled and admitted that Crystal blabbed about it the first time she met them at the mailbox.

"And we still love you," Gordo said.

"Well thanks. But I know I'm a horrible risk-taker."

Gordo protested. "That's not true. Look how brave you were to audition for that band, how you toured all over the country. You gotta have courage to do that."

"And how you eventually got out of Crystal's car, and found a great job and an internship and learned to navigate all over the city to write music reviews," Doug added. "Give yourself credit, Margie. What's holding you back from signing that contract?"

I considered the two main reasons: my Dad's reaction when

I tell him and my concern for Doug's health. I shared only one. "Well…truth is I'm worried about you, Doug," I said, draining the hot dogs for the pièce de résistance. "What if your doctors recommend that you don't travel this summer?"

"Oh Margie. 'Lay aside life-harming heaviness, And entertain a cheerful disposition.'"

I laughed. "And there it is."

Chuckling at himself, Doug suddenly turned serious. "We have to see what happens with me, but you've got to sign the damned contract!"

The three of us huddled around the tiny kitchen table eating mac and cheese with hot dogs and a side of applesauce – fine dining on the cheap, New York-style. I noticed Doug only picked at his food throughout the dinner. Granted, it wasn't the most appealing meal. Immediately after we finished eating, he gave Gordo "that look" that I had learned meant "It's time to go." *Like in any family, we're close enough to not take offense with quick exits.*

****

The next morning, I received a frightening call from Gordo. "I'm at the hospital. It's Doug. He's too weak. Please…can you? You gotta come." I threw on a pair of sweatpants, a sweater, and sneakers. Grabbing my purse, I ran to the corner of 65th and First Avenue to hail a taxi. At seven-thirty on a Saturday morning, it didn't take long to flag down a cab.

"Memorial Sloan Kettering at 1275 York Avenue, please," I said, catching my breath.

Gordo sounded exhausted and pitiful on the phone. I wanted to be there for him. Random thoughts flashed through my mind as I fought back tears, sniffles, and stupid hiccups. *God, Doug didn't seem too bad at dinner – no appetite but not weak. What happened? Was he putting up a mask, trying to act like he was healthier than he was? That's so like him.* I stared out the taxi window, not really taking in the streetscape whizzing along, collecting my energy to focus on my two dear friends.

I arrived at the hospital and connected with Gordo in the visiting area. We isolated ourselves, sinking into yellow upholstered chairs as he reported that Doug's condition had stabilized although he remained extremely weak. In addition to pneumonia, doctors explained that Doug's illness had progressed to what they believed was a cancer called Kaposi Sarcoma. More pokes and x-rays and blood tests *might* confirm this.

Gordo tried to spit back the report for me. "They're saying they found that the swelling in Doug's neck had gotten worse, and there's a bunch of lumps in other parts of his body." He dropped his head and stared at the floor before continuing. "There are also dark lesions on his back and neck. Oh Margie, I knew about 'em. A few had been there for a couple years, but they started getting worse. Then lesions formed on his legs…but I didn't wanna…I wanted to pretend they weren't there, Margie." He choked back a sob. "I'm a terrible coward. I know what they mean. He's getting real bad."

I grabbed his hand. "Can the doctors do anything for him, Gordo?"

"They don't know what to do. There's nothing to fix this…"

One of Doug's doctors came out and pulled Gordo away for a consult. *Too sudden…these symptoms came on fast.* A few minutes later, Gordo waved at me, indicating that I could go into Doug's room for a short visit. I followed him into a sterile-feeling room – white walls, white curtains surrounding the bed, white bedside table, and white blankets and sheets covering my friend whose head rested on a white pillow.

Doug's voice barely squeaked out, "Greetings."

I scooted around the foot of Doug's hospital bed and stood to his right, while Gordo remained closest to the door. Doug's hospital gown draped loosely around his collar bone, revealing two dark lesions radiating from his back to the side of his neck. *Ah, Doug's ascots served dual purpose.* "What are you doing lying around, Doug?" I teased.

Gordo intervened. "Now, now. Doug's simply resting up for the summer, that's all. He'll be bossing around those actors in no time."

"Aw, time...," Doug said in a whisper. Gordo moved closer to the bed, and I leaned in to hear him better. "'...time is like a fashionable host, that slightly shakes his parting guest by th' hand.' I'm afraid I'm running out of time."

I smiled softly in an attempt to disguise my breaking heart.

****

I visited Doug at the hospital every chance I could – evenings after work, lunch hours, I even called in sick one day to spend extra time with him. Alissa and Miguel visited, too. They were my support system as much as Gordo's and Doug's. *That's what families do.* I loved it when the five of us were all together, despite the antiseptic surroundings. Some days we hugged silently; other times we told silly stories and laughed. Mostly Doug smiled, more and more too weak to speak.

My emotions were on high alert and super "in the moment" – I didn't have time to think about the future. I couldn't think about Miguel leaving or how much it was tearing me up inside. In fact, I barely spoke to Miguel at all during those hospital visits – we could only hold on to each other. *Am I purposely avoiding talking to him, or do I simply not have the strength?* All I could think about was "Get Doug better. He's got to get better. Of course, he'll get better!" Each day I convinced myself that he looked stronger, that his color had improved, that his voice was clearer. *He's sipping a bit more water today. His cheeks are rosier today. His grip on my hand feels stronger today. He must be getting better today.*

And then…Doug died. *Devastation.*

# 25

# Backtracking

*April, 1983*

The world was safe and familiar under the covers in my bedroom in Church Creek. At eleven o'clock in the morning, I should have been up and out of bed, but no one was bothering me. I heard Mom whisper to Dad, "Let her be. She needs time."

I flashed back to the hospital and Doug's raspy voice in my head uttering, "…time is like a fashionable host, that slightly shakes his parting guest by th' hand." I whispered, "Good night, sweet prince." *Doug would appreciate that.* I couldn't shake the image of poor Gordo sitting in the hospital attempting to grasp a future without his life partner. They'd been together for seven years, practically a married couple. They created a home together, completely committed to each other. They lit up when the other one came into a room. *What an amazing example of a loving couple!*

After Doug died, my world fell apart. The reality of Crystal's fate, Miguel prepping for his departure for Iowa, the end of my idealized summer theater adventure with my friend – these all came crashing down at once. It was too much to navigate.

I didn't realize how much Crystal's spiraling behavior, our group confrontation, and her parent's abrupt whisking her off to rehab had affected me until after she was gone. The apartment's quietness closed in on me. My ears began to ring, my pulse raced. I supposed these were the after effects of the constant stress I'd been experiencing whenever Crystal was around. Stress I hadn't even realized.

I continued to push away the thought of Miguel leaving for Iowa – shoving it deep in the back of my mind. With all that went on at the hospital and Doug's death and the memorial service and...well, it was easier to stick my head in the sand and avoid dealing with the reality that Miguel had been packing up his apartment and taking care of final details. The slightest image of him getting into a car and driving over the George Washington Bridge and out of New York City caused a throbbing pain in my chest and tears to well up in my eyes.

We had come to an understanding about our relationship but still...I couldn't deny what was in my heart, how strongly I felt about him. Why didn't we ever communicate these emotions to each other? Would that have made a difference in how this turned out for us? Maybe we knew that expressing those feelings would make the leaving hurt even more. I was losing the best relationship that I'd ever known. Dealing with more emptiness...I didn't know if I could handle the darkness that began to seep into my psyche.

And my writing career...where was that really going? The whole Playwright-in-Residence thing at Red Barn Theater was a shaky plan at best. *Was I more excited about working with Doug or exploring a new direction for my writing? Was complacency setting in again or was this simply an emotional set back?* I couldn't even think about the Red Barn Theater without conjuring an image of Doug. Poor Doug. It was all too awful seeing him wither away in that dreary hospital bed, moaning in pain, and feeling utterly helpless and useless as his friend.

Friends dying. People breaking the law. Roommates freaking out. Trying to invest in a relationship but being pulled in different directions. Making career plans but never being sure. Every move feeling risky. A parent creating constant obstacles. And the city suddenly seeming too loud, too bright, too chaotic, and well…too much.

I quit New York.

I had no more energy to give. I wanted to shout from the top of the Empire State Building: "You win Broom Man and Typing Paper Man. You win frightening cockroaches. You win stinky garbage all over the sidewalks and graffiti-filled subway trains with schedules that still confuse me. You win freakin' cold, icy days in February when the streets become wind tunnels. You win tourists who push and shove or stop suddenly in the middle of the sidewalk for no apparent reason. You win stupid A.I.D.S." *No, not that…A.I.D.S. doesn't get to win. We can't let that happen.*

Exhausted by the disintegration of my second family and my New York City world, I made the rash decision to throw in the proverbial towel. I packed my bags, left an apologetic letter for Mr. Mason with a Radio City page attempting to explain what had happened and why I was heading back to Maryland's Eastern Shore, and mailed my unsigned Red Barn Theater contract back to Mr. Tarkington with an equally pitiful explanation. I taped a note addressed to Gordo and Alissa on Gordo's apartment door, knowing that I couldn't face them – especially Gordo. I apologized for abandoning him but how could I help him when I was a freakin' mess? Worse, I asked them to deliver a goodbye letter to Miguel for me. *Geez, what kind of family member steals off without a proper goodbye? What sort of girlfriend doesn't say goodbye to her boyfriend face-to-face? A cowardly, stressed, exhausted, depressed one, I'm afraid.*

I retreated to the only place I knew to be safe – my childhood bedroom. It may sound crazy, but then I felt crazy. My arrival in Church Creek had been the answer to Dad's prayers. He didn't waste a moment before he laid into the error of my ways and his plans for my future. Neither approach aided in my recovery from the pain running through my heart and body. I knew returning home would come with consequences, including Dad's daily lectures. That's how far into the dark abyss I had fallen.

"I'm glad ya finally came your senses, Margaret," he'd start in. "That New York City was never the right place for ya. You're smart and pretty. Wastin' your youth up there with your silly writin' notions. Gawd, you're…"

His rants washed over me and faded into the background. I'd heard it all before – stay in Church Creek, marry a local guy, stay in close proximity, think about having kids. I knew he was trying to manipulate me to do his bidding. Emotionally drained and exhausted, I couldn't fight him this time. For days I curled up in my childhood bed – the safest place I thought I could be.

****

The smell of Mom's Salisbury steak and gravy wafted up the staircase. Deciding I needed nourishment beyond Chamomile tea and blueberry muffins on a bed tray, I finally dragged myself downstairs to the dinner table. Mom had all the fixings: fluffy mashed potatoes, green beans she had put up from her summer garden, hot dinner rolls, and double chocolate cake for dessert. My stomach rumbled. *I guess I'm hungrier than I realized.*

Mom tried to jumpstart the dinner conversation. "I have a little present for you, Margaret." She handed me a leather-bound journal with a nice strap – a thoughtful gift. "Maybe a bit of writing might cheer you up."

I took the journal and set it aside. "That's nice, Mom. I'll think about it."

She continued her attempts. "You've received several phone calls from your New York friends. Messages are on the telephone table."

"Uh huh," I mumbled.

As hard as Mom tried to pry conversation out of me, she failed. I had no interest in dredging up my New York life.

"A girl named Alissa called several times. She sounds nice. Didn't she sound nice?" Mom directed that last question to my Dad who shoveled mashed potatoes into his mouth. Once he realized that Mom was giving him a "cue," he swallowed his mouthful to do his part.

"Nice, right." He gulped down the remainder of his milk. "And I took a call from a Gordo. Now there's a fine young man. Bet he's from Texas with that accent. Seemed like quite a manly sorta guy."

I almost choked on my Salisbury steak. "Um, yep! You'd like him, Dad." *Now there's a meeting I'd love to see. Gordo and Dad chatting in our Early American living room. Not awkward at all!*

****

The warm April weather persuaded me to pry myself out of bed, get dressed, and take a walk down to the estuary that butts up near our property. I brought along the new journal Mom gave me in the hopes I'd find inspiration to write again. It took all my strength to walk a short distance. Sitting on a fallen log, I gazed out at the water and took a few deep breaths. The creek and its surrounding world filled the air: water babbling as the current carried it over rocks along the shore; rustling young leaves as a gentle wind pulsed; bird tweets, chirps, and trills as they communicated with each other.

I flashed on a memory of New York City's birds, few though

they were. I remembered the visiting sparrows on the windowsill of our sixth-floor apartment and wondered how those crazy birds knew they had found a softy like me living there. I pictured the usual suspects who flew around Central Park – cardinals, blue jays, wrens, and gold finches. I summoned up images of older folks who spent their days on park benches throughout the city, tossing seed to the silver-gray pigeons. Birds always brought a sense of calm to me – their flight, their songs, their nesting habits. I began thinking that if a huge city like New York could maintain a bird habitat, maybe there was hope for the world at large. *Could there still be hope for me there?*

I opened the journal, poised to explore these feelings further…but nothing. I tried to write a sentence, a phrase, a single word…anything. *Maybe a sketch to get my creative juices flowing?* Nothing. I felt as if I was a bird clamoring to fly but whose wings had been clipped. I couldn't take flight. One thing about living in New York, its energy fed a creative freedom in me. *That NYC artists' energy Miguel alluded to…is that energy something I need, crave, require now?*

****

Several days later, the April morning sunshine filled my bedroom. A voice calling my name pulled me out of my deep sleep. Rubbing my eyes and stretching my arms overhead, I eased into consciousness. "Margaret! Phone for you!" Mom's voice called from downstairs. "It's Miguel."

*Miguel? He should be nearly ready to move to Iowa for his summer writing program about now.* "I'll be right there. Tell him to hold on." I grabbed my light cotton robe and hopped down the stairs three at a time. Mom held out the receiver and quietly exited out the front door.

Me: Miguel? Are you alright?

Miguel: I called to ask the same of you. All I got was a *loco* letter – no goodbye. Now I hear you are not taking any calls from your friends? That you gave up the apartment, your Radio City job, the Playwright's Residency, all of it? What is going on, Margie? I am worried about you.

Me: Oh, Miguel…My life is falling apart. I'm…I don't know. Numb.

Miguel: But you were looking forward to the summer theater playwriting, yes?

Me: I can't go without…Anyway, that's weird. I thought you didn't think much of me writing kids' plays…remember?

Miguel: Yes, I remember, but I also told you many times that you have talent. Do you remember that? What are you doing back home?

Me: I don't know….I don't know what I'm doing. When Doug died and you were getting ready to leave for Iowa, reality hit me. I fell apart. New York closed in too much, became too heavy. I had to get away.

Miguel: *Ay Bendito*. I wish I could have done more to help you. You did not seem to want me to bother you…Well…I hope you are still writing.

*(long pause)*

Me: Look, I'm sure you have tons of last-minute packing to do. Good luck, Miguel. Drop a postcard from Iowa.

Miguel: Margie, please—

Me: I gotta go. Good luck.

Hurriedly, I hung up the receiver before my voice cracked. Hearing him speak – his slight accent, the mention of writing… it was all too much. A floodgate of feelings and memories gushed as well as tears. The writing group, Dr. R.'s constant encouragement and challenges, creative discoveries and pivots, that New York energy, Miguel's kindness and patience, my wonderful New York family – it flooded into my mind and heart. *I'm not strong enough to deal with this now.*

I tried to control my urge to break down in tears using the breathing method that had been successful in the past. Breath in "Relax;" breath out "Release." But I couldn't concentrate. Instead, uneven panting took over while images of Miguel and Doug and Gordo crowded my thoughts. Sobbing, I ran upstairs to the security of my childhood cocoon, throwing the covers over my head.

# 26

# Dead End

*May, 1983*

By early May, Dad's constant droning had worn me down. I agreed to work at Dad's general store again, stocking shelves, covering the register when he had a merchandise pick up, pricing items as they came into the store. Dad grinned nonstop, having succeeded in his plan to have me under his thumb. *I wouldn't be surprised if he's vetting local guys as potential "gentleman callers" – Good Lord!* At least he was drinking less – definitely a positive.

Weeks of mindless busy work took away the sting of missing Alissa, Gordo, Crystal, and Miguel; and especially the pain of losing Doug. Aw Doug…I'd never had a friend who'd died before. And what a shitty way to leave this earth! *Why couldn't they help you? You simply faded away.* I worried about Gordo. Was he next? Was he afraid about his own fate? These thoughts filled me with heartbreak and guilt. *How was he holding up without Doug? I'm a horrible friend to have abandoned him. How could I have…? Ah…I'm incredibly exhausted…*

I grabbed a handful of gum packages from a cardboard box and jammed them onto the shelf, pushing thoughts of Doug and Gordo out of my mind. *Mindless busy work, Margie. Keep at it.* I shoved down thoughts of Miguel, probably already on the road to Iowa – walking out of my life forever!

In my bedroom the next morning, I assessed the day ahead as I prepped for breakfast and my walk across the road to the general store. *Another May morning, another day.* Once downstairs at the kitchen table, Mom mentioned that she had news she was sure would interest me.

"I read that the band those friends of yours play in, what's it called? Magic something or other...Well anyway, it's playing in Salsbury this weekend. It's not that far from here. You should go, Margie."

"You mean Jimmy and Chaz's band, Magic Eight?"

While it might have been fun to see them, what would I say? "Hi guys. Guess what? I totally blew it in New York City – freaked out – couldn't hack it. I'm back in Church Creek working at my Dad's general store. Living life to the max!"

I looked down at my muffin. "That's nice, Mom, but I don't think so. I don't feel up to it."

"You need to get out and have fun. All you do is mope around. I'm worried about you."

"I work at the general store. Isn't that what Dad wanted? I'm safe at home. Isn't that what you wanted." I heard the edge in my voice. *Oh crap…*

"Margaret, that's not fair. I told you I wanted you to live your life and not worry about Dad and me."

I took a deep breath and gently released it. "Sorry. You're right. And I did try…." Tears moistened my eyes. Not wanting to make a scene, I took a last gulp of coffee and stood up. "Gotta go." *Okay, maybe she is attempting to cheer me up, but I can't muster the strength to explain how I'm feeling right now.*

I hiked the short distance to the general store. When I got there, Dad was already sweeping the back storage room floor.

"Great, you're here."

I sighed. "Yeah, Dad. I'm here every day."

Dad gave an odd look. I'd almost call it sympathetic. "Look Margaret, ya may not agree with my reasons for not wantin' ya to live in the city. But I want ya to know I appreciate ya helpin' out here at the store. I like havin' my girl around."

"Sure Dad." I simply couldn't offer much more.

He smiled ever so slightly. "Okay then. I'm drivin' to Baltimore to pick up a load of discounted soda that never got delivered. Need ya to man the store for most of the day." He handed me the broom. Before leaving, he turned and said, "Ya know, Margaret, you've grown into quite a responsible gal." Shocked and confused by this totally out of character sentiment coming from him, all I could do was muster a teeny smile.

That morning, I attended to mundane tasks that had become my life – finished the sweeping, stocked the canned goods shelves, organized the dairy case, and waited on two customers – Mrs. Johnson needed a gallon of milk and Michael Brewster bought a pack of Camels. The eleven o'clock boredom crept in. I decided to sweep the outside porch and get a breath of fresh air.

Glancing across the road toward our house, I spotted Mom and another person approaching the store. *Who the heck is that walking with Mom? Someone from church, maybe?* Between the morning sun's angle and the oddness of Mom visiting the store, I couldn't get a good read. I continued sweeping until they got closer. It didn't take too long before I recognized the other person. I dropped the broom.

"Miguel!"

We ran to each other without hesitation and embraced, speaking at the same time. "What are you…," "I had to see you before…," "I'm happy you're…," "I need to tell you…." We laughed, took a breath, and embraced each other for a long time.

Mom smiled and turned to walk home.

I began first. "I'm happy to see you, Miguel, but I don't understand. Shouldn't you be on your way to Iowa?"

"My cousin is driving me to Iowa, and I begged him to take a detour to Church Creek to bring me here. I needed to see you."

"I'm glad you did."

Miguel adjusted his glasses and looked at the general store. "Hm, this is where you work now? Are you happy here?"

"It fills the time…" I knew he'd be asking me about my writing next and I cringed at the question. But he surprised me.

"Margie, I came because I am worried about you. I understand what you said on the phone – your world was shaken when Doug died. Okay, you came home for a rest but now it is time to get on with it."

"It's more than Doug's death, Miguel. It's this overwhelming…well, fear."

"What do you fear, Margie? Explain this to me."

I wasn't sure if I could put my feelings into words since I had kept them bottled up for too long. Miguel reached for my hand and led me to the porch step, where we sat together. I looked into Miguel's soft brown eyes, feeling his warmth and trust. In the safety of his presence, the words flowed out of me.

"First, I was afraid to go to the summer theater without Doug. I had pictured exactly how the experience would be and when he died…I wasn't only sad but that whole image shattered. He advocated for my plays. What if no one else at the theater thinks they are any good?" I took a deep breath. "What if you're right, Miguel? What if writing children's plays is a waste of time and talent? I have no idea what I'm doing with my writing career."

A slight frown appeared on Miguel's face, but he nodded, encouraging me to continue.

"And then, there's the fear of what might happen after the summer, all the unknowns, the risks. Do I even want to return to New York? What would I do there? Continue writing music reviews as a freelancer? Be a secretary for the rest of my life? Be a playwright? It all seems too risky. New York is hard; it can sap your energy. Then when you layer on all the rest of it…I became overwhelmed."

"Ah, I see," Miguel said. "But Margie, think about this… about how courageous you have already been in dealing with these fears. You moved to New York, found a job, got a writing internship and a freelance job that even Gwendoln was jealous of, and discovered a passion for playwriting. Living in the city can be hard, yes. But look at what you accomplished already."

"That's true. Thank you for the reminder."

Miguel looked straight into my eyes and became serious. "Now there is one thing in your thinking that I must correct because I might be to blame."

"I doubt that, Miguel."

"No, listen to me. You tried to explain about the value of writing plays for children, but I did not understand. I saw your passion, yes, but told you the plays were silly. That was wrong of me, Margie. You were right."

The seriousness of Miguel's tone caught me off guard. "What brought about this change of heart? You were quite adamant that I should give up writing Children's Theater plays, as I remember?" I chuckled, trying to lighten the mood.

Miguel remained somber, glancing into the distance. "It was Doug. In one of his stronger moments in the hospital, he talked about the summer theater and how he wished he could see your plays on the stage. He made me understand what you tried to explain to me – the importance of the messages to the young people, how child audiences are the readers and audiences and citizens of the future." *Dear Doug, always my advocate.* "Margie, I am sorry I was such a *cariduro*."

"A what?"

"*Ay, cariduro*…a stubborn person. Shameful. But truly, you must do what you are passionate about…without doubts."

"Without doubts…Hm." I took in those words. As usual, Miguel found the perfect phrase to cut right to my soul. "Thank you for sharing this with me. It means everything."

We sat quietly, holding hands and gazing at the trees across the street. My heart beat rapidly as I dreaded the words, "It is time for me to leave now." I knew I had more in my heart but was afraid to begin a conversation that might get cut short. *Is Miguel sensing my anxiety or is it solely my shallow breathing tipping him off?*

"Is something else bothering you, Margie?"

*Oh boy! Hold it together.* I stared at the ground, tears welling up in my eyes. "If I did go back to New York, who would even be there to return to? Doug is gone, Crystal's gone, and…especially now…you'll be gone. I blame New York – it's too much, Miguel."

"We are still your second family."

His words touched me, but I cautiously probed. "How can you be a part of my support system when you'll be doing radical things in Iowa?"

"Iowa is not forever…don't forget that, Margie. I'll be coming back to New York for holidays and between semesters. I hope you'll be there doing what you love."

Miguel's words were lovely and reassuring, but I knew I continued to hold back. He sensed it too.

"Something else, Margie?" he asked.

"Yes, although this is harder to say." I took a deep breath to fortify myself. "I never thanked you for helping me face my horrible secret about that sexual assault with that band member years ago. You were amazingly patient and kind with your willingness to let our relationship grow slowly, to check in and make sure I felt safe and protected the few times we were close..."

"Sweet Margie, that was...is...because I care about you."

"Yes, Miguel. I know this. But now I'm afraid that...well, maybe not afraid, more regretful that, we never said all the things we needed to say, we never brought the relationship to next level. Will we be able to survive the distance between Iowa and New York? Is this the end of the most wonderful relationship I've ever known?"

Miguel smiled, lightening up my gloomy outlook. "You know, Margie, you do worry a lot. We do not know what the future brings to us, but I do know one thing: I love you."

Any remaining resistance released from my body, my mind, and my heart. "Oh Miguel, I love you too." Miguel took me in his arms, firmly pulling me close to him, and caressed my back. Pulling away slightly, he lifted my chin toward his face and kissed me, softly stroking my cheek. He stood and stepped back, allowing me to collect my senses, before breaking into a radiant smile. As he turned to walk away, I drew in a quick breath, stifling a sob. *I know in my heart and soul we will be together again.*

****

The day after Miguel's visit, I awoke lighter and more invigorated. I propped myself up in bed and opened the new journal Mom had given me. Overwhelmed with the desire to write, I recorded my thoughts.

Reflections on a May morning

*I've met many interesting people during the last several years and each are amazing. I'm not the only person who has faced self-doubt and fear and risky situations. Think about Jimmy and Chaz having to search for new horn jobs after the end of King Vido's Swing Band, when those positions were scarce. They trudged on, confident that something would turn up. And what about Amy and the tough situations she's had to deal with – an unplanned pregnancy, not wanting to give her baby up for adoption, succumbing to alcoholism? She may be filled with anger, but at least she's fighting her way back. And then there's Gordo's story of coming to NYC at age seventeen with eighty bucks to his name after being kicked out of house by an abusive father. Talk about dealing with risk without turning back. Now Gordo is facing the rest of his life without his partner. Crystal is facing the uncertainty of rehab, one that Alissa has tackled before. And even Miguel's next chapter, going to Iowa City to begin a writing program where he knows absolutely no one, which takes a lot of courage and confidence. All these people in my life have faced their fears. I ran away from NYC because of doubt and pain. But what am I going to do moving forward? Maybe those feelings are exactly what I need to experience to be a more compassionate writer. And as much as I love my roots here on Maryland's Eastern Shore - my Choptank River, my waterfowl, and walks along the estuaries - it seems that I equally crave NYC's energy to jump start and inspire my writing - in whatever form it may take in the future. Thank you, dear sweet Miguel, for reminding me of this.*

What Miguel said the day before rang true. Even more, I left the safety of my small town to tour the country as a singer, expanding my world view – for better or for worse. I grew to question, explore, and accept people, cultures, and ideas different from the way I was raised. *Heck, I even learned to appreciate punk music!* I couldn't allow myself to be paralyzed by unknown fears. What kind of life would that be? I also couldn't allow myself to fall back into complacency. But mostly, I couldn't allow my career or life choices to be dictated by anyone other than my own heart. It was time to deal with that situation.

I pulled on a pair of jeans and a tee shirt and rushed downstairs to breakfast. Mom and Dad sat at the kitchen table, sipping coffee.

"You're up early. And you look pretty chipper," Mom said.

Dad sipped his morning brew. "That's good 'cuz there's plenty to do at the store. I brought back a ton of cases of soda from Baltimore yesterday and it all needs pricin'."

"Sorry Dad, but I won't be available today. I have my own list of things to do."

"I don't understand."

"Look Dad. I don't want to argue this morning. And I don't want to hold these resentful feelings toward you or the store anymore." I walked over to his chair and knelt down next to him, placing a hand on his knee. Initially he recoiled, surprised by my sudden closeness, but once we locked eyes, I felt he'd listen. "I need you to understand that I'm an adult now. And your love and acceptance of me can't be conditional anymore."

"Conditional?"

"Yes, Dad. Conditional on how you want me to behave, where you want me to live and work, how you want me to worship, what kind of man you want me to marry, when you want me to procreate. I mean, for goodness sake…I'm a twenty-eight-year old adult!"

Mom covered her mouth, as she suppressed a smile. Dad's face grew serious, not in an angry way, but more thoughtful, even calm.

I addressed both Mom and Dad. "I need to have a choice about my career decisions, about who I might marry – if at all – and about when or even if I want to have children. And you may not like my choices, Dad. I never said this before, but being able to make these decisions for myself is important to me. I'd like to be able to discuss them with you without arguing. But I can't let you or anyone dictate my next steps anymore."

I searched Dad's face for a reaction. I could see the wheels turning behind his eyes as he considered my words.

"Look, Dad, I know you're stressed out about things with the general store; and I don't want to cause you more problems – I really don't. And I've never told you before, but I appreciate how hard you've worked all these years to make the store a success."

The slightest smile spread across Dad's face. "I appreciate that, I do."

I continued. "And for my part, maybe I've been too tough on you, Dad. I know that you and Mom have my back, but as an adult, I need to start dealing with the consequences of my own decisions, the ups and the downs, and figure things out. It's time that I stop running home any time the going gets tough." Mom let a small gasp. "Don't worry, Mom…I'll still come home for holidays whenever I can."

After a pause that seemed to last an eternity, Dad finally spoke. "Well, now…much as I hate to admit it…some of what you're sayin' makes sense, Margaret. Sure, I had my fears about ya livin' in that city, but I guess I had more fears about ya leavin' your Mom and me. You're not my little girl anymore – maybe I gotta start convincin' myself of it. That's something I can try to work on."

Mom smiled, then added, "You are a talented young woman with a lot of options in front of her."

"And you can stop your worryin' about the store," Dad said. "I'm workin' on a deal with young Frank – ya know, your old beau."

"Geez…we only went out a couple of times!" I protested.

"Anyway, he's got an idea to lease half the store for a bait shop. We'll see." Then Dad reached down, wrapped his arms around me, and gave me a warm hug. He whispered in my ear, "Whatever ya do, and however it turns out, your mother and I'll be here."

"That means a lot." I reached into my pocket and pressed a folded piece of paper into his hand. "I want you to have this, Dad." He unfolded the origami crane that the Asian woman had given me at the anti-nukes protest in Central Park. "It's a symbol for a long peaceful life and prosperity." He smiled.

I left Mom and Dad to talk. I had plenty to do – calls to make, letters to mail, and journal entries to write. *It's time to chart my next course.*

# 27

# Pivoting

*June, 1983*

I appeared at the Silver Star Diner's door, suitcase in one hand and two canvas bags draped over my shoulders. Alissa gasped when she spotted me. Putting my finger to my lips to signal "quiet," I sneaked up behind Gordo, sitting at his favorite window booth hunched over the latest edition of *The New York Times*. Leaning in, I planted a kiss on his cheek. Once he recovered and recognized me, Gordo jumped up and we hugged for several minutes, both attempting to subdue sobs. We failed miserably.

"I know asking 'How are you doing?' is ridiculous, Gordo. You and Doug are on my mind all the time."

"I appreciate that. I do." Gordo exhaled. "I miss him every minute. The worst is being in that apartment without him. Ask Alissa. I've been spending a lotta time here at the diner."

As we slid back into the booth, I grabbed his hand across the table. I hoped he knew how much my heart ached for him. Our quiet moment was interrupted by Alissa as she rushed over for a hug, coffee pot in hand. When we pulled back, I noticed tears welling up in her eyes, her tough exterior exposing a soft core.

"You surprised the crap outta me, girl. You get me?" Gordo and I laughed at Alissa's greeting.

Once our chuckles subsided, Gordo asked, "What the heck

are you doing here, Margie? Not that I'm not happy as all get out to see you."

"Well…I'm hoping to crash on your sofa for a couple days, for one thing."

"Sure. Sure. You know you're family."

Overhearing my request, Alissa chimed in. "No need for that. You're staying with me. I've got a spare bed!"

"Uh, thanks for the offer, but I don't remember you even having a sofa in your 91th Street apartment, let alone a spare bed." Alissa and Gordo gave each other a smug smile followed by snickers. "Okay, you two," I said. "Let me in on the secret."

Alissa grinned from one multi-pierced ear to the other. "I've moved into the big time. No more bogus bathtub in the kitchen for this girl."

"And we at the pitiful East 65th Street brownstone couldn't be happier to have her!" Gordo added.

"What? I'm confused. Tell me the whole story."

"It's simple," Alissa said. "I've been saving up to get myself out of that bathtub-in-the-kitchen efficiency forever. When we got your note, I jumped on the building's Super, used my charms, showed him the cash with a little extra for his effort, and snagged your apartment, you get me? Gordo and I decided…'You never know if Margie might come back.'"

"Are you? Are you coming back?" Gordo asked as Alissa rested her head on my shoulder, her now platinum blonde hair falling over her face.

"I'm not exactly sure," I said. "But I have made a radical decision about my life. I am moving forward, not backward."

Alissa and Gordo nodded, encouraging me to continue.

"I'm tired of distractions, playing it safe, letting parental pressure get in the way of my creative journey. I decided that I have to take risks, and if I fall on my face, then I'll simply pick myself up, brush myself off, and start over."

Alissa placed her hand on top of Gordo and my clasped hands. "Like I've been telling ya...You gotta loosen up. Now you're getting it!"

****

I opened my eyes the next morning and for a brief second had to reacclimate. Then I felt it...a surge, a heat, a buzz...that New York energy. I stretched in bed, letting the vibe soak in until I was struck by something unexpected...the sound of guitar strumming and soft singing. Throwing on a light robe, I followed the music to the kitchen where I found Alissa. I watched her grooving on her music for several minutes, smiling at the transformation in front of my eyes. Tough-as-nails-Alissa pouring out her heart in a bluesy soulful song.

"Sounds great."

"Coffee's on the stove. Bagels and cream cheese on the table," she said as she continued to strum.

I poured a cup of coffee and walked over to the window. Three sparrows were munching on bagel crumbs, carefully scattered by Alissa. "I see the bird feeding tradition has been continued."

Alissa smiled. "I couldn't let them starve, could I?" After a big slurp of coffee, she blurted, "Now spill it. What's the deal with you and Miguel? Is he in or out?"

I had to laugh at the concise way Alissa stated things. "Totally 'in.' He's amazing. Did you know he stopped to visit me in Church Creek on his way to Iowa?"

"That's totally bitchin'!"

"I probably wouldn't be back in New York if not for Miguel. The deal is: We're going to stay in touch, do the long distance thing, and keep supporting each other's writing careers. We are realists. We know it won't be easy while he's away at school in Iowa, but we're also in love."

"Aw...kind of sappy, but I like you two together, so it's okay. And what's the plan for the summer?"

"I'm hoping I can fix it with Mr. Tarkington. I already mailed him a letter from Church Creek explaining the whole fiasco and we spoke on the phone. Sounds like he's willing to talk to me about the summer theater. I'm meeting him today at his apartment on East 27th Street.

"Do you think he'll still hire you on at the summer theater?

"Who knows? He said on the phone he had an idea to discuss with me. That's what we're going to talk about. I don't know where this summer stock experience might take me, but I'll never know unless I try."

****

I arrived at Mr. Tarkington's high-rise apartment at two o'clock and took the elevator to the fifteenth floor. He opened the door, pipe dangling from his mouth, and led me to the living room with a gorgeous East River vista.

"What a view!" I said as I positioned myself on a camel-colored leather chair. The entire room could have popped off the pages of *Architectural Digest* – the floor to ceiling curtains on hidden tracks covering every inch of wall space, the matching leather chairs and sofa, the glass with gold trimmed coffee table. Even the fragrance of cherry tobacco seemed appropriate – not too academic, but masculine enough. *Now this is New York chic. Extremely high-end and impressive!*

"Thanks for seeing me today, Mr. Tarkington. I'm sorry for leaving you hanging about the Playwright-in-Residence position. As I explained in my letter, Doug's illness, his death... it all got to me."

"Understandable, Margie. I hope you understood that I had to move on and hire someone else for the position. But if you are serious about working with Red Barn Theater this summer, I did have an idea."

"I'd like to hear it."

Mr. Tarkington filled the bowl of his pipe with tobacco from a glass jar sitting on an end table. "I like your work. My idea is to hire you as an Assistant Playwright-in-Residence and to add other duties. These might include a few hours a week in the Box Office and helping out with marketing. You wouldn't get all your plays produced, but I could guarantee at least one production on stage this summer. And after last summer's fiasco with the guy I hired, you never know what will happen…you may end up taking over the role for the whole season. I know it's not what you had originally hoped but it's a start."

"This sounds wonderful."

"Great. Take a few minutes to look over the contract now, and if you're okay with it, sign it, and we have a deal." He continued the tamp and refill process with his pipe while I read and signed the contract. "Excellent, Margie. I'll expect to see you at the theater in Plymouth on Sunday. And no surprises, okay?"

****

The following day, I toured Manhattan taking in the sights as a tourist and a semi-New Yorker. At the same time, I found myself navigating my memories and circumventing any fears, doubts, and even my nervousness about the future. Central Park, the Museum of Modern Art, Caffe Reggio, SoHo, the Village, Washington Square Park, St. Patrick's Cathedral, and Rockefeller Center all held strong images of times spent with Miguel and my dear friends or times spent wrestling with my anxiety about my future during the past two years.

The toughest stop on my self-guided tour was Radio City Music Hall. I couldn't bring myself to enter or face Miss Chambers or Mr. Mason. I let my cowardly letter do the explaining for me and hoped it would suffice. Instead, I sat on a wall across Sixth Avenue facing the marquee and took in my beloved Radio City Music Hall. At that moment, I not only grieved Doug's passing, but also the fact that I had let go of the coolest job I had ever known. It represented beauty in a city marred by ugliness. It represented a place where I was surrounded by constant creativity. My position represented security. But as heartbreaking as it was…as risky as it was… if I planned on having a writing career, I had to let go of this secure job where I'd be too tempted to climb the corporate ladder rather than focus on my artistic career. *Thank you and goodbye, Radio City Music Hall, you beauty.*

****

Gordo and Alissa insisted on helping me lug my suitcase, a large shoulder bag, and my canvas writing bag to the Port Authority on 41st Street and Eighth Avenue. They wanted to see me off despite the early morning departure of my bus to Massachusetts. To tell the truth, it warmed my heart that they came to say goodbye.

"I know you got your ticket to Boston," Alissa said, "but make sure you get off in Plymouth, you get me? Pay attention."

I laughed. "Since when have you become a mother hen?"

"Shut up! Remember, you've got an apartment and a roommate waiting for you at East 65th Street when summer's over, got it?"

Gordo gave my suitcase and the shoulder bag to the driver to stow in the baggage area under the bus. I hugged them both before boarding and hobbling down the narrow aisle to the first available seat with a free window. Pressing my face against the glass, I focused on Gordo and Alissa standing on the curb in front of the bus, waving like a couple of goofy toddlers. *What lovable nerds!* The sound of folding doors closing, the bus driver's muffled announcement over the p.a. system, and the whoosh of brakes releasing meant it was time to go.

After a final wave to Gordo and Alissa as the bus pulled out of its space and onto the streets of New York, I pulled my journal out of my canvas bag.

> *Temporary Goodbye NYC*
>
> *Waved to my second family, knowing that whatever happens they will be a part of my life. And how wonderful that I have the love of a special man. This also fills me with excitement for whatever that future may hold. I'm looking forward to my summer as an opportunity to explore the next phase of my writing/playwriting journey. Thinking back on my first music interview for SoHo Weekly News with Ann Magnuson at Club 57, something she said has stuck with me. I had asked, "How are you able to get away with these more outrageous performances?" I remember how she became quite animated when she answered. The gist was this: "Because we don't let anyone tell us 'no'... don't let poverty stop our artists from realizing their dreams."*

*I recall her words often. True creative types don't let critics or poverty or a father's demands or self-doubts tell them no. Artists trust their gut and their art. When will I let go of fear or other people's expectations and fully trust my creative impulses? I plan to put my New York energy-inspired creations to the test and see where they may lead me.*

I closed my journal and gazed out the window as the bus carried me closer to the next chapter of my writing career. In my two years in New York, I experienced a lot – some good, some bad, and some fabulous, as Doug would say. Even though I thought I had come a great distance as a woman who could speak up and express herself, the move to New York taught me that a huge obstacle to my personal growth remained – communicating with my Dad and facing my own fears. And it was on me to stop hiding and address these. I learned to overcome writing complacency and stop letting fear paralyze me, figuring out a way to navigate through it, even if it meant leaning on my New York family. I have Miguel to thank for many things, most importantly, for helping me overcome my fear of intimacy in such a beautiful way and for introducing me to New York's creative energy. I've discovered that when fear and self-doubt consumed me to point of becoming immobile, I needed to force myself to take a step, even a baby step. Or in some cases…to simply get out of the car!

The End

# Author's Note

True confessions…I've never written music reviews of band gigs, but I *have* written plays, including Children's Theater plays, as Margie does. I've never lived in a small town on Maryland's Eastern Shore, but I *have* lived in New York City in the early 1980s, as Margie does. I've never waitressed at a diner, but I *did* work as a receptionist at the famed Radio City Music Hall, as Margie does. In my two Retro fictions, I am an example of the type of writer who "writes what she knows" and then researches the heck out of the rest.

Many situations, named places, and even people in this book are supported by historical research. I utilized sources such as *The New York Times* archives covering NYC's arts and music scene between 1981 – 1983, articles and advertisements from *SoHo Weekly News* and *The Village Voice*, books (both fiction and nonfiction), and interviews. Specifically:

- Research about Radio City Music Hall (RCMH) included Charles Francisco's *The Radio City Music Hall* (E. P. Dutton, 1979); a wonderful interview conducted via email with a former RCMH page, Neil Byrne; and many articles from *The New York Times* archives.
- References to the receptionist job at RCMH were recreated partially from memories of my own experience as a receptionist from September 1980 through May 1982, including descriptions of the Art Deco furnishings and decorations,

the offices in the Executive Suite, and navigating around the building and the entire Rockefeller Center complex. Where there were memory gaps, I filled in with document research.

- The RCMH productions and events mentioned in this book all occurred during the 1981 through 1983 time period and were well researched. These included: the RCMH production of *America*, the *Christmas Spectacular*, and the "Night of 100 Stars" special event. However, it should be noted that Miss Chambers and Mr. Mason are completely fictionalized characters as are the positions of Vice President of Finance and Chief Executive Officer. Choreographer, Violet Holmes was real, however.
- *SoHo Weekly News* was a real alternative newspaper covering news and arts specifically for the SoHo neighborhood of Manhattan. References to the real Josh Freidman keep these scenes authentic. I fictionalized an assignment editor, Phil, with whom Margie interacted. The *SoHo Weekly News* offices were located at 111 Spring Street, and indeed the operation shut down in March 1982.
- Club 57 was a real East Village, "members only" club located in the basement of Holy Cross Church and founded by Ann Magnuson. Ann's experimental no wave "band," Pulsallama, did perform there as described. I paraphrased pieces from real interviews given by Ms. Magnuson and other members of the Pulsallama band into this scene to give readers an understanding of the philosophy behind the no wave work. While Pulsallama first performed at Club 57 as a 13-piece percussion ensemble as early as 1980, I could find no historical record of additional performances at this venue and the probability of Ann being involved

with Pulsallama beyond 1981 is doubtful. For the sake of my storyline, I created a performance on October 2, 1981 for Margie's first writing assignment for her *SoHo Weekly News* internship and included Ann.

- *The Village Voice* was a popular publication covering the arts scene and more. Robert Chistgau was the real Senior Editor and Music Critic. I created a fictional junior editor, Joe Reedy to whom Margie reported for the sake of the story. However, the 1982 Ramones' performance at My Father's Place was reviewed in *The Village Voice* as was the 1982 Beastie Boys performance at CBGB.
- CBGB, a famous music venue in the Village, stands for country-bluegrass-blues, although eventually the venue hosted music of many genres, including punk, new wave, and no wave. My description of this venue for the book was based on historical articles and images of the period.
- References to club venues, ABC No Rio and Space 2B, in the East Village and Lower East Side, respectively, were real locations and based on researched descriptions.
- Doug's Off-Off Broadway theater is typical of storefront-type theaters of the time. I modelled Doug's theater after the New York Theater Workshop, a real Off-Broadway theater in the East Village during the 1970s and 80s.
- SoHo Playhouse is a real Off-Broadway theater located at 15 Vandam Street in the SoHo neighborhood. The theater currently offers both main stage and theater for young audiences productions. I was unable to determine a specific date when the theater introduced children's performances into their season. For the sake of the story's timeline, I created a fictional matinee production of *Sleeping Beauty* in 1982.

In addition to its arts themes, *Navigating Her Next Chapter* explores several important historical events occurring in the early 1980s, including the frightening beginnings of a disease among the gay community and beyond that baffled the medical professionals and perplexed the government. As we now know, the disease was eventually identified as HIV/AIDS. In addition, a second epidemic manifested – the cocaine addiction crisis – which swept up every type of person – from the stock exchange financiers to the blue collar worker to the naive student. Having witnessed these two issues first-hand during my own time in New York in the early 1980s, these themes found their way into the book, filtered through Margie's eyes. Adding to my own memories, the writing is supported by historical research, interviews, and supplemental reading, specifically:

The HIV/AIDS research includes interviews and perusal of articles and websites including: https://www.hiv.gov/hiv-basics/overview/history/hiv-and-aids-timeline, as well as *The New York Times* archives, much of which is paraphrased within the book.

I also drew from the memories of my interactions with friends I've known through the years who have succumbed to this dreadful disease. Their spirit lives on in my heart.

For research into the cocaine crisis and specifically cocaine smuggling in New York City in the early 1980s, I relied on *The New York Times* archives. For better understanding about addiction and its symptoms, I used two documents: "Drugs, Brains, and Behavior: The Science of Addiction." NIH National Institute on Drug Abuse, July 2014 and *Street Drugs…A Drug Identification Guide*. Publishers Group West, LLC., 2022. I also consulted with Linda Auerback, a professional Substance Abuse Prevention Supervisor (now retired but still very active in local drug awareness and prevention activities), to review aspects of

Crystal's cocaine addiction and Alissa's post rehab experience in the manuscript. Also note: The Mountain Manor Treatment Center in Baltimore is a real rehab facility. The novel *Bright Lights, Big City* by Jay McInerney as well as the 1988 film by the same title, starring Michael J. Fox and Kiefer Sutherland (screenplay by Jay McInerney) provided useful color. I'd like to take a moment to include the following: If you or someone you know is struggling with drug or alcohol addiction, please consider seeking help by calling 988, the National Hotline for all mental health and substance abuse issues. It's sponsored through SAMHSA.

Finally, a third theme woven into *Navigating Her Next Chapter* focuses on the residual effects of Margie being sexual assaulted in book one, *That Summer She Found Her Voice*. To accurately and sensitively handle the writing of these scenes, I consulted the Mayo Clinic's online site for information about PTSD symptoms that can result from sexual assault. These include emotional deregulation as well as the following: a strong startle reaction, touch triggers, or memory flashbacks causing the sexual trauma victim to shut down. I learned that it is helpful for victims and their intimate partners to openly communicate and identify triggers in order to build a trusting relationship. I encourage readers that if you or someone you know is struggling, please consider seeking help and know that you are not alone.

I thank you for reading *Navigating Her Next Chapter: A Retro Novel* and following my writer's journey. As with all my writing, it is my hope that this book will be a catalyst for conversation. I am grateful for your support.

# Acknowledgments

I am incredibly fortunate to be surrounded by so many capable colleagues who make the journey from idea to publishing a pleasurable one. Not the least of these are the amazing team and my publisher, Kevin Atticks, at Apprentice House Press.

But even before the manuscript reached the publisher, I interacted with generous and helpful experts who assisted in my writing process. They must be acknowledged and thanked.

For early research, I'd like to thank Linda Auerback, retired Substance Abuse Prevention Supervisor at the Carroll County Health Department. Linda took the time to answer my many questions, lent me excellent resource materials, and read an early revision of the manuscript in order to provide specific feedback on my depiction of the drug crisis in the time period of the book, the drug addiction scenes, and the impact of drug addiction on the other characters.

Additionally, I'd like to thank Dr. Lisandra De Jesus, Dean of Student Affairs at Carroll Community College, for her time, feedback, and recommendations on additional reading specific to the character of Miguel and the Puerto Rican community in New York City in the 1970s and 80s. Her insights were invaluable.

I'd like to express my thanks to the amazing *New York Times* bestselling historical fiction author Fiona Davis. Through her generous willingness to exchange a series of emails, she shared a research resource about Radio City Music Hall, which led me to Neil Byrne, a former RCMH usher during the 1960s. Thank you, Neil, for answering many of my questions about the usher program at RCMH and the wonderful vintage photos you shared. (Isn't it wonderful how this chain of inquiry works?)

Gratitude also goes out to Stephanie Diorio at the New York Transit Museum for her input and confirmation about vintage subway schedules and maps specific to the early 1980s. We both had fun researching period documents for historical accuracy.

Thank you to Bill Toscano for the time he spent with me both answering interview questions about life in New York in the 1980s as well as providing amazing feedback after reading an early revision of the manuscript. Another excellent in-person resource!

I am grateful to my other advance readers who provided lovely praise as well as thoughtful feedback: Carol Cahill, Flo McCahon, Hamilton Clancy, and Mary Lavin Kendall.

Sarah Witcher and Lynn Davidson at Maryland Department of Natural Resources confirmed historical data on birds of Maryland's Eastern Shore in the early 1980s. Thank you both for this information. In addition, thank you to Sean McCandless for several discussions about the effects of DDT on Maryland's Eastern Shore bird populations in the early 1980s. Because of these wonderful naturalists' expertise, I learned that my references in early revisions to certain birds on the Eastern Shore during 1982 and 1983 were completely wrong – a perfect example of important research that required me to cut an entire section of the manuscript. (Yep…sometimes research leads to a writer's heartbreak, but I'm a stickler for accuracy!)

Many thanks to my developmental editor, Barbara Van Aken, for her insightful questions on my early draft and a subsequent revision. I appreciate the way she gently but firmly pushes me to explore my characters more deeply – each time urging me to go beyond my self-imposed comfort zone.

To the Maryland Writers' Association, the Eastern Shore Writers' Association, and the Authors Guild, thank you for your support and many resources. These professional writers' organizations are essential to me. They allow me to grow and develop as a writer. I am grateful to them everyday.

Finally, and always, I thank my wonderful husband, Don McCombie, for standing by me throughout this and all my writerly projects.

# About the Author

Jean Burgess is a writer, editor, playwright, and workshop presenter. As a former professional stage actor and director, many of her written works relate to the performing arts, including her debut novel, *That Summer She Found Her Voice: A Retro Novel.* Her nonfiction, *Collaborative Stage Directing,* was published by Routledge in 2019. Before diving into a writing career, Jean taught theater and speech communications on both the secondary and college levels for twenty-three years. She holds an M.A. in Theater from Northwestern University and a Ph.D. in Educational Theater from New York University.

Themes of friendship, finding love, family dynamics, career challenges, and more make *Navigating Her Next Chapter: A Retro Novel* a great Book Club choice. A discussion guide and other materials are available on Jean's website.

Please check out Jean's website to stay up to date with her writing activities by signing up for her monthly newsletter on any webpage. https://www.jeanburgessauthor.com

Interested in reading more about Margie's life in the first book of this Retro Series?

Use this QR code to purchase *That Summer She Found Her Voice: A Retro Novel* in any format:

Apprentice House Press is the country's only campus-based, student-staffed book publishing company. Directed by professors and industry professionals, it is a nonprofit activity of the Communication Department at Loyola University Maryland.

Using state-of-the-art technology and an experiential learning model of education, Apprentice House publishes books in untraditional ways. This dual responsibility as publishers and educators creates an unprecedented collaborative environment among faculty and students, while teaching tomorrow's editors, designers, and marketers.

Eclectic and provocative, Apprentice House titles intend to entertain as well as spark dialogue on a variety of topics. Financial contributions to sustain the press's work are welcomed. Contributions are tax deductible to the fullest extent allowed by the IRS.

To learn more about Apprentice House books or to obtain submission guidelines, please visit www.apprenticehouse.com.

Apprentice House Press
Communication Department
Loyola University Maryland
4501 N. Charles Street
Baltimore, MD 21210
Ph: 410-617-5265
info@apprenticehouse.com • www.apprenticehouse.com

www.ingramcontent.com/pod-product-compliance
Lightning Source LLC
LaVergne TN
LVHW010604100826
845148LV00014B/2841

* 9 7 8 1 6 2 7 2 0 6 2 7 3 *